REAP &
REPENT

BOOK I OF THE REAPER SERIES

LISA MEDLEY

Reap & Repent:
Book One of the Reaper Series © 2015 Lisa Medley

ISBN: 978-0-9908856-3-4

Cover and formatting by Sweet 'N Spicy Designs
http://sweetnspicydesigns.com

First printing March 2014 by Harlequin E

Published in the United States of America

Lisa Medley

http://www.lisa-medley.com

DEDICATION

To my husband and daughter for believing in me and eating more Ramen noodles for dinner than is nutritionally sound so I could write instead of cook.

PROLOGUE

What does a guy have to do around here to get some service? Deacon Walker marveled as he glared at the undulating queue of grotesque reapers in front of him.

For all that's holy, move the hell along already.

It had been a long week, and it wasn't over yet. He needed to make at least one more pass through the hospital circuit before he could call it a day. He could already feel the tug of a freshly departed soul. *Again.* People were dropping like flies lately.

He massaged his brow, trying to soothe his exhausted patience as the line inched forward at a snail's pace.

He was worn thin. Over the past few weeks, three demon soul poachers had popped up in his fair city of Meridian like poisonous mushrooms after a hard rain.

While it wasn't unheard of for one to slip out from Hell every now and then, three was a nightmare.

When it got topside, a demon's M.O. was to steal a

human body, poach a few souls from the dead and dying, and then make its merry way back to Hell, taking its host's soul along for the ride. The only way to save the souls a poacher was carrying was to behead the host with a scythe. Not a pretty thing to do, but the poor suckers were too far gone by then to survive anyway. No human could withstand the pressures of being ridden by a demon. And it was worth it to save a handful of souls, not to mention inconveniencing the demon.

Deacon refused to lose any souls from his territory. At all. So far the score was Deacon, 3. Demons, 0.

As a reaper, carrying souls to Purgatory for judgment was his job and he wasn't about to cede his territory to poachers who used up their hosts like they were disposable Tupperware. So now, in addition to his normal day job, he also had to keep an eye out for more demon invaders.

While demons burned through most human hosts in a matter of days, some in a matter of hours, they had discovered long ago that under the right circumstances they could ride a reaper. Of course, they couldn't just worm their way in like they did with humans—they had to be *invited.* But once a deal was struck? They were in.

And reapers? Yeah, they could hang on for decades inside a reaper. Deacon knew that fact firsthand. His stomach twisted at the thought, but he shook it off, looking ahead with a heavy sigh.

Seriously, this line? Still. Not. Moving?

God, he needed a freakin' vacation. Extended. He dragged a hand through his hair in frustration as his mind flipped through postcard-esque locations of reapings past. He snarled at the thought of New Orleans in summer. He would definitely want to go someplace cool—cool as in frigid, not hip. He was sick of the heat, and it was only the beginning of summer in the semitropical Midwest.

Come to think of it, he was sick of a lot of things.

This place was high on the list. It was as hot as...well, Hell actually. Or at least what he imagined Hell to be, although he'd never actually been there. Thank God. Steam rose from random cracks in the stone floor of the underground station, veiling the place in a humid sulfur stench.

He pushed forward, finally making his way to the front to deposit his cargo of souls. He didn't bother chatting. In. Out. Move on. It was a motto that served him well.

Mission completed, he hustled through the crowd, forgoing the bar-side frivolity of some of the more socially inclined reapers and their small talk about their glory days in the field or—even better—the missteps of the newest reapers. Newbies often tested their limits to humorous if not disastrous effect at least once in their early careers. That was exactly why new reapers had mentors or at least worked in teams. From all the laughter, he could tell that the stories were good ones. It didn't tempt him.

He slapped his palm against the black granite monolith and flashed out of Purgatory to what he prayed was his last stop of the day.

CHAPTER ONE

"What color is my light?" Ruth Scott's mother asked her as soon as she stepped into the hospital room. Not "Hello" or "How was graduation?" or any of the normal niceties polite people employed.

Ruth didn't try to soften it for her. "White."

Silence filled the space between them. The time for talk was over. Her mother turned to face the wall. They stayed that way for a long time—together, but so far apart that Ruth might as well not have been there.

She didn't *want* to be there. Not in this city, not in this hospital and definitely not in her dying mother's room. Estranged or not, she wasn't happy that her mother's life was ending.

Uncomfortable with both the silence and the ergonomically uninclined chair, Ruth stared out into the night, waiting for her mother to fall asleep. The soft whoosh of machinery and rapid beeps of monitors filled the space between them. There were a lot of things that she could have said to her mother. Things she probably *should* have said. But even now, listening to her mother's life come to a slow end, her father was the one she thought about.

Ruth knew when people were dying. Ever since she was a little girl, she'd been able to see the light around people. Now she knew what it meant. Each person was surrounded by an aura that reflected his or her life energy. Auras waned and waxed, changing according to feelings and circumstances, like a personal mood ring. The colors of the living ran the gamut, but the dying? Their auras were bright white—the absence of color, the absence of life.

She hadn't always known that her ability was abnormal. The first time she made the connection was the day of her father's death.

She and her family had been on their way to church when a blinding white glow suddenly descended upon him. By the time they arrived, she told him that his light was so bright white she couldn't even look at him. It burned brighter and brighter still, becoming a supernova. The three of them walked into the sanctuary, hand in hand in hand, and then her father collapsed in a heap on the church floor. He died of a brain aneurism before he hit the ground. The light snuffed out as quickly as it had appeared, and the typical chaos associated with death in a public place ensued.

As he lay dead on the church floor, surrounded by feverishly whispered prayers, weeping parishioners and a man leaning over him attempting CPR, Ruth saw her mother's light transform to a muddy brown.

Over the years, Ruth had told her parents over and over again about the light she saw around people. Her father had responded with humorous indulgence, saying that while other children had imaginary friends, their daughter was more inventive. But her mother was deeply superstitious. Each time Ruth mentioned someone's light, she hushed her. She didn't seem to believe in

Ruth's visions any more than her husband did, but she feared them nonetheless. That day in church, her superstitions transformed into a wariness of Ruth. Mary Scott no longer denied her daughter's abilities, but Ruth quickly learned that her mother's denial had been better than her belief. Ruth knew what she was thinking: *Where could such a talent come from? Surely nowhere good.*

The muddy brown Mary's light developed on the day her husband died became the predominant color of her aura for the rest of her life. Ruth now associated it with an unsettled and negative spirit.

Because of her mother's superstitious terror, most of Ruth's early knowledge of auras had come from trial and error. She'd figured things out on her own. The meaning of a white aura had been clearly and indelibly stamped upon her psyche: white equals death. Her few attempts at quizzing her mother about other possible color meanings had ended badly, causing Mary to retreat further into herself, pulling away when Ruth needed her most. The reserved yet caring mother Ruth remembered from her childhood was replaced with a depressed, fearful shell of a woman, who seemed to hate her own daughter.

As a result, Ruth did what any kid would do. She stopped talking about it. Her mother didn't ask, and she didn't tell. Ruth knew that if she wanted to learn what the colors meant, she'd have to discover the answers on her own. Which she did. Eventually. But the burning question, even now, was what she was supposed to *do* with that knowledge.

Ruth rubbed her eyes to stop the flow of memories and disappointments. She crossed over to the bed and peered down upon her mother. Nothing was going to change the past. And for her mother, the future was all but over. Things could have gone differently. *Should* have gone differently. She felt a twinge of guilt at not trying harder to hide her ability from her mother over the years. Sometimes, particularly in her teenage years, she had even taunted her with it. The way her mother had cringed from her spot-on aura readings had made her feel powerful…and lonely.

The white glow around Mary's body intensified tenfold as Ruth stood by her bedside. She took Mary's hand in hers and the light crackled like a Fourth of July sparkler as her mother's body rose and fell with her last breath, then stilled.

The monitor flatlined and set off a fluster of activity as Mary Scott passed out of this world.

Ruth placed her mother's hand upon her chest, then kissed her forehead as the last of her light faded away. A bustle of nurses and hospital staff hurried into the room and tended to her dead mother's remaining needs.

There were forms to fill out, questions to answer and arrangements to make, all of which took several more hours and a myriad of phone calls to complete. When Ruth finally walked out into the hospital hallway, she was physically and emotionally exhausted.

As she hurried down the hospital corridor, she kept her eyes fixed on the floor, watching the green and white tile squares slide past as she made her way to the exit. The auras in a hospital were more disconcerting than anywhere she had ever frequented. With white (death) being the predominant color throughout the hospice ward, she didn't want to look around her any more than was absolutely necessary.

As she rounded the corner of the hallway, she slammed into a rock wall of a man dressed in black scrubs. Startled, she directed her gaze up, up, up his torso until she locked on to a pair of ice-gray eyes. His hands gripped her upper arms, preventing her from stumbling.

Flustered, she began to sputter an automatic

apology. But then she noticed something that shocked her silent. He had no aura. None.

She gaped at him, staring for what must have been an aeon before she finally returned to her senses and looked away. He probably thought she was an escaped mental patient, but what explanation could she possibly offer? It wasn't exactly normal to ask a stranger about his aura (or lack thereof). That was something crazy people did.

He gave her a questioning look, his eyebrows raised, his dark hair falling across one eye. Shrugging her shoulders from his steadying hold, she skirted around him without explanation, because there wasn't one. She knew it was rude, but she was finished with people for the day.

Even this strange—and strangely beautiful—man.

Who had no freakin' aura!

At another time, another place, she might have submitted to her curiosity and tried to find out why he had no light. As it was, she just wanted to be alone.

* * *

Deacon was shaken. Being a reaper, he was not easily undone. He should have pursued the girl, questioned her. Truth was, he had been so surprised by her missing aura and the way she'd pinned him to the floor with her doe-eyed stare, he hadn't been able to think straight. At the time, he'd consoled himself with the lie that she'd been too fast. That she'd scurried away into the bustle of hospital activity before he'd had time to respond.

But now, after the fact, even he couldn't make himself believe that bullshit. Something else was going on.

He'd been on his way to retrieve a soul, the one he'd

felt tugging at him from Purgatory, when he literally ran into her. She was beautiful: petite, with long, curly dark hair and pale, smooth skin.

Basically, he knew just one thing about her...she wasn't human. Even if her nonexistent aura hadn't been a dead giveaway, he would have known that from the way she'd looked right at him.

Reapers naturally repelled the attention of "normals" when they were on the job, and could turn on the charm if necessary, manipulating subtle changes in humans' auras to bend them to their will. Most of the time, they could pass by completely unnoticed. Not invisible exactly, but certainly less than memorable.

She'd definitely noticed him, and then some.

What the hell?

When he walked into the hospital room after their encounter, he was surprised to find that the dead woman's soul had been detached but not reaped. He'd assumed the girl was a reaper. Because of all the supernatural beasties in his known universe, only reapers didn't have auras.

So if she isn't a reaper, what is she?

He procured the prize, and then checked the visitor log on the way out. *Ruth Scott* had been the last visitor of Mary Scott, the soul he'd retrieved. The girl was the daughter? He would have followed her, but she was already long gone. The dead and dying he could track; the living were trickier.

He'd have to go old school to find her.

The mother's house?

The living always gathered at the deceased's residence at some point. He could bide his time if necessary, but he would find her again. And question her. Something wasn't right.

If she was a reaper, she'd failed to do her job. Considering the state of things lately, he would have been informed if another legitimate reaper had been assigned to his territory.

If she was some new type of poacher, he was even more confused.

So many questions. The last thing he needed was to be distracted from his job. Bad things happened when a guy got distracted.

CHAPTER TWO

Ruth walked into her apartment and stared at the answering machine blinking on the kitchen bar. She didn't carry a cell phone. It was just another bill to pay, and honestly, she didn't have any friends who would bother calling her anyway. Punching the button to play back the message, she already knew what it would be about.

It had only been a few hours since her mother's death and already people were following up with her about the various minutiae that needed to be addressed. It was amazing how many details had to be considered by the living on behalf of the dead.

Luckily, her mother's no-frills life would carry through to her death. She'd left a letter detailing her wishes—cremation, burial beside her husband and no service.

Easy enough. All Ruth had left to do was sign some paperwork.

Mother is dead.

Ruth had watched the white light of her mother's

aura fade to nothing, winking out like a burned-up star. And yet she still couldn't quite wrap her head around it.

Her mother had been sick for many months, and she'd expected that she'd feel something more when her light faded away. Surprisingly, the thing she felt most keenly was regret.

She sat at the bar with her head in her hands, trying to figure out what to do next. Then, from the corner of her eye, she caught sight of her favorite and most precious family photo on her faux hearth: her and her father standing in front of a bulletin board in her second-grade classroom after she'd won the spelling bee.

She'd never been good with people, but she had always loved words. Her father had been the same way, and he'd spent hours reading aloud to her while her mother worked nights as an RN in Meridian. He'd even penned a few short stories for her himself, filling her in as the heroine every time. She had so many good memories of her father.

Ruth smiled as she surveyed her piles and piles of books stacked in tall vertical columns along the walls like a Verizon cell signal because she lacked the appropriate handyman skills to construct even a makeshift bookshelf.

She felt a strong pull of nostalgia for her early childhood, back when she and her father and mother had been a real family, and before she even realized it, she was packing. What she needed now was to be close to those few good memories. They were all she had left. She loaded what she could into her father's old Lincoln Continental, from floor to roof to trunk, and headed south into the growing darkness.

She was going home, and she wasn't coming back.

* * *

Later on that night, she pulled down the long tree-lined driveway to her childhood home. It was small and cozy and...small.

A bungalow, she supposed.

Realtors would undoubtedly use words like *charming* and *quaint* to describe it. It was actually a turn-of-the-century rock-sided house. Ruth always thought of it as a giraffe house because the large, flat sandstones that were mortared to its frame on every side made it look like a prehistoric giraffe.

This house had once represented the hopes and dreams of her parents. Now it was much like her mother had become: functional but barely. It boasted all the basic trappings of a home—plumbing, electricity, furniture—but it lacked any sort of warmth or personality because her mother had ceased to exude either of those qualities after her father's death. Still, there *were* good memories here, as well—they were what had drawn her home.

Parking her car in the open-fronted double garage behind the house, she grabbed the first of several armloads of belongings and carried it inside. She retrieved her things one trip after another, leaving them in a heap in the living room until she could decide what to do with them. A crushing heaviness settled into her chest as she surveyed the house. It had been quite a long time since she'd been home, preferring to avoid her mother's disdain.

Her heart lurched as she looked around the living room. All of the little touches and reminders of her father were gone: the gilded painting of the Last Supper he'd always loved and made up stories about, his collection of leather-bound classics, and the framed and autographed photo of Harper Lee. After his death, her mother hadn't been able to bear looking at his things anymore, and she'd stowed them all away. It had been heartbreaking for Ruth.

Her motivation waned and exhaustion took her over as she sank down into the overstuffed chocolate-colored sofa, feeling foolish for thinking home would fill the empty hole she felt growing inside her. Everything caught up to her and brought her to a halt.

Both of her parents were dead, and she had no living relatives. She was truly alone.

Rolling into a tight ball, she rested her head on the arm of the couch for a pillow.

The cicadas in the trees outside buzzed loudly, their calls penetrating through the rock walls. The noise became a din in her head. The rhythmic buzz lulled her into a dreamless sleep: a welcome break from her emotional and physical exhaustion.

* * *

Deacon flashed into the small rural cemetery and waited for his eyes to adjust to the moonlight. It was dark in the countryside. He'd decided to try the Scott house tonight. In case he could get that lucky.

After the week he'd finished, he was pretty confident luck was not on his side. He was not a patient man, and this was an inconvenient trip. The address was in the middle of nowhere, nearly thirty miles from his regular hunting grounds. Plus it was *two miles* from the nearest cemetery. He could have chosen a more conventional mode of travel than the consecrated subway reapers used to get around, but nothing was faster. Even with the walk.

He really didn't want to make this trip very many times. If she didn't show up, he'd have to track her down another way, but that would take even *more* time. Time he couldn't afford to waste. Souls piled up if you weren't diligent. And while the souls of the newly dead pulled at him, that feeling began to fade after a day, or sometimes even a few hours, making them more difficult to track down. If too much time went by, it was all but impossible to find them unless you practically stumbled upon them. The lost and lingering souls were called sleepers. He'd found a few in his day, but it was like picking a needle out of a haystack.

Even one day off would create an uncomfortable backlog. Most territories the size of Deacon's were serviced by a team of reapers, but he was single-minded in his work. He didn't take vacations. He didn't socialize. He worked.

As a result, he drew attention—good and bad—but all of it unwanted. What he really wanted was to be left alone to do his job. His profession was not necessarily enjoyable, but the intense and pressing nature of the work didn't leave him with much time to ruminate on things. He spent zero time in his head because it was almost constantly occupied with detecting, locating and transporting souls. The rest of the time was devoted to sleep even if it was an hour or two at a time.

Because he'd been on the job for a long time, his body didn't require as much nourishment as it once had—a benefit of being a seasoned reaper. But all this demon hunting was wearing him out, and it was taking a lot more energy than usual to fuel his body.

Seasoned, he scoffed, as he exited through the wrought-iron gate of the cemetery.

Disgruntled, he stalked down the secluded driveway, his steps crunching against the gravel. At least it would be quiet here—maybe he could get a few hours of sleep while he waited for her to show. As he reached the house, he stopped. There was a car in the garage and a light on in the house.

Looks like this might be my lucky night after all.

* * *

The unpleasant sensation of being watched jerked Ruth awake. Her fear was confirmed by the presence of "No-Light Black-Scrub Man" in the chair opposite her.

What the hell?

She scrambled up and over the couch, landing hard on the wood floor behind it. Without taking the time to regroup, she raced toward the back door. Her legs operated solely on instructions from her adrenal glands as she clambered forward in slow motion.

She was reaching for the knob when Scrub Man suddenly appeared in front of her. She crashed into him. Again. The man was built like a concrete dam, and the air rushed out of her lungs on the impact.

He grabbed her shoulders to steady her, his hands growing warm around her upper arms. The heat flowed down her arms and up her neck, relaxation pouring over her like a hot bath as her legs turned squishy.

Ruth tried to fight the growing heaviness of her eyelids, which clearly had no natural cause. Conflicted by the urge to run and the calming effect he was imposing on her, she slumped forward toward the floor. *Toward him.* Scrub Man scooped her up and carried her to the couch.

After easing her down onto the cushions, he backed away to the hearth. Her body immediately mourned the loss of contact as the warmth of his touch faded.

Sitting across from her, he leaned forward, alert and coiled. "Ruth, I'm not here to hurt you. I just want to talk." *Uh-huh.*

The warm fuzzies lingered, tingling up and down her nerve ends. Shaking her head to clear the fog, she considered her options, gauging the distance to the front door.

Fight or flight?

"Ruth, look at me. Please."

Against her good judgment, she peered up at him, studying him for the first time. His dark black hair, a little too long on top, drooped into a wave across one eye as he leaned forward, his intentions unclear. Dark stubble covered his sharp, angled jawline, accenting high cheekbones. The hot glare of his bright blue-green eyes pierced through her, making her more self-conscious than afraid. She guessed that he was in his late twenties, perhaps early thirties. The sleeves of his scrubs cut into his chiseled biceps.

He must have been just over six feet tall because her head had barely reached under his chin when he'd held her. A silver chain disappeared down the front of his shirt. She couldn't see what dangled from it, if anything. With slow caution, she pulled herself together.

"Thank you." He smiled, and her heart betrayed her by doing a little clinch in her chest. "I want to ask you a few questions and explain why I'm here," he said. "But I can't do that if you're going to sit over there plotting ways to kill me or escape. Do you think you can sit there, nice and calm, for a few minutes?"

She nodded unenthusiastically. She didn't trust her voice not to break if she said it out loud. There was no use in screaming. The nearest neighbor was a good mile away; the next was farther.

"Ruth, my name is Deacon. You might have noticed that I have some rather unusual abilities. For one, I'm very fast when I want to be. For another, I can affect your mood by touch, which I did just now to calm you. I don't want to hurt you, but I *do* need to know a few things. What are you?"

What am I? Uh, a girl would be a good start. What the hell?

She shook her head side to side, indicating "No."

"No, you don't understand? Or no, you don't know

21

what you are?" he asked, obviously growing frustrated. She shook her head again.

"Okay, this isn't going to work unless you speak. I don't read minds, you know."

Good to know, she thought. What came out was, "I don't understand."

"When we ran into each other at the hospital, you had no aura. *What* are you? Are you a reaper? An angel? Christ on a crutch, you aren't a valkyrie, are you?" he asked, running a hand through his hair, pushing it away from his face. "I'm betting no on the angel front because the Reiki energy doesn't seem to work on angels. So *what* are you?"

"A student. Or, I was a student. Now I'm just... I don't know what you're talking about—angels and reapers and valkyries. I'm...human?"

"You are more than human."

"I'm not. What do you want with me?"

"I want answers. In the hospital, I sensed something about you when we met... Your mother was Mary Scott. Correct? She died in that hospital room while you were there?"

"I didn't do that. It wasn't my fault," she blurted out.

"Okaaay," he proceeded cautiously. "Did you touch her before you left?"

She considered him, her mouth going dry. She *had* touched her. She'd given her that final kiss on the forehead. "Yes," she whispered.

Ruth couldn't look at him as she began to realize what all of this might mean. Had her bizarre handicap really killed her father, and now her mother, too? She was a killer.

"You're not a killer," he said, rolling his eyes.

"I thought you couldn't read minds!" She sobbed, tears choking her throat closed.

It's my fault. I AM a killer.

"You're not," he insisted. "I think you're a reaper, like me."

Her heart started beating faster and her vision started to go blurry around the edges. The whole room sped down a black chute into darkness. She was going to pass out. She was going to pass out with a strange supernatural man in her house.

God help me.

CHAPTER THREE

Ruth woke slowly, taking an internal inventory before she opened her eyes. It felt as if all of her clothes were still on, and there were no apparent missing or bloody bits.

That's a plus.

Sitting across from her, now somewhat less patiently, was Scrub Man, or Deacon, if that was really his name. The gravity of her situation crashed down on her. "Do you think we could try this again?" he asked, sighing. "I came to reap your mother's soul. When I ran into you in the hallway and saw that you had no aura, I assumed that you were a reaper like me. But when I got into the room, and her soul was detached but unreaped, I was confused. I collected her soul and took it for processing. And then I came here to figure out what you are... Ruth, you're more than human. Only reapers have no auras. Have you experienced anything out of the ordinary before now? Any sign that you might have special abilities?"

Ruth was flat-out dumbfounded.

He thinks I'm a reaper?

She was torn over how much to tell him. She wanted to talk about her gifts with someone who might actually understand. Maybe "reaper" was as good an explanation as any for what she could do, but how could she trust a man who'd stalked her and broken into her house? Of course, if he had planned on hurting her or doing more than chitchatting, he'd already had ample opportunity. She closed her eyes and dove in.

"I'm just a girl...but I can see people's auras. And I know that the light around someone turns white when they're close to death." She shifted, uncomfortable now that she'd gushed her crazy all over him.

"What else do you know about the colors?"

"Yellow is happy, green is peaceful, mustard is angry, brown is unhappy, and red is I-want-to-get-down-your-pants-then-steal-all-your-cookies. But that's all. I'm not anything. I can only guess at everything else," she lied. She knew a *lot* about auras and their colors. Too much maybe. Trying to decode the colors and their meanings had been one of her first research projects. It was what had set her on her nonexistent career path.

"Ruth, if you can see auras, you already know that you're more than *just* a girl. And if you touched anyone else with a white aura, you might have hindered their passing by detaching their souls prematurely, making them difficult to retrieve. If that happened, their souls are likely still near their bodies. I reaped your mother's soul. Have you ever knowingly touched anyone else who has a white aura?"

She hesitated. "My father maybe? When he died, it was the first time I realized what the white aura meant."

Deacon sighed. "Anyone else?"

Ruth picked nervously at her fingernails. "No, I don't think so. Ever since then I've tried to stay away from people. I keep to myself. I don't like knowing every little thing about how strangers are feeling, or worse, people I know. I feel compelled to tell them things because of what I see. Like that they should probably get their crap in order and make up with their loved ones because they're about to *die*. Stuff that I'm smart enough to know will land me right in the nut house if I don't shut up about it."

Deacon sat quietly for several long minutes, probing her with his sharp eyes. Ruth squirmed under his scrutiny. She didn't like being looked at, period, let alone this intensely. She felt as if he was counting her pores or wondering if her size-eight skin might fit well into his collection.

"Where is your father buried?"

"Why? You aren't thinking of digging him up, are you?" She tried not to scream the words at him.

"I'm not going to dig him up...not exactly." Deacon rose to pace the floor in front of her. "We need to go see if his soul is still hanging around. If it is, he'll be stuck haunting his grave until he's collected. I assume he's been dead for quite some time now? He's not going to be too happy about that. They never are."

Ruth tried to process this random new development in her overstuffed brain. It wasn't computing. Up until twenty minutes ago, she'd managed to keep her secret in a nice tight box in the back of her mind. Now that box was opening like Pandora herself had peeled back the lid.

Maybe I am going crazy.

She tried to keep it together, but the effort strained against her throat, threatening to come out in a nice loud scream at any second. Deacon approached her cautiously and held out his hand.

"Take my hand, Ruth."

"Why?"

"I can help calm you."

She took it. God help her, but she did. His hand was warm and comfortable. Familiar even. She didn't know how else to explain it, but holding his hand seemed like a perfectly sane and acceptable antidote to the insanity that was building inside her.

Her brain was in conflict with her body. His touch made her feel better: warm, but not fuzzy this time. Clear. Sure. Content. Yet, her adrenaline refused to entirely release its grip.

Be afraid, it warned.

He pulled her to her feet and into his chest in an embrace. She let him.

She curled into him like a kitten, and he felt so good against her that she wanted to purr. The longer he lingered, the better he began to smell, too. Like cedar trees and fresh earth. Ruth closed her eyes and breathed him in. She hadn't been this close to a man in a long, long, long time.

Dangerous.

She relaxed so much that her inhibitions were in danger of failing. That was what pulled her out of her stupor, and she jerked back. "What are you doing to me?" she whispered.

"I'm calming you. I won't make you do anything you don't want to do, Ruth. Let me help you relax."

He led her back to the couch, and they both sat. He pulled her snug against his chest, and they sat there for a long moment, him pumping the happy juice through her until a pale orange glow surrounded both of them. It occurred to her that she should be asking more questions, like how come he had suddenly become a human glow stick for starters. Instead she relaxed into him. It was nice in that scary "what the hell am I doing with this strange man" sort of way. She was letting go, and he was holding her.

And damn if it didn't feel good.

* * *

Deacon had no idea what he was doing here, on a couch with his arms wrapped around the girl he'd suspected of being a poacher up until twenty minutes ago.

This is wrong.

One thing was for damn sure, she wasn't a poacher. He knew all too well that poachers could possess *anyone*—no matter how nice or normal or sane—if they found the right in, but Ruth showed no signs of possession.

Still, Deacon had let his inhibitions down to the point of stupidity tonight. He needed to figure out her game and be done with her, one way or another. He had work to do. There was no telling how many, if any, demons still roamed the city. Not to mention the souls that pulled at him incessantly even as he sat here on this couch, his arms around a strange woman.

So soft and warm.

Sure, it had been a little easier for him to juice her into submission than it should have been if she was a reaper. On the other hand, the fact that she wasn't a blabbering vegetable after the amount of juice he'd already poured into her also proved she was more than human.

So what other explanation was there?

His gut told him she was an untrained reaper.

CHAPTER FOUR

I must have dozed off, Ruth thought. She opened her eyes, slowly absorbing the fact that she was still on the couch, and the early afternoon sunlight was streaming in through the window. She'd somehow managed to sleep half the day away. The smell of bacon cooking in the kitchen filled the room. The day before came back to her in fuzzy bits and pieces. Her mother dying. The Scrub Man. Reapers. She got up and padded into the kitchen in the clothes she had now worn for two days. Deacon, the reaper, was flipping eggs on her mother's stove. Surreal.

"Hope you're hungry," he said. "You'll need to keep eating to maintain your energy. That's one thing about being a reaper—most of the same human rules apply, you just get some benefits, too," he said, a smirk on his face.

"Seriously, I don't know why you keep calling me that. I have no idea what you're talking about." In the light of day, she still wasn't buying the whole reaper thing. But she knew one thing for sure: *Deacon* was more than human.

That energy mojo trick is not normal.

It wasn't that she was dismissing the possibilities of what he was offering outright. Her own experience was proof that not everything was black-and-white.

Most people said that they didn't believe in the supernatural, but if they believed in God, they should at least believe in the possibility of everything else. If God, then why not other supernatural entities: Satan? Angels? Demons? Vampires? Werewolves? Reapers? It was a slippery slope for sure. Open one door and no telling *what* might come through it.

Regardless, Ruth wasn't ready to take it all on face value or the word of the very fine man who was cooking her breakfast. But she had to admit that he had some admirable points.

"You might as well accept it so that we can move ahead, Ruth. Unless, of course, you have a better explanation?" She shook her head no and stared down at his plate longingly. She hadn't eaten since breakfast yesterday.

"So, do you know where your father is buried?"

"Of course I do."

Deacon popped a bite of bacon into his mouth. "Let's go there after breakfast to see if he's hanging around." He filled a plate for her.

"You mean we don't have to wait until the stroke of midnight or have a séance or take an Ouija board or anything?" She was a little disappointed with the whole thing. She'd expected something…more.

"We'll go see if his soul is there. It all depends on whether or not you detached it accidentally when he died. If his soul made it with him to the cemetery, it will still be there. Let's hope he's been reaped. If not, we'll reap him. It'll be fine. Trust me."

Clearly, he was delusional.

Her urge to bolt from the house was only staid by

the plate of oh-so-crispy bacon and eggs he placed on the table for her. "Oh sure, no problem, trust you. I don't even *know* you, and until yesterday my life was fine, and now …?"

"Fine? Really? You said yourself that you stay away from people because you can't stand to read their auras. You were estranged from your own mother and from what I can deduce you have no family or friends. I'd say you are far from fine."

"Who are you to judge me? You don't know what it's been like. I thought I killed my father. And now you're telling me that I may have trapped or *lost* his soul? How do you think that makes me feel? Let me tell you. It makes me feel like shit. It makes me feel tired and like shit. I don't know what the point of all of this is, but I'm already damn tired of playing."

Ruth flopped down hard into a chair at the table, suddenly overcome with emotion. She put her head down on her arms. Hot tears welled in her eyes, and she could not keep them from leaking out. She was mad and sad and hurt. And most of all, she was really, really tired.

Deacon put a hand on the back of her head and pushed some happy juice into her. Maybe if she could learn *that* little method of self-medicating, she could pull it together. She didn't know why she was picking now to fall apart.

Maybe I found the fault line in my brain.

"It's going to be okay, Ruth. I'll help you through this."

"Why?" she sobbed. "Why do you want to? Aren't you just cleaning up a mess? My mess?"

"Yes, but we need good reapers. Besides, I could use the help. You seem like a good kid and…hell, maybe you can work with me. Once you're up to speed, of course." His voice trailed off but he kept his hand on her hair.

She looked up at him. She must look like a hot mess. Her mascara, which had probably smeared around on her face in her sleep, had most likely starting running and was even now pooling in dark semicircles under her eyes. Her nose was stuffed up from stifling her emotions, and she hadn't looked in a mirror since Friday morning. She could only imagine what her hair looked like.

A frizzy, wild Chewbacca mess, I'm sure.

He knelt beside her, putting an arm around her, and pulled her toward him. "Hey," he said softly.

She peeked up. He lifted her chin with his hand and looked into her tear-blurred eyes. "It *will* be okay, I promise." She prayed he was right.

He leaned in and pressed his soft, warm lips against her forehead. She closed her eyes, soaking it in. It was a tremendous relief that she couldn't see his aura and know his true feelings—whether he liked her or just pitied her. As he brushed his lips down to the corner of her eye, he lingered on the salty bits there, his hot breath breezing against her skin. All of her bones were melting. She didn't feel the push of his calming mojo, only his breath, his lips and his hand on the back of her neck, pulling her to him.

Parting her lips, she sucked in a shuddering gasp as his mouth found hers. She thought she might ignite into a puddle of fire. His kiss was firm and earnest. Torn between wanting to consume him and wanting to run away—*stranger, delicious, dangerous*—she settled somewhere in the middle, and kissed him back.

Reluctantly, he pulled away, rested his forehead against hers and sighed. She felt like Jell-O. *My first kiss,* she thought. Of course, it wasn't her *very* first kiss. She was twenty-seven after all. But it was the first one she'd experienced without an ounce of dread.

Flitting thoughts of Rob Carmichael's eighth-grade advances in an empty classroom at the Methodist church dance—soggy wet lips, roaming hands and a hot red aura—filled her mind. This kiss was nothing like that one had been.

This kiss was wonderful. She hoped it wasn't a pity kiss because, she realized with surprise, she would like a few more of his kisses. He stood, leaving her dazed. His face was a puzzle she couldn't solve.

"I shouldn't have done that …" He backed away.

Great, she thought.

"But I'm glad I did." He smiled. "Now eat your breakfast so that we can go Free Willy," he said, ruffling her hair. Ruth's father's name was not Willy. But she ate her bacon with a smile on her face.

* * *

Panther Valley Cemetery was an old rural cemetery in York County, Arkansas, that was a couple of hours from Ruth's home. They'd been delayed because Ruth had needed to follow up on the inquiries regarding her mother's passing. It was probably a good thing they were heading to the cemetery now, so that she could check on things before her mother's interment.

The Scott family had been buried here for centuries. No matter how far from home they roamed during their lives, this was where they were buried. It was a tradition repeated throughout the rural cemeteries. Even if they fought like cats and dogs during their days above ground, all the chicks finally came home to roost in the end. A few surnames dominated the headstones: Bailey, Monroe and Scott. Hundreds of similar cemeteries dotted the state. Since it was a week before Memorial Day, the grounds were neat and clipped, and even in the growing darkness she could tell the grass around the headstones had been trimmed to perfection by the caretaker. The grounds were empty of visitors as they pulled up and through the gate.

The entire area was rural and unpopulated, and on the long drive in, they'd been surrounded by rolling green hills, waist deep with the first growth of fescue of the year. A lush green line of trees demarked the borders of Panther Creek.

The good thing about cemeteries was that only the visitors had auras. Ruth couldn't see auras around animals or other living things, which she considered a small but welcome blessing. She couldn't even imagine how distracting *that* would be.

Deacon followed her into the cemetery to search for her father's headstone. She shone her key chain light left then right, trying to remember the layout of the family plots. The cemetery was small, and once she got a feel for things, the stone was easy to find. The earth on top was packed down, grass and weeds covering the grave in spotty patches.

"This is it," she said, brushing grass clippings from the front of the stone. She wished she had brought some flowers. She wasn't exactly a frequent visitor.

Including her father's burial, this was her second visit to the site. Ever.

She would likely never have visited again except to bury her mother if not for this latest development. She didn't see the point of visiting graves. It wasn't like the dead kept a register of visitors, and she didn't need to see his headstone to think about him. But being here without flowers, particularly the week before Memorial Day, felt disrespectful.

Deacon knelt and studied the ground in front of the headstone.

"Can you step back from the grave?" he asked. "If his soul hasn't been reaped, I don't want your energy to interfere with the process." Ruth stepped back.

He spread his palms out over the earth and pressed down against the packed ground. It was nearly pitch-dark now, and the heat of the late spring day radiated off the ground and stones. Ruth felt clammy thanks to the high humidity. It wouldn't be too many more days until the summer heat conspired with that devil humidity to cook up a nice greenhouse effect that would make Al Gore weep.

The mid-South in summer. Was there anything worse?

A soft orange glow radiated from Deacon's hands. It shimmered and rose from him in waves like the heat off an amusement park's asphalt in August. But instead of heat, a cold, edgy blast built around them, increasing until the ground trembled and shifted. The next thing she knew, she was looking at a husk of gray light glistening and forming into something that looked remarkably like her father. The apparition hovered over the grave before them. Deacon had somehow wrenched her father from his grave—or at least a part of him.

His soul?

Her stomach rolled, and she swallowed down the lump that formed in her throat.

This is my *fault.*

Deacon leaned back on his heels and rolled up to his feet. Both of them looked at Ruth's ghost father, who stared back. He looked confused and unsure. She didn't know that she could blame him. A long, silent moment passed. Ruth heard a truck rumbling in the distance, its exhaust pipes announcing its arrival long before its headlights appeared on the horizon. She looked at Deacon, wondering what was going to happen next.

"Do we need to hide him?"

"No one else can see him," Deacon said. "Be cool. I think that truck's about to pass us."

The truck rounded the corner, its high beams sweeping only the farthest edge of the property as it continued down the road, its aftermarket exhaust pipes thundering into the distance.

Rednecks.

She breathed out a sigh of relief, her heart rabbiting in her chest.

"Ruth, I'm going to reap him because I don't want your first time to be with a family member. That's messed up. Keep a hand on me and maintain contact. After I reap him, I'm going to bring him straight to Purgatory, and you can tag along for the ride if you're touching me. At least I'm pretty sure you can. If you truly are a reaper, it won't be a problem. If you aren't…well, I guess you'll have to wait for me to get back, or go on home without me. It's going to be a hell of an initiation, but if not now, when?"

Ruth's father stared at her as Deacon spoke. She thought that perhaps she could detect the smallest spark of recognition in his eyes. "Can he hear me?"

"He can, but I don't know how much he can understand after all this time, or if he remembers anything from being alive," he said, waiting patiently. "He can't speak or communicate with you… He's an untethered soul. His sentience began to fade as soon as his soul detached. He needs to be processed."

Tears filled her eyes as she took a tentative step toward her father. She wanted to embrace him, but that would have been useless under the circumstances. Not to mention impossible—she could see straight through him.

"Daddy, it's me, Ruth. I'm so sorry you've been here all this time. I didn't know. I still don't understand any of this, but this man is here to help you pass over. Don't be afraid. You'll be with Mother soon. She just passed. I hope you can find peace and be together again."

Her father still looked confused, but he was staring at her so intently, she figured that maybe he had at least enough awareness to know they were here to help him. "Touch my back," Deacon said. "Don't break contact until I've reaped him, and then we'll go immediately."

Ruth placed her open palm against Deacon's black scrub top. Deacon reached his glowing hands forward and made contact with her ghost father, whose shape shimmered and dissolved into a glittering gray stream. When Deacon inhaled, what was left of her father flowed forward into him through his sternum, vanishing like water down a drain. Her hand grew cold and painful against his back, but she didn't let go. Deacon shuddered and consumed her father. When he turned to look at her, his blue-green eyes were icy gray.

"Let's go."

Deacon stepped off the grave and pulled Ruth into an embrace after surveying the road to make sure no one else was headed their way. "Hold on."

He reached out and placed his hand on top of the headstone.

The headstones and the entire cemetery shimmered, and she lost the vertical hold on her vision as everything began to swirl into a vortex around her.

I'm going to be sick.

She closed her eyes and waited for it to pass as they spun and slid down, down, down.

CHAPTER FIVE

Ruth opened her eyes to complete and utter chaos. There were creatures everywhere. She would have been hard-pressed to prove most of them were now or ever had been human. It was like the cantina scene in *Star Wars* without the fun band. Ruth's mouth gaped open. It was dark, foggy and damp in the long underground chamber where they'd landed, like some kind of subterranean cave. She'd never seen anything like it.

It was a depot of sorts, it seemed, and there were long tunnels crisscrossing every which way, disappearing into the stone walls. Her mouth still agape, Ruth followed Deacon into what appeared to be the main hall, where the floors and ceilings were also rough stone, and light from an unseen source flowed down through strategically positioned skylights along the ceiling. Reapers were everywhere: men and women but also a disturbing number of...well, *monsters* was the word that came to mind.

There was so much to take in that it was overwhelming. Chiseled placards demarked the top of each tunnel in a language she didn't understand. And at each end of the main channel, huge platforms rose above the fray. Sitting on stone thrones upon the platforms were two very similar-looking men who looked like angels, complete with flowing purple robes and wings.

Deacon took her hand and dragged her along behind him. "Keep up."

"Don't worry."

She did *not* want to be down here alone, wherever here was. They rushed through the throng of creatures, large and small, human and otherwise, toward the opposite end of the channel and the angel who was sitting there. They were almost there when someone called out behind them.

"Walker? What the hell? I thought you would have cashed in by now," the man said. Deacon spun around, pushing Ruth behind him. "Kylen," Deacon said, grimacing and barely containing his obvious disgust. He clearly wasn't happy to see the guy. "I've been...occupied."

"I can see that," he said, leaning over to give Ruth a slimy once-over look. "Who is she?"

"We're bringing in a sleeper," Deacon said, changing the subject.

"A sleeper? Wonder how I missed that one?"

"It doesn't matter," Deacon said, forging ahead.

"Put up a good fight at least?" Kylen asked with inappropriate enthusiasm.

"What are you doing down here? Have you grown tired of your ride?"

"Oh, no. I just like to keep a finger on the pulse of things. Network. Mingle." He winked, then directed a disturbing smile Ruth's way.

"Right." Deacon pulled Ruth away from Kylen, leading her the last few paces to the platform.

A line of mixed creatures wound in front of them.

Ruth had no idea what some of them were. Of the ten or so in front of them, two looked passably human. The rest were all variety of sizes and degrees of grotesqueness. One great slobbering gelatinous mass in front of them, who was Deacon's height, but twice his girth, turned to assess her. His wet reptilian skin shimmered and glistened as his Ping-Pong-sized lizard eyes looked her up and down, then locked on to hers. She looked away and snugged up closer to Deacon.

"Eyes on the prize, asshole," Deacon said to the thing through gritted teeth. Mr. Lovely turned back around with a grunt.

Otherwise, there was no chitchat in the line. She wondered if all these things even spoke the same language.

Deacon leaned over and whispered, "Try not to freak out—this will get easier. This is Purgatory—a way station. It's a neutral zone. A no-man's-land of sorts. All reapers can meet here and interact, but there can be no conflict. It's a forced détente essentially. Pray you don't see most of these creatures on the topside."

She couldn't imagine any situation where she would.

"The guy in the purple robe is the angel Rashnu. The guy on the other end of the station? Also Rashnu. He's split himself into two because he doesn't trust anyone else to do the job right. He's the sorter. The gates of Hell and Heaven are locked up tight. No soul gets through Purgatory except with his blessing. He's rarely wrong, but once in a while a soul gets kicked back and…well, let's hope that doesn't happen today."

The line inched forward. She watched as the reapers approached the angel Rashnu and wished she could hear the exchange between them. From where she was standing, she was close enough to get the gist of it. The reaper approached and spewed forth its cargo, which floated down and assumed its original shape. The deposits held their ghostly form for a few moments, and then Rashnu waved his open palm in front of them, and they were sucked away down one of the various tunnels carved into either side of the station's stone walls. The contrasting colors of the walls clearly indicated which tunnels led to which eternal resting place. Left was lovely, and lightly colored markings and symbols adorned the wall. The right side? Not so much. It looked like street gangs had tagged the entire wall from stem to stern. The souls streamed away in a smoky mist ranging in color from black to white and everything in between.

"Are all of them reapers?"

"Yes, there are a lot of different races represented down here. I can give you a crash course later. But stay quiet for now—Rashnu hates disrespect."

Ruth zipped her lip, and they shuffled forward again. Deacon was up to bat. Ruth tried to look small and insignificant behind him, which was not much of a stretch. Rashnu bored a hole through Deacon, and then she felt his gaze settle on her.

"Forward!" the angel bellowed.

She was frozen in place. Deacon hesitated for a second then swung her around in front of him.

Lamb to the slaughter. Thanks.

"Just when I thought it was going to be another boring day in Purgatory." Rashnu scowled. "What do we have here? Speak, reaper. Name yourself."

Ruth wasn't sure if he was asking her or Deacon, since she didn't think she qualified as a card-carrying reaper yet. Deacon gave her a nudge in the ribs, encouraging her to answer.

"Ru… Ruth," she stuttered.

"Well, RuRuth, why are you presenting yourself in Purgatory this day? This is very unusual. I think Dante was the last to cross through here uninvited and that was…a while ago." Rashnu glowered. "We don't do visitors. And you don't appear quite suicidal." Rashnu arched an eyebrow and threw a withering glance at Deacon.

"I brought her. She's a reaper, but she's untrained. She grew up without the proper guidance. I'm...mentoring her. I brought you her father today for processing. He's a sleeper—his soul has been untethered for fifteen years." Deacon didn't bow before the angel, but he did cast his eyes downward in an act of submission.

Rashnu seemed to consider his options as the people—and creatures—behind them shuffled, growing agitated by the delay. One look from Rashnu, and they all stopped in their tracks. Ruth didn't know what power the angel held over them, but even the insane-looking creatures obviously had a healthy respect for him that seemed a lot like fear.

How some of those things could fear anything considering how terrifying they looked themselves, she had no idea. She certainly didn't want to incur the wrath of Rashnu, though, or any of the rest of them for that matter. Mostly, she wanted to go home.

Like, now.

Rashnu motioned Deacon forward and her father's soul began to purge from him. For a brief moment, her father reformed before Rashnu. The angel waved a glowing blue hand at him for a little longer than he had with previous customers, and then her father streamed up and away, toward a chimney in the center of the station. Her father disappeared into the "good" chimney, if appearances could be trusted.

Deacon fell to his knees and a sharp gasp sounded from the line of reapers waiting behind them. Trying to recover, he did a face plant instead. Realizing that he needed a hand, she bent to help him.

"Are you okay?" she asked, trying to get her weight

under his shoulders and ease him to his feet.

"The latent ones are always the toughest." He smiled weakly.

Rashnu looked as if he was ready to smite them both to dust at any moment. He was obviously done with the drama. And frankly, Ruth was, too. She didn't like having all of those creepy crawlies at her back, and her spine tingled at the thought of them. The air felt thick and dangerous.

"Now…about this *new* reaper." Rashnu waved his hand and the people—and things—in line turned in unison, making their way to the other end of the station, leaving them alone before him.

"So, Deacon, you are offering to mentor the girl?"

Deacon got to his feet and gave Rashnu a long look before nodding what seemed to be a rather reluctant *yes.*

"Very well. This is, of course, not standard procedure, but if you're willing to take responsibility for her and her actions for the entirety of her training, I'll approve it. There won't be another official training session until next summer since everyone has been occupied with…activities. However…she is completely in your charge. Understood?"

"Understood."

"Come, Ruth. You will not receive your scythe until you've proven that your training is complete. If Deacon continues to fulfill his duties and exterminate his territory of its current *visitors,* you won't be needed for hunting demons anytime soon. It will be up to Deacon to determine when your training is complete."

Deacon placed his hand on the small of her back and urged her forward, toward Rashnu. She felt tiny next to the angel as he towered over her. He was much taller than Deacon and the ridiculous purple robe didn't make him any less imposing. His dark hair was shoulder length and wavy, and his face was so smooth and flawless.

"Well, Ruth, let's see what you've got." He took her face between his palms and tilted her head upward, his green eyes locking on to hers. His gaze bore into her as his palms grew warm against her face, and she watched as a white radiance began to envelop her. Everything faded away except for her and Rashnu, and try as she might, she couldn't break the hold his gaze had upon her.

Memories flipped through her head as if he was turning pages in her mind, rewinding her personal history one chapter at a time. Many of them she'd forgotten—some were good, some were bad, but all were familiar once they floated to the surface, retrieved from the closet of her mind. Familiar, that is, until a different reel began to play.

One that wasn't her own.

Abruptly, Rashnu detached from her and stepped back a pace. His eyes had gone large and round with wonder, but they quickly narrowed and his surprise was replaced with what appeared to be concern.

"Well?" Deacon asked.

"Interesting." He aimed an inscrutable glance at Deacon. "Good luck."

Rashnu raised his robes off the floor a few inches and climbed the short set of stairs back onto his raised podium. He was just the sort of guy who enjoyed lording over people. Or reapers, as the case might be.

Confusion shot through her as she tried to shake the images he'd pulled through her conscience. Especially the ones that weren't hers.

So much for not being able to read minds.

Had Deacon lied to her about that or was Rashnu the only one who could do it?

She wasn't surprised by the angel's reaction. He wasn't the first seer to be repelled by her. When she was sixteen, she'd gone to a tarot card reader in the hopes of getting some good news about her love life after yet another failed boyfriend attempt. Carlos Sanchez, with his mustard aura and anger issues…so not the one. Again.

It had gotten so bad that she'd nearly given up because she couldn't help judging boys based on their auras, which eliminated about 99 percent of the boys she met. Even if they made it past the initial meet and greet and things progressed, she could always tell when they were trying to deceive her with promises and lies, which, with teenage boys, turned out to be often.

The more tangled their lies became, the more swirled and muddied their auras grew, until she bailed in frustration. She would have given anything to turn off her aura vision and be oblivious, just like the rest of her freshmen class.

The tarot reader had taken Ruth's money, shuffled her cards and then promptly pronounced the session to be at an end when the Death card was the first to appear. Ruth wasn't a card reader, but she knew the Grim Reaper when she saw him. Or so she'd thought.

As she hurried Ruth out the door, the woman had been visibly shaken, and she'd taken care not to touch her client. The encounter had confirmed the suspicions that had kept Ruth up at night throughout the years. Something was very, very wrong with her.

And now? Now a fierce and feared supernatural beastie was giving her the brush-off? Really?

Deacon took her hand and pulled her toward the monolith where they'd arrived. She didn't know what the plan was, but she was all for a quick exit.

"That was fun." Kylen fell in step beside them.

"Ya think?" Deacon replied.

"Hey, man, just makin' conversation here. We never talk anymore. So what's the story with Snow White here? She a freelancer? I wouldn't mind teaching her a thing or two." Kylen winked lasciviously at Ruth.

She shuddered.

He looked human...but everything was a bit off about him. His movements were a little too jerky, his speech a little too staccato. He was the same height as Deacon, but his blond hair was nearly white, in stark contrast to his disturbing black eyes. His black pupils took up most of his ocular landscape—a thin ring of dark purple rimmed the outside edge of his pupil and another even thinner band of white shone at the outermost corners.

Creepy.

"Thanks for the concern, Kylen, but I've got it covered." Deacon hurried Ruth toward the other end of the terminal.

"I'll bet you do," Kylen said, his eyes never leaving Ruth's face. He winked again and laughed to himself as he walked away and faded into the crowd.

"What was that all about?"

"Later," Deacon said, urging her along, his hand pushing against the small of her back. "We need to get out of here. Now."

"Absolutely."

As they passed through the crowd, Ruth was careful not to brush against any of the creatures. The one thing they all had in common was their complete lack of auras. Now that she actually wanted to read the people around her, she had nothing to go on, nada. It was less than reassuring. They stepped up to a large stone monolith that resembled a scaled-down stone from Easter Island. Markings and unrecognizable symbols covered most of its smooth surface all the way around. The word *Sanskrit* popped into her mind.

"Grab on," Deacon said, curling an arm around her waist.

When she was firmly in his grasp, he slapped a hand on the marker and everything grew swimmy around her again. They zoomed back up from Purgatory, landing smack in front of her father's grave.

* * *

Judging by the pitch-black sky, it was very late when they landed topside, but she was relieved to see something familiar again. Even if it was a cemetery. She bent over and lost the lunch she hadn't had onto the ground beside the grave.

Motion sickness?

Deacon put a hand on her back and pushed happy juice into her. "It gets easier."

She didn't know if that was more comforting or alarming. She also didn't know if she even wanted to ever experience any of this again, let alone grow accustomed to it. He rubbed his hand across her back in slow circles.

"We need to get back," he said, taking her hand and pulling her toward the car. "I need food, and it wouldn't hurt you to eat, too."

Her stomach still felt queasy after her vomiting episode, and food was the very last thing on her mind. She was pretty sure he wouldn't want to kiss her again anytime soon.

As they headed to her Continental, Deacon reached for the keys. She handed them over without complaint. It had been a long, strange day, and she didn't trust herself to get them back to the house in one piece. As he started the car, she noticed that the dash clock flashed 9:35 p.m. They'd been at the Purgatory way station for two hours.

I guess time flies when you're having fun.

CHAPTER SIX

Deacon was conflicted as he drove them home. Ruth had now officially been recognized as a reaper even if she was still in training. How had his life gotten so topsy-turvy in such a short time?

Now that she'd made it to and from Purgatory, things would change for her. Her powers, which had been mostly latent for all these years, would begin to activate.

He swore to himself. It was the absolute worst time for Kylen to have surfaced.

Once, Kylen had been Deacon's best friend and fellow reaper, but for the past century he had been possessed by a demon soul poacher. At least once a decade, Kylen's demon showed up to taunt Deacon. He would carve a path of destruction all around him before falling off the radar again.

Deacon had done what he could to save Kylen, consulting with his superiors and finally a local coven to try to free his friend from the demon who held him. But the only way he could do that was if he found out the demon's name…or, of course, killed its host.

As in beheaded him.

Demons could animate a human body as long as it still held some energy, but they wore out quickly. Only two things killed a reaper: completely depleting his or her energy, or decapitation.

Demons had figured out long ago that as long as they kept their reaper host fed *and* protected, they could ride him or her indefinitely. A reaper's natural Reiki energy would continue to heal his or her body from virtually any injury. Minus beheading, of course.

If Deacon hadn't chased out the three Meridian demons himself, he would have sworn Kylen was to blame for the soul poaching in the area. Kylen was certainly capable of that level of carnage all on his own. He'd done it before through the years. Repeatedly. The difference this time was… Deacon suddenly had someone to lose.

And now that Kylen knew there was someone who might mean something to him… Deacon feared that he might endanger Ruth.

Something about the girl was compelling. She had no idea what she was in for, and since she had never been trained, her powers weren't developed. He needed to keep Kylen as far away from her as possible. Kylen couldn't hurt her in Purgatory, but topside…well, she was vulnerable.

How had this happened? Some reapers were born into their work, others trained for it if they exhibited latent supernatural abilities, including the ability to manipulate auras, travel the consecrated subway, and respond to the pull of the dead and dying. Still, the reaper pool was a tight-knit and closed society. Normals didn't regularly fall into its waters or off the radar like Ruth apparently had. Regardless, there were damn few female reapers. Most women with a talent for reaping were trained as valkyries, a prestigious and precarious job. They could carry many more souls than the average reaper, and as a result were constantly summoned to one battlefield after another.

No rest for the weary.

There were millions of reapers scattered across earth, each manning their own little piece of the pie. Deacon worked a territory he'd claimed many years ago. He'd been drawn to the quiet and seclusion of Meridian...he'd had all the drama he wanted for a very long time after Kylen's possession.

His ongoing battle with Kylen was personal, and he knew the stakes were high, not just for him but for anyone he cared about. It was dangerous to let anyone close to him with Kylen lurking about. He knew it.

So what was he doing with this girl? Had he really told Rashnu he planned to mentor her? It would slow him down. No doubt about it. And it would put her at risk, too.

Stupid.

He should walk away now. If she'd made it this long without using her gifts, she could just wait until the next training course opened up in Purgatory. Or she could keep living her life the way she'd been living it. Her sad, lonely, pathetic life. Why did he even care about that? Why had he kissed her?

Damn it.

They drove along in silence as a fresh ulcer began to eat at the pit of his stomach, and he pondered why exactly he felt so compelled to protect someone he'd only just met.

After a long drive, they finally arrived back in Meridian. A quick trip through the drive-through for food was a necessary delay. The grocery shopping still hadn't happened, and neither of them was in any kind of shape to dine in. The car dash clock read a quarter to midnight as they wound down Ruth's driveway.

As they got out of the car and headed up the driveway to the house, Deacon paused and listened intently, trying to pinpoint an unusual sound in the darkness of the woods around them.

"What is it? Did something follow us out of there?" Ruth fidgeted nervously, edging closer to him.

"No," he said, less than convinced. "There's nothing out there. It's just the frogs. They're so freakin' loud out here."

"Oh, they're just spring peepers looking for love."

"I'm not used to the noisiness in the country. I guess I don't spend much time away from work."

"People must die out here, too?"

"Sure, but there usually isn't any reason to linger." His hand pressed against the small of her back, urging her toward the house. "Let's get inside. Those frogs are creeping me out."

* * *

Ruth opened the door to the back porch, kicking off her Nike shoes before padding into the kitchen. Tossing her empty fast-food bag toward the trash can, she realized that Deacon hadn't touched his yet. He'd been pretty intent on not careening them off one of the many curves on the way to her house. She got the impression that he didn't do a lot of driving.

She pointed to the table. "May as well sit down and eat."

Deacon hesitated in the doorway. "I should go."

"Oh, no, you don't," she said, her voice rising, edged with anger. "You open up a whole new world of crap for me, drag me to Hell and back, and now you think you're just going to leave me? *Now?* At midnight? Alone? I don't think so. You're staying right here and answering some questions, of which I have plenty."

Ruth's face felt flushed as she finished her tirade. The food she'd eaten was crap, but she *was* starting to feel a little better. So much so that she wasn't about to back down. He had best plant his ass at that kitchen table because he wasn't going anywhere without doing some serious explaining first.

Deacon raised his eyebrows at her as she got her second wind. He started toward her, but she raised one hand in a dismissive "talk to the hand" motion she'd seen the sorority girls at school use to great effect.

"You are *not* juicing me! I want to feel what I feel: the good, the bad and the ugly." She repeated, "Do. Not. Juice. Me." He sat down at the table with a grin on his face, pulling out his fast-food bag.

"I'm going to go take a shower. When I get back, you sure as hell better be here, or I swear to God I'll ..." She actually didn't have an ultimatum to threaten. She was hoping the possibility of incurring further wrath was enough. She'd never spoken to anyone like that, but then she'd never had reason to before. She was entering one uncharted territory after another tonight.

Her exceptional intelligence hadn't exactly been showcased in the past twenty-four hours, but she was ready to channel her inner badass if need be.

I know I did not see a smirk on his face, she thought as she turned in the direction of the master bathroom.

"It was Purgatory."

She whipped around. "What?"

"Purgatory. Not Hell. I dragged you to Purgatory and back. Trust me, babe. If you'd been dragged to Hell and back, you wouldn't be nearly so feisty." She harrumphed and stomped off to shower.

CHAPTER SEVEN

Deacon admired her spirit. She was spunky.

Unstable but spunky.

He finished his fast food while she showered and resisted the urge to walk in there and …

What the hell was wrong with him?

He threw his trash into her bin and occupied himself with inventorying her food situation. She had no idea how all of this was going to affect her. Tolerance came with time, and right now she wasn't going to have the luxury of either tolerance or time. She was practically a child. A beautiful, sexy, unstable…*Shut the hell up!*

Food. Make the grocery list!

He pilfered through her cabinets, then the fridge, making a mental inventory. Finally, he found a notebook and pen and began a real list.

* * *

Ruth spent a good fifteen minutes under the hot water, letting it wash away the day's events. Seeing her

53

father again after all these years, even in his unearthly state, had been amazing. And jarring. Her heart hurt as memories of him filled her mind.

She knew he'd had much bigger hopes for his family and this home than had come to fruition. Her father had wanted a large family, and when that hadn't happened because of fertility issues, they'd adopted her as an infant through the Catholic Church. One child had turned out to be enough for her mother, but her father invented imaginary siblings for her and had told her hundreds of stories about their adventures through the years.

The house came with nearly ten acres, and all of it was woods. The small yard was already growing into an out-of-control mess in the few days since her mother had checked into the hospital. Between the clover and the thistles, there didn't appear to be much actual grass out there anymore. Still, she'd at least need to mow a path to and from the house.

There was a lot of work to be done. Much more than she could handle. Luckily for her, she had no pesky job prospects to distract her. The thought of a job working with the public was terrifying, and as she'd neared graduation with a PhD in Information Technology, she'd found herself procrastinating and making no inquires…which had landed her exactly where she was now: jobless.

Her dream was to work in the bowels of a huge library far away from the public in research or reference or maybe even doing paid research for clients. So far, she'd been a perpetual student.

Face-to-face communication with people was unbearable for her, which was a lesson she'd learned over and over throughout the years. Their auras were too distracting and confusing. It was like trying to have a conversation with completely naked strangers.

When her professor had walked into one of her first-semester classes with an unmistakable white aura, she'd had a panic attack. She'd caused such a disturbance that someone called an ambulance, and she wound up making a brief visit to the mental health ward. Her school psychologist, to whom, of course, she lied, eventually diagnosed her as agoraphobic, which helped her secure online classes for most of the remaining semesters.

Since then, she'd been a shut-in, and when her mother got ill, it had been easy to push off job hunting. Now what was to become of her? This whole reaper business was boggling. Was it even a real job? Did they actually get paid?

Good grief.

As the water turned cold, she put the brakes on that train of thought and started mentally assembling a rather long to-do list. She left the shower, dried off and got dressed. After a haphazard attempt at detangling her hair, she gave up.

* * *

When she returned to the kitchen, Deacon appeared to be making a list of his own. She was pleased and more than a little relieved that he had yielded to her threat and stuck around. Rummaging through the cabinets for an after-midnight snack, she was surprised to realize that she already had the munchies again. Settling on the only piece of fruit in the house, a soft, blackened banana, curiosity got the best of her, and she peeked over his shoulder.

"What's up with the list?"

"Grocery list," he said, leaning back in his chair. "You're going to need a good stash of high-calorie foods on hand for post-reaping replenishment. Fast food is the best because it's super high in calories, but you may not always be able to stop somewhere. These will do in a pinch. You're going to need to carry a backpack with you with plenty of portable snacks in it and probably a change of clothes."

She glanced down at the list and whistled after a moment. "Who are you? Bob Harper's evil twin?"

The list consisted of peanut butter, Snickers bars, chocolate, avocados, energy drinks, bacon, beef jerky, mac and cheese, nuts, mashed potatoes, lots of frozen dinners, and meat, meat, meat.

"You gotta be kidding me. If I eat all of that every week, I'll be five hundred pounds. They'll have to cut my dead and bloated body out of the house with the Jaws of Life. Seriously, I saw it on The Learning Channel."

"Ruth, each time you reap or travel through the network, you'll need to replenish. The process will burn thousands of calories each time, especially reaping. You might do six reapings in one day. What are you, about a size eight? Maybe a hundred and fifteen pounds soaking wet? Eighteen hundred calories a day will *maintain* that. Subtract six thousand plus calories a day, and you'll be a bone sack in a week."

She considered this revelation. There were a lot of negatives to being able to see auras. All of her life, she had only seen it as a hindrance. She'd spent years thinking she might be dangerous and avoiding people because of it. As a result, she had become the campus cat lady…without the cats. And now, *today,* at twenty-seven, she was finding out that she could eat as much as she wanted without repercussions because she was a reaper. She knew a gaggle of sorority girls at the university who would have *killed* for that opportunity. Of course, most of their calories would have been liquid, but still. On the food front, all she could see was an upside.

It's good to know the rules.

"So, what happens if I don't eat? Will it kill me?"

"No, but you'll grow weaker and weaker. If you go too long without replenishing yourself, you'll most likely be rendered immobile, which will leave you vulnerable to attack. Reapers *can* be killed, Ruth. We aren't immortal, but we are close. After you've reaped enough souls, your body will transition, and you won't expend quite as many calories when you're working. You may even develop some enhanced abilities similar to the ones you've already seen me use. Yours may be the same or they might be different. We'll have to see how it plays out. It might take more than a hundred reapings before *anything* unusual happens."

He had her attention. "What *can* kill us?"

"If your life force becomes too depleted through lack of nutrition or if you carry too many souls for too long, your energy could be completely and irretrievably exhausted, and you would die."

"What would happen to the souls?"

"The souls would leave your body along with your own. If you were lucky enough to die where a reaper could get to them, they would be reaped. If not …"

"They could become sleepers? Like my father?"

"Yes. But it's a situation that you can easily avoid. We're able to heal ourselves as well as others, but not if we are completely drained ourselves."

Ruth leaned forward, excited. "So you can heal people?"

"No, our energy is too strong for humans. We can use light pulses to manipulate them when necessary, but if we use too much reaper mojo, they'll permanently short-circuit. You'll want to use your energy sparingly until we know how it affects you. We are at our weakest point when we reap and our own bodies are filled with the souls of the dead. The good news is that it's pretty damn hard to die accidentally. The bad news is that you'll be putting yourself in danger if you let yourself get too depleted. That's when you're at your most vulnerable. If your soul is drawn out when you're in that state, it's game over. That and …"

"What?"

"Beheading."

Ruth shivered. "How long can I live?" Feeling suddenly ravenous, she poured Raisin Bran cereal into the biggest bowl she could find, only to realize there wasn't any milk.

"Most of us stay in the business for around two hundred years. That's the average. There's no forced retirement, but most reapers tend to flame out around then, so there are some retirement options."

"Like what?" she asked, giving up on the dry cereal and going for the peanut butter straight out of the jar. She needed comfort food. Now.

"Well, some choose to pass on to the afterlife to be with their friends and family. They get a new body, and after a pretty lengthy process to cleanse their souls, they move on. Others who want a change of career apply for ascension. If they're chosen, they train to become a low-level Guardian Angel or to transcend to one of the higher levels of Heaven, if they qualify. Others want out of the service side of the industry altogether and choose…a darker path." Deacon shifted in his chair, clearly uncomfortable with the direction of the conversation.

"How much darker can you get than being a grim reaper?"

"We're just reapers. There's only one Grim. He was the first reaper, which was fine until the population got out of control. Now there are millions of us. Grim doesn't even reap anymore."

"Have you seen him?"

"No."

"Then how do you know he exists?"

"Do you believe in God, Ruth?"

"Of course."

"Have you ever seen him?"

"No."

"You believe because you have faith. It's the same with Grim. I believe in him."

They both sat for a while, lost in their thoughts. It was almost impossible to absorb, yet Ruth's brain was soaking it up like a sponge. The possibilities seemed endless, and she was excited that there was so much to learn. If this was all true, what else didn't she know? It was crazy and dangerous and exciting and right all at the same time.

She felt as though she'd spent her entire life wondering why she was different and what it meant. Now she felt as if a door was being opened for her, ready to reveal answer after answer if she was only willing to look.

"How old are you?"

He hesitated and drew a hand through his hair, smoothing it away from his eyes. "Two hundred and six."

Wow, no wonder he looks so tired.

She could not wrap her mind around that because the man sitting at her kitchen table didn't look as if he could be more than a few years north of thirty.

Weathered? Yes. Tired? Definitely. But more than two centuries old?

No. It would probably have been easier to accept if he had long gray hair and a Dumbledore beard, but Deacon Walker, the man, the *reaper,* before her? That was tough to believe.

Now that the peanut butter was starting to work its magic on her brain cells, she felt as if she was beginning to piece some of the events of the last thirty-six hours into a more acceptable framework. The puzzle was starting to come together.

"Why do you look so young? And is that why Kylen said he thought you might have cashed in? Because you're two hundred and six? And while we're on the subject, what *exactly* is Kylen? Those eyes were not…human."

Deacon let out an exasperated sigh. "Do we have to cover the entire history of the netherworld tonight? One of the benefits of being a reaper is that we stop physically aging after our first reaping. But much like this conversation, it's still exhausting. After reaping a sleeper and taking a hitchhiker to Purgatory and back, being interrogated by *you* is intolerable. Besides eating, we also need sleep to rejuvenate. Seriously, no more tonight."

Ruth felt chastised, but one thing he was going to have to learn about her, and soon, was that she was nothing if not persistent. She was willing to let it go for now, but she didn't graduate with a PhD without learning a few things about finding the answers to hard questions.

"Fine," she said, slamming the now empty jar of peanut butter down onto the counter. "You can shower down the hall if you want. I don't have any clothes you can change into, but you can clean up in there. The house has three bedrooms. You can sleep in my mother's room, on the futon in the junk room or on the couch. It's your choice. But don't think this is over …"

Deacon made eye contact with her. His eyes had brightened back to blue-green, she noticed—they were no longer the icy gray they'd turned while he was carrying her father's soul.

He gave her a curt nod. "Thank you."

"You're welcome. Good night."

"Good night."

CHAPTER EIGHT

Ruth tossed and turned. How would she ever fall asleep with a man—that man—in the next room? What was he *doing* in there? Why had she insisted that he stay?

Every instinct told her she was being foolish. She'd only known him for a day and a half, and he was certainly not human.

Or at least not just *human.*

A million questions plagued her, and she wished she had some sleeping pills or a stiff drink to calm herself down. Her mother had neither in the house.

When her mind wasn't busy adding to an ever-growing list of questions, it kept returning to the image of her father's ghost and everything that had happened in Purgatory. How had things come to this? Had her parents known she was different even before she admitted to seeing auras? She replayed her memories in her mind, trying to see them in the new light of the knowledge that had been awakened in her. Her parents had seemed so shocked that day in the car when she'd kept harping on about that white light. Although she'd mentioned the lights before, the brightness of her father's that day had been overwhelming. Clearly her ability wasn't normal, but they couldn't have known she was different even as an infant.

Could they have?

And what of the "memories" Rashnu had unearthed? Where had *those* come from? A woman with dark curly hair and sad eyes, standing with a large group of people around a bonfire?

She wanted to turn her mind off. Shut it down. She wanted a little relief, if only for a while. It was just too much. Way, way too much. Ridiculous actually. The stuff of fairy tales *or nightmares,* she thought. *Yes, nightmares.* And the man in the next room? What about him? Was he the prince or the villain of this story? Time would tell. She prayed for the prince because if villains kissed that good, she was screwed. Utterly and completely.

* * *

Deacon tossed and turned on the couch. Ruth had given a blanket to him before disappearing into her room. He pulled it over himself. He usually slept in the nude, but that wasn't going to work out here on the couch in a strange woman's house. He settled for taking his shirt off. At least the scrub bottoms were loose and comfy. The couch sucked. He needed to sleep in a bed. His bed...or hers.

Shut up already, he told himself.

He could have slept in her mother's bed, he supposed. She'd offered, but that seemed...weird.

Like this whole situation isn't weird?

Hell, he was never going to fall asleep out here. Now that Ruth was out of sight, he kept thinking about how much work he was missing...and it wasn't like someone else would pick up the slack. His work was compounding like the interest on bad credit. In the hundred or so square miles he covered, there were six to ten deaths a day. He could carry as many as six souls at a time, more in an emergency, but it left him more vulnerable than he liked. Even though he was a workaholic and didn't take very good care of himself, he didn't have a death wish anymore…most days. He'd reaped one soul today. He should be out working now. Meridian's population of a quarter million people cycled in and out, living and dying on a daily basis.

At least he had job security.

The good news was that it paid well. In fact, he'd never wanted in his life. Then again, he'd never really wanted much of anything to begin with—material possessions were meaningless to him, and he'd always preferred to travel light, especially after the whole Kylen debacle. The idea of planting roots and developing attachments had utterly lost its appeal. While he hadn't exactly rooted himself in Meridian, he had found himself lingering in spite of the occasional fantasy of falling off the map on some permanent vacation.

He could feel the tug of detaching souls, but if he didn't rejuvenate himself with some sleep, he couldn't adequately confront Kylen. And tomorrow, he was planning to draw him out while he caught up on work. He needed to be strong for that. But despite his total and utter exhaustion, he wasn't about to fall to sleep here on the couch.

On Ruth's couch.

He feared that his inability to sleep had more to do with her than the dubious comfort of her furniture or his guilt over his job. Damn, he was in trouble.

* * *

When Ruth woke up the next morning, it felt decadently late. She halfheartedly opened her eyes and did a fast recap in her head. Stretching, she let her weight sink heavily into the mattress. It was a child's bed. The cheap twin mattress had worn out its springs long ago. Her mother hadn't spared any extravagance on herself or the house, let alone on Ruth. Mary Scott hadn't exactly been frugal—more apathetic. She'd never recovered from her husband's death. Without any hobbies or close friends, she had poured all her energy into her work as an RN at the very hospital where she eventually died. There wasn't even cable or internet at this house, for God's sake.

Given how far the house was from town, Ruth wasn't even sure those were options, but one of the first things she planned to do today was find out and get some groceries. Thinking of Deacon was enough to motivate her to get out of bed and head for the bathroom. She went through the motions of brushing out her hair and scrubbing her face and teeth. Digging through her suitcase, she found an old T-shirt and shorts. She hadn't even had time to unpack, and her to-do list was getting longer and longer.

Heading to the kitchen, she stopped, drawing in a surprised breath when she caught sight of Deacon's prone form on the couch. One arm was thrown over his face and eyes in an effort to fend off the growing light beaming through the living room window. The other arm was resting across what might well have been the most beautiful bare stomach and chest she had seen outside of a celebrity magazine. Not that she read that trash.

Mercifully, he still had his scrub bottoms on, but his feet were bare. God help her, but that was the icing on the couch cake as far as she was concerned. She had an almost overwhelming desire to start rubbing her face against his chest like a cat, but that would *not* be an appropriate reaction.

He must have felt her staring at him because he shifted a little, and then opened his eyes.

"Morning." His sleepy gaze sent a shiver of pleasure down her spine. He was tan and lean and hard in what appeared to be all the right places. With the morning light bouncing off him, he almost seemed to have a halo around him.

"Morning," Ruth managed to choke out. Then, because all she wanted to do was stare at him some more, she spun around and headed into the kitchen.

"There's no milk, and I don't think there's too much to eat in the kitchen unless you want peanut butter out of the jar," she said, unscrewing the lid and peering inside the empty jar. "Or maybe not even that. I need to go to town, run some errands and get moving on that grocery list you made for me. You're welcome to stay or..." She let the *or* hang in the air. She wasn't sure what she wanted him to do: stay or go. Last night she'd planned to grill him to the nth degree, but this morning, in the light of day, things seemed less dire. There would be plenty of time for questions later. Probably.

"I've got to get home. I need to get changed and replenish my backpack," he said, crossing over to her. "I don't suppose you have a newspaper this morning?"

"Nope. Why?"

"I need to work. Today. The souls are piling up. It would be easier to read the obits and catch up that way than have to feel my way at this point."

"Okaaaay, so do you want me to drive you? How exactly did you get here, by the way? I didn't see a car parked anywhere." Things had happened so fast since Deacon had shown up at her house that she hadn't even stopped to consider how he had gotten there.

"I used the network. I checked the hospital chart and found your mother's address. You were listed as next of kin. I figured that I might find you here. I was lucky I found you sooner rather than later. I came up in Good Springs Cemetery about two miles from here, then... I walked."

"Well that seems inconvenient."

"Not most of the time. I reap in the city, so it's pretty easy to move around. I can move from consecrated ground to consecrated ground through the network. There's practically a church, chapel, cemetery or funeral home on every other block in the city. It's out here in the rural areas that things get more...complicated. You'll need to have your home consecrated so you can travel back here more easily." He grabbed his scrub shirt off the end of the couch and pulled it on, covering that beautiful chest.

"How am I supposed to do that?" she asked, pretty sure that there wasn't a Yellow Pages heading.

"A bishop or a witch has to do it. It's easier to get a witch than a bishop. Bishops ask way too many questions. If they only knew... Don't worry, I know a guy."

Well of course he did.

"When your home is consecrated you can travel to any other consecrated ground from here. It will also be circumscribed so that nothing can come in or out without your permission. As long as you're within the consecrated circle of your home, you'll be safe, unless you break the circle and allow something inside or bring it in with you. Mind you, that doesn't mean they can't be waiting around the borders for you to leave. You're going to have to start being more careful."

Ruth shuddered, remembering the "things" she'd seen in Purgatory. She was pretty sure she was safe in the daylight. Why she thought that made any difference she didn't know, but it sure was easier to have a positive attitude about things when the sun was shining.

"I wouldn't object if you wanted to drop me off at Good Springs on your way." Deacon scooped up a handful of dry cereal. "I'll meet you back here at dark with my guy. We'll get this place locked up tight."

"All right," she said, unsure.

"Do you have any weapons?"

Ruth didn't even try to hide her shock. "I have pepper spray."

"Pepper spray won't cut it. Salt spray might help, but pepper is useless. How about a backpack? Do you at least have a backpack you can carry with you? I can find a few weapons for you to use until we get you some training."

She rummaged through the pile in the living room and found her backpack. It was still full of books and notebooks from school. It was hard to believe that part of her life was over now. Stacking them into yet another pile, she handed him the bag.

He rummaged around the kitchen, pulling open cabinet doors and drawers, then piled a few things onto the kitchen table—a silver serving knife, a can of iodized salt and a cast-iron pot hook from the back porch.

"This is all I could come up with right now, but it will be a deterrent if you have any trouble." Deacon tossed the backpack on top of the collection.

"What kind of trouble are you expecting me to have?" she asked, feeling more and more uneasy despite the sunny day. In fact, she was beginning to think that tagging along with him all day might be a better plan. Cowardly, but she wasn't feeling all that heroic at the moment.

"Probably nothing. By tonight we'll be all set. Do your thing today, and if any odd beasties approach you, pull out this silver knife. Silver will hurt most supernaturals and even kill a few. It takes a lot longer and a lot more energy to heal a silver wound. But you probably won't even have to use it. Think of it as insurance. Here ..." He poured a handful of salt into his hand and walked over to her. He grabbed hold of the waistband of her shorts and pulled her to him. She braced her forearms against his chest between them, unsure of his intentions or what she was supposed to do. He leaned in, his face mere inches from hers, and then she felt him slide his hand into her pocket...and fill it with salt.

"Fill up the other one, too," he said with a wink. "If things get hairy and something or someone supernatural is bothering you, throw a handful of salt right into its eyes. It won't kill it, but it will have a much more satisfying effect than pepper spray."

He walked over to the sink and opened the bottom cabinet doors. Retrieving a bottle of Windex cleaner, he poured the blue liquid down the drain. Turning on the hot water, he let it run until it was nice and steamy while he funneled salt into the bottle. He filled it with the hot water, screwed the spray top back on and shook up the contents.

"We'll spray this around the perimeter of your car floorboards and along your window ledges, dashboard and back glass. It's a barrier at best, but most things won't want to cross it."

Most? That was not very reassuring.

"You're talking about the things we saw in Purgatory? Why would they even care about me? I never knew they existed until yesterday." Her heart raced and a light sweat beaded on her forehead and lower back.

"Those 'things' have always been here. But now that you've been to Purgatory, the reaper in you has been awakened. You'll be able to see past their disguises to what they truly look like. Angels and demons look mostly human, but there are some subspecies of demons and other things that are...not. I don't have time to draw you a family tree here... Just try not to attract attention to yourself."

She was torn between wanting to curl up on the couch and sleep until dark and getting pissed off. She realized as an afterthought that she didn't much like being ordered around.

She was also not particularly brave. She hadn't ever needed to be. As long as she stayed out of crowds and away from people, she could pretty much avoid having to deal with her fear of auras and what they might mean. Most of her fears up until now had been more abstract anyway. Now she was about to come face-to-face with God knew how many bogeymen.

Ruth threw the ridiculous collection of stuff into her backpack with a little more than the necessary roughness, and then stuffed her purse in, too. Perturbed by his bossiness, she grabbed the spray bottle without another word and headed for the back door.

Deacon appeared between her and the door. "Let me go first...please."

"No problem," she said curtly.

Better for his face to get eaten off first than mine.

Deacon walked outside into the beautiful May morning and stood on the bottom step, looking over at the trees. He closed his eyes and spread out his arms, palms up. His palms glowed faintly as light emanated out in tendrils, drifting toward the line of trees. As the light faded, he opened his eyes.

"It's safe. Let's go."

They walked over to the car, where he opened up all four of the doors of the Continental. "Bottle?" he asked.

She handed it to him, and he set about dousing her car with his homemade concoction. He used the entire bottle, which left her with a soggy carpet and a dripping interior.

Nice.

"It'll dry. Then only the salt will be left. Don't worry about it—it won't hurt anything." Martha Stewart he was not.

Ruth was skeptical as to its effectiveness, but considering the potential alternative, she wasn't going to bicker over salt stains.

She drove them to Good Springs Cemetery, and he got out. Walking around to the driver's side, he bent down and leaned in close through her window.

"I'll be back before dark. Make sure you are, too. And stay inside the house. Get some more salt while you're out. A lot. And put it in an unbroken line along all your window sashes and across all of your doorways when you get back. We'll talk more tonight."

He lingered longer than necessary in the window and for a second, she thought he was going to kiss her again. After a moment's hesitation, he turned and walked through the Good Springs archway. He didn't even look back as he grabbed hold of the first headstone he came to and swirled and shimmered in a mini tornado until *poof,* he was gone. Just like that.

Ruth rolled up her window and locked the doors. All of them. She was not ashamed to admit that she was more than a little scared. As far as she could tell at the moment, there wasn't anything to actually *be* scared of in her immediate vicinity.

It's the things you can't see.

She backed her big-ass car out of the cemetery and headed into town with the radio blasting so that she couldn't think too much.

CHAPTER NINE

Deacon didn't dally in collecting his things from home. He changed, reloaded his backpack, and then went straight to the hospital to begin his usual rounds. He worried about leaving Ruth, but he was eager to lure in Kylen…and the last thing he wanted was for his former friend to be anywhere near Ruth.

The pull of the detached souls he'd missed the day before had already begun to fade. Sometimes the feeling lasted for days, others only hours. Because the more stagnant souls were harder to track down, he took the easy way out and checked the newspapers when necessary.

Use it if you've got it.

Technology was wonderful. Back when he had officially been installed as a reaper in the mid-1800s, finding missed souls had been damn near impossible. For one thing, the world was much less populated and hiding a body was an easy thing for enterprising criminals. It was usually a matter of dumb luck to stumble upon a sleeper. Everything moved slower back then—the news, the transportation…life.

He quickly learned not to let things slide. When he felt the tug, he went.

These days, with so many reapers and so few uninhabited places, it was rare to come across a sleeper. They were something of a hobby that he only actively pursued during downtimes if business was slow. Finding them was like combing a beach for pirate booty with a metal detector. Slow, laborious and rarely fruitful. Of course, there hadn't been too many slow times in the business of death since he'd become a reaper.

War after war had kept them all occupied. But World War One was the last war that he'd actively participated in. He put a lid on that memory and stuffed it back down where it belonged. This was no time to indulge in bitter memories.

Deacon strode the halls of the hospital. While he should track down the stale souls first, the pull here was too strong to ignore. He entered the room of a middle-aged female patient who lingered near death, clinging to life at the precarious mercy of tubes, wires and machines. The quiet whoosh of a breathing machine mimicked the beat of her long-dead heart. It wouldn't be much longer.

He sat in the chair across from her bed, watching her white glow pulsate, and waited. Impatiently.

God, he was a dick sometimes.

Was he really too busy to sit for a few minutes and wait for this woman to pass?

The real problem with any sort of downtime was it was the perfect opportunity for way too much *introspection.*

It wasn't like the future of the universe depended on him or that he was the only reaper who could do these things.

That would be ridiculous. Reapers weren't some sort

of Santa of Death, delivering the sweet or terrible hereafter one night a year to everyone on the planet. Death came often and in a variety of ways. It amused him that the normals still thought, after all these millennia, that there was one Grim Reaper.

As he'd told Ruth, there *was* a Grim Reaper, but he was more of a figurehead now. Grim had been the first reaper. When Eve persuaded Adam to eat the forbidden fruit and they gained knowledge, God decreed that mankind and all of his creation would suffer for their indiscretions and eventually die. Ashes to ashes, dust to dust and all that.

But something had to be done with their souls.

Purgatory was formed. Grim was designated as the middleman, ferrying the souls there to be sorted, naughty and nice, and then sent on to their destiny. It all worked splendidly. Until the population got out of hand.

Now, Grim had lots of help.

The reapers had needed to grow exponentially with the proliferation of mankind. And today? With nearly seven billion people on the planet? Yeah, they were busy.

Then there were the *other* creatures, as well. God was such a hoarder; he couldn't part with his wonderful and terrible prototypes for man. Not to mention the results of various matchups gone haywire. A whole new class of monsters and abominations emerged from *their* unholy unions and aligned with one side or the other.

Good or evil.

The results were wraiths, shifters, vampires, gremlins, giants and all manner of creatures. God had once halfheartedly tried to destroy them with the flood, along with the world's wicked humans, in the hopes of starting fresh. But most of them were resilient, and when they survived his efforts, he promised them salvation…*if* they earned it through obedience and service to him.

Regardless, everything had a soul.

Except demons and imps, which were born of Hell. Lucifer's creations.

And every soul had to be reaped, including the monsters. Each species had their own reapers—one or thousands, depending on their population. And each reaper had his or her own territory.

He liked Meridian because there was less reaper political drama here than…well most everywhere else he had ever worked. He deserved the rest. But the past few weeks had been anything but calm and restful… And now Kylen was back again.

He had stayed away longer than usual this time. Deacon had almost suspected his death, and wouldn't that have been a relief after all these years. Especially if it wasn't by his own hand.

But he was certain he would have known. Sharing energy formed a connection over time, and throughout the years Deacon and Kylen had taken many opportunities to heal and sustain each other with their light. Their connection was strong enough that if Kylen had passed, Deacon would have felt the loss. As long as Kylen had his soul, no matter how black it had become, Deacon would be linked to him even if he didn't know exactly where the reaper was.

He rose to pace around the small hospital room, his anxiety over Kylen's whereabouts growing. Kylen's appearance dragged up memories better left alone. Memories like the battle in Kosovo.

And Kara …

Deacon, Kylen and Kara had grown up together and graduated from the same training class in 1833. Deacon and Kylen had always been competitive with each other, and with Kara, their competitiveness switched to hyperdrive. They'd both vied for her attention, but as soon as it became clear which way the wind was blowing, Deacon backed off. Still, his feelings hadn't changed.

Kylen and Kara had spent many good years together. Hell, the three of them had. But when they were pulled to that battlefield in Kosovo, everything changed. More than thirty thousand dead in a less than a month. It had taken nearly a fourth of that many reapers and a handful of valkyries, including Kara, reaping around the clock to take care of the souls of the departed.

And when Kara died on that battlefield, Kylen's and Deacon's lives were changed forever ...

A steady, high-pitched beep rang out in Deacon's ears, shaking him from his reflections and snapping his attention back to the task at hand. Hospital staff hurried into the room, administering various treatments on the woman, but Deacon watched as her soul floated up from the shell of her body and reformed beside the bed.

He rose and walked over to collect her, unseen by the nurses who bustled by him.

Hers would be the first of many souls collected on this long, long day.

* * *

Ruth drove west toward town, trying not to process or analyze things too closely. Even with the loud driving beat of AC/DC blasting through her speakers, it was impossible not to replay her recent experiences in her mind.

Huntsbury was a small-town suburb of Meridian, about twenty-five miles away, with a population hovering near five thousand. She could accomplish nearly everything she needed to there.

Her first stop was at the funeral home to sign the

paperwork she'd arranged over the phone with the hospital before all this reaper craziness had ensued. Since her mother had already made all of the arrangements, and had opted not to have a graveside service, there wasn't much else to do in the short term. Her mother would be in the ground the day after Memorial Day.

That mission completed, she headed to the grocery store.

Though she ordered pretty much everything else over the internet, she had yet to figure out how to do her grocery shopping online in a way that wasn't cost prohibitive. The last thing she felt like dealing with right now were uncomfortable auras…and God forbid if she saw a white one. Now that she knew she was supposed to do something about that, she'd feel compelled to help in some way. Too bad, she wasn't sure exactly how. But she was determined that this would go smoothly. No eye contact, no awkward conversations with well-meaning locals who knew about her recent loss. In. Out. No problem.

She played that mantra through her brain on repeat as she pushed a cart in from the parking lot toward the store. She decided to start in the produce section because even though she was more than willing to get the things Deacon had suggested, she also didn't want to throw her diet to hell just yet.

Picking out some nice strawberries, grapes and bananas for good measure, she tossed in lettuce, hothouse tomatoes and avocados as a pure act of rebellion. She never bought avocados because they were so high fat, but hey, a girl had to live a little.

Very little, she thought. She was pathetic.

Making her way around to the meat counter, she considered some steaks for grilling. Out of the corner of her eye, she caught a glimpse of something odd through the glass window leading into the cold cutting room of the butcher shop. The butcher was covered in blood, which might have been expected, but all of the skin on his face, neck and hands was rotting off in black fleshy chunks. His cheekbones protruded through in shiny white contrast.

How the three ladies who were perusing the chops and pork butts weren't running screaming down the aisle in a state of terror, she had no idea. As he discussed the merits of different meat cuts with them, an especially loose bit of flesh dangled from his jaw, flopping to and fro. Ruth almost lost her stomach all over the display case. As she backed away, the creature looked straight at her and took a step toward the glass, as if he was maybe going to speak to her.

She scurried off to the dairy for milk before the T-bone lady released him from her barrage of demands. Since he didn't seem to be following her, Ruth hoofed it up and down the aisles, tossing things into her basket in haste, forgetting to consult her list. Her heart wasn't in it anymore.

By the time she got to the checkout, she thought her heart might beat out of her chest. She was pretty sure it had to sound like "The Tell-Tale Heart" to everyone in her immediate proximity. Other than the sweat breaking out across her back and forehead and the shaky hand that swiped her ATM card through the scanner, she tried not to draw too much attention to herself.

She declined the grocery boy's help and hustled her purchases to the car by herself. Shaken, she threw everything into the trunk and slammed it down. She debated the merits of heading home versus finishing her errands as she locked herself into her car. She wanted so badly to forget all of this…to just go home and get under the covers until Deacon came back. But no, this was her new reality, and she needed to be brave. Steeling herself, she started the engine and headed over to the phone company to see about getting her DSL hooked up.

Rummaging with one hand as she drove, she dug the silver knife out of her backpack and moved it to her jacket pocket. It was too warm for a jacket, but the monstrous butcher had shaken her sunny-day confidence. If she couldn't trust her butcher to be human, whom could she trust? She was definitely asking Deacon what the heck that thing was when she saw him next.

ComTel was five minutes across town, but it was almost noon, and she knew they would shut down for lunch. Her own stomach growled loudly. Deacon hadn't been kidding about the food thing. Her appetite was on hyperdrive. So not appropriate under the circumstances.

After pulling in under the little awning at a nearby drive-up burger joint, she called in her order: two extra-long chili cheese dogs with double-cheese-covered tots. Comfort food was what she needed. She finished it all off in a matter of minutes, licking the cheese from the wrapper while contemplating busting into the groceries in the trunk.

That was when she remembered that in her haste to leave the grocery store, it had totally slipped her mind to buy ice for her cooler. That was one rule about living in the country that she had almost forgotten: always carry a cooler for cold groceries.

She gathered up her trash and left it on the little tray by the intercom before pulling across the street to Stop & Go to buy a bag of ice. Sliding her key into the trunk latch, she raised the lid and set the ice inside the trunk bed. She scrambled through her random packed groceries. The bagger boy had flung her purchases into the paper bags without any organization. She sorted out the cold items, stuffing them into the cooler. As she emptied the ice from the bag over them, a chill ran up her spine that had nothing to do with her task. She whipped around to find Kylen standing behind her in the parking lot.

She dropped the ice bag and slammed the cooler lid shut. Taking a quick look around the busy lot to see if anyone might be able to come to her rescue, she debated between fight or flight once again as she backed up against the Lincoln. She slid one hand into her shorts pocket, fisting her car keys in the other.

"Busy day?" Kylen asked, grinning. "Where's your keeper?"

"What are you?" she asked, trying to keep the stutter of her heart from her voice. She didn't see any point in beating around the bush.

"Well that's a little rude, isn't it?" he asked, closing the gap between them. "A customer, of course. Ask anyone here …"

He looked human, but his eyes gave him away…and there was something more, something intangible. But maybe she was the only one who could see that?

That was the question. Since no one was screaming or running in terror, he probably looked nondescript to everyone else, like another customer in the lot. She eased around to the driver's side, pushing the trunk closed on her way.

"What's your hurry? We just got started."

"I don't want any trouble, Kylen." Nervous, she scanned the parking lot again for a possible ally. "I have cold stuff in the trunk and errands to run. If you want Deacon, I'm sure you know how to find him."

"You know my name? How sweet. Then I guess Deacon's told you about me?" He eased up closer and cocked his head at an odd angle that made his eyes look even creepier…if that were even possible.

"I heard him call you by your name when we were in…down…below," she said, unable to call it what it was: Purgatory.

He was right in her face now. Uncomfortable and scared, she palmed the knife in her jacket pocket, wondering when and whether she should show it or use it. Kylen slid a dry hand down the side of her cheek and around the back of her neck, pulling her closer to his face. She stiffened and vacillated between stabbing him through her jacket pocket and screaming.

He was so close. She could hurt him at least. Screaming might also be effective, but either of those options would lead to lots of questions, possibly a confrontation with the police, and the rest of the day would be toast. Besides, she had no explanation that would not land her under "observation" for several hours, if not longer.

She released the knife. Instead, she slid her hand into her pants pocket and extracted a handful of salt, hurling it directly into his eyes. He cursed and bellowed like a wounded animal, clawing at his face. She pushed him hard, and he stumbled far enough backward that she was able to get the Lincoln's big-ass door open and scramble inside. Slamming the door shut, she popped the electric locks. She turned the motor over, slammed the car into Reverse and peeled out of the parking lot and onto Main Street.

ComTel was going to have to wait. She was done. Heading home, she wondered if Kylen had a car or if he could travel like Deacon. One thing was comforting. He probably didn't know where she lived, or he would already have come by. She hoped his eyes wouldn't work too well for a while. That much salt in a normal person's eyes wouldn't feel all that great, and he was so not normal. In fact, he had seemed particularly averse to it.

Her hands trembled as she gripped the steering wheel and tried to keep from pressing the gas pedal all the way to the floor. She'd had enough fun for one day. She had food, snacks, coffee, the Meridian and Huntsbury papers, and an entertainment magazine...not that she read that trash.

CHAPTER TEN

It was after 1:30 p.m. when she got home. The front page of the Huntsbury paper indicated that sunset would be at 8:02 p.m. It was going to be a long afternoon. She didn't know if Deacon had meant that he'd be back after dark or at sunset. Either way, she seriously wished for a giant intimidating pet dog to escort her in and out of the house while she unloaded her groceries. Nervous, she worked quickly. Her errands in town were far from complete, but the encounters with the butcher and Kylen had snuffed out her fragile tolerance for public contact of any kind, human or otherwise.

Unloading her grocery bags into yet another pile on her kitchen table, she locked the doors, then set about the task of salting the house even before she put away her cold stuff. She didn't feel up to walking down the stairs and into the dark, dirt-floored cellar, so she opted to salt the doorway at the top of the stairs. If anything tried to get in through the tiny window down there, it would hopefully stop at the top of the stairs.

Ruth wished for the umpteenth time that the DSL

was hooked up. That should have been her first stop instead of her third. Oh, how she would have loved to look "salt barriers" up on Google for a second opinion. Even *one* more source would have made her feel better about its effectiveness. Of course, it had incapacitated Kylen for long enough for her to get away, but she wasn't so confident that it would stop him from walking into her house. Some real-world evidence of its success would have made her more of a believer. There were plenty of people on the internet message boards who would have been more than happy to share their stories, good and bad.

When she finished salting the last window, she mumbled a sloppy prayer, hoping it wasn't too little, too late. She hadn't prayed since before her father died.

She knew her father had wanted her to grow up in the church. She remembered enjoying it when she was small, and they were a real family. But after her father's death, her mother had refused to bring her back to church. God had never again been mentioned in their house. It was as if her mother had thought they were cursed because of Ruth's abilities. After what she'd seen over the past couple of days, it seemed a lot more likely that if *those* things existed, God probably did, too.

She did a quick final walk through the house to make sure she hadn't missed anything. The house had what could have been a cozy front living area with a fireplace and two front windows that looked out on a good-sized covered porch. The three bedrooms were off to the right side of the living area. The master bedroom and bath had of course been her mother's. The second bedroom was hers, and it was also connected to a small bathroom. The third and smallest bedroom had become the junk room. She hadn't even had time to change the sheets, let alone go through any of her mother's personal effects. Later, she would box up the clothes and take them to the Goodwill in Meridian.

The living area opened into an eat-in kitchen where a small half wall somewhat divided the room. The dining area sat to the left and the kitchen to the right. Both sides had small windows, one behind the tiny kitchen table and the other over the kitchen sink. The kitchen led into the back mudroom area, where the washer and dryer were kept, and out to the back door.

Another door in the laundry room led down to the basement and root cellar. She was pretty sure she would take her chances with a tornado before she would ever take refuge down there. Unfortunately, the fuse box was in the cellar... She hoped those fuses lasted forever.

The house itself sat three quarters of a mile from the main gravel road at the back of the wooded property. The driveway was long and overgrown enough that very few people wandered down it by accident.

It was secluded, which had seemed like a much nicer benefit before her world had been flipped upside down.

Gathering the cooler's contents, she placed them into the fridge and freezer. She systematically put away the remaining groceries, which left her in a quandary about what to do next. There was still a long time until dark. She debated between tackling the pile of stuff she had brought back from school and making a decent dinner. Her stomach growled at the thought.

Hungry again? Already?

It grumbled even louder in answer.

Decision made, she opted for food and went about putting together a killer lasagna thanks to one of her few on-campus classes, Culinary 104. It wouldn't be ready for an hour or two, so she and Deacon could have dinner together. Besides, it was always better after it sat for a while and was reheated. She snacked on cheese while she worked. Nothing said comfort food like pasta, meat and cheese. She even had garlic bread, which, under the circumstances, she was going to consider a potential weapon, as well.

The occult had never been a topic of interest to her—she'd had her hands full of enough weirdness given her ability—so she only had the most rudimentary ideas about all things paranormal. What she did know, or *thought* she knew, came from bits and pieces she'd read in the numerous literary classes she had taken over the years. She'd kept every textbook she had ever used, including all of her Norton Anthologies. There were stories and poems about the occult sprinkled through every time period the anthologies covered. Unfortunately, the short stories or poems were the only works offered in their entirety. All of the other entries were selected snapshots of much larger works. Most students, including her, had not read very many of those works in their entirety.

She scanned through her mental card catalog, trying to remember anything that might be relevant, as she finished assembling the lasagna. Distracted by the pull of the anthologies in a pile on the floor, the stories began to feel less and less like fiction. One in particular nagged at her, Dante's *The Divine Comedy.* The angel Rashnu had mentioned Dante... Had he planted that seed on purpose? She had read small bits of all three sections—*Inferno, Purgatorio,* and *Paradiso*—in the past, and she had the feeling that Dante would have much more to offer on the subject than Wordsworth or Whitman.

If only my DSL worked ...

Ruth set the timer on the oven and walked into the living room, surveying the mess. Deciding to tackle the "pile" of her belongings and then her mother's room, she got to work. Her mother's bed was much better than the one in her room, and once she got settled into the master bedroom, she knew she'd feel better. In fact, she *already* felt better. As her fear subsided, she could almost pretend that the events of the morning had all been in her imagination… almost.

She spent the rest of the afternoon working on her two giant projects, getting so involved in them that she forgot to worry. The buzzer rang, indicating her lasagna was finished, and she took it out to cool before stuffing it into her now overflowing fridge. It was nice to have food in the house, and she looked forward to digging into the lasagna when Deacon made it back.

Making good progress on the house, she fitted clean sheets onto her mother's bed.

My bed.

Tonight, she would sleep there and move forward.

Exhausted and disgusted by the idea of cleaning one more thing, she slumped down on the couch around 6:00 p.m. and decided to try to rest a little before Deacon got back. Reaching for a book from the pile, she tried to read, but felt her eyelids grow heavy three pages in.

CHAPTER ELEVEN

Deacon flashed into Purgatory, exhausted and starving. He'd been ferrying souls in since early in the morning, and this place was a freakin' zoo now. As he purged his twenty-first soul, he breathed a well-earned sigh of relief. Somehow, he had managed to catch up, but the day hadn't been without its challenges. Two souls had been missing. Poached.

He had a pretty good idea who was responsible. Kylen.

What was even more disturbing was that he hadn't encountered him all day. Where was he? When Kylen had shown up in the past, he hadn't missed an opportunity to taunt Deacon, particularly when Deacon was on the job. Today, he had stayed far away. The more he worried the problem over in his mind, the more he felt that it was vital for him to be with Ruth and to train her. She was far too vulnerable now that life as usual was over for her.

She should have been trained from the moment her ability to read auras had emerged. Every reaper he knew had at least one reaper parent who had passed down the gift. Ruth was an apparent anomaly. Neither her mother nor her father had been reapers. He should know. He'd now reaped them both in the course of two days. Puzzling.

Something was off about the whole situation. He hadn't mentioned it to Ruth, who had more than enough on her plate. He would have to figure it out on his own, and the sooner the better. Ignorance made you weak and vulnerable to attack. The thought of Ruth being attacked made him want to punch something.

He would do everything in his power to protect her, and if need be, he'd take her wherever he went from now on to keep her safe. A surge of possessiveness coursed through him. He hadn't felt this way about a woman in a long time. Nearly a hundred years to be exact. It was disconcerting. What was she doing at this very moment? Was she safe? Had Kylen been bothering her? Fear and guilt squirmed into the back of his mind as he made his way through the sea of reapers to the stone monolith portal.

Deacon's emotions were mixed. He'd already failed one woman he cared about. Kara. He hadn't been able to protect her. His heart couldn't afford for history to repeat itself. After a brief conversation earlier in the day, Nate, his witch friend, had agreed to come over to Ruth's house tonight to consecrate it. Deacon had kept the reasons to himself...he had always operated on a need-to-know basis with Nate.

Life, or at least the transportation problem, would get a little less complicated after Ruth's house was a stop on the consecrated subway. Or so he hoped. When he placed his hand on the portal, he felt the familiar tug as the consecrated subway sucked him in and spun him toward Good Springs Cemetery.

He materialized in the middle of the grounds and

watched the sun set as he made his way along the two miles of gravel road leading to Ruth's house.

* * *

Ruth's eyes sprang open to a clattering racket as something crashed down her chimney, landing on the hearth in front of her in a burst of sooty dust. It took her eyes a few seconds to connect with her brain and formulate a response to the slimiest, foulest-smelling toadlike creature she could ever have imagined. The thing rose from the ashes to its full height of two feet, shook itself like a wet dog, and bared an impressive and terrifying array of needle-pointed, three-inch-long teeth. Its hissing broke Ruth from her paralyzed stupor. She lunged and snatched the iron poker off the face of the fireplace.

Without another thought, she sprang forward and speared the beast through its middle.

It let out a little "humpf," squatted and dissolved into a smoking pile of gooey, chunky debris on her stone hearth. Ruth's hands and legs trembled so violently she marveled that she was still vertical.

What the hell? Salt!

She had forgotten about the chimney and fireplace. On rubbery legs, she stumbled to the kitchen and snatched up the box of salt, giving the entire hearth a good dousing. The remainder she poured directly on the still-steaming blob for good measure. She'd seen enough movies to know that dead wasn't always dead.

Her heart felt as if it was going to break loose from its anchors and go its own way. When a strong noxious odor wafted up from the thing's remains, she gagged but willed herself not to vomit.

One mess to clean up is more than enough.

As she watched the blob on the hearth for any signs

of life, she realized that the sun had set, and the house was bathed in twilight. Reaching for the lamp on the end table, she turned it on along with every other light she could reach, all without taking her eyes off the blob.

Covered in sticky goo, the poker trembled in her hand. She peeked at the clock: 8:30 p.m.

She prayed Deacon would show up sooner rather than later because she wasn't sure how many more surprises she could take in one day.

After twenty agonizingly slow minutes, she caught a glimpse of movement along the driveway. Relieved to see that it was Deacon, she resisted the urge to run to him. Sidestepping the still-smoldering black ooze, she unlocked the front door and waited impatiently, keeping her eyes glued to the blob.

She opened the door, sparing Deacon a sideways glance and a lackluster greeting, "Hey."

"Hey. Sorry it's taken so long. Can you break the salt line so I can come through?"

So it keeps him out, too? Interesting.

She scuffed a foot through the salt, breaking the line.

He took a deep breath, looked Ruth up and down, and was through the door in a heartbeat. Something about her expression must have tipped him off because he immediately scanned the room, his eyes fierce.

"What the hell?" he asked, as he took in the hearth.

"You tell me."

She was ready for some explanations...and backup. All of her bravery had been exhausted for the day. He reached for the poker she hadn't realized she was still clutching in her hand. A huge burden lifted from her as she released it.

"Did you do that? With this?" He pointed the makeshift weapon toward the blob on the hearth.

She hoped the blob hadn't been a friend of his but quickly decided that if it had been, and he hadn't wanted it dead, he should have warned her. Specifically.

"Yes," she said, her voice shaking.

He stared hard at her, the corners of his mouth and eyes wrinkling into concerned lines.

"Are you okay?" he asked, inspecting her with clinical attention. "Did any of it get on you?"

"No, none of it got on me. Is it dead?" she asked, trying to still her trembling limbs.

Deacon walked over and stabbed at the gelatinous pile with the poker. "Oh, yeah. It's more than dead. You salted it *after* I'm guessing?"

"Yes," she said, her voice faltering. "I forgot to salt the hearth. I didn't think of the chimney. I fell asleep on the couch and woke up when that thing slid down and…plopped out."

Deacon smiled. He looked as if he was on the verge of chuckling, but she thought better of him when he didn't. She didn't find any of this funny. At all.

"What the hell is it, and how do I clean it up?"

"It's an imp," Deacon said incredulously. "A demon's spy. Any idea how it found you?"

She considered that.

"It must have followed me home from Huntsbury this morning. It was not a good day."

"What happened?"

"Can we get rid of that first?" she asked, pointing to the blob.

"Sure." Deacon laid the poker on the hearth and walked to the back porch, returning with a bucket and dust pan. He grabbed bleach and a scrub brush on the way.

She was happy to sit back and let him work. In fact, she had never been so happy to see another person in her entire life. Relaxing a bit, she felt the tears well up in her eyes. She let out a little sniffle.

"Sorry," she said, rubbing her face on her sleeve.

"Don't be sorry. You did a great job here. It's not every day someone sends an imp after you," he said, poking at the pile.

Ruth shook her head in disbelief.

"The iron poker was just right, Ruth," he continued. "And the salt finished the job. Still... I'm sorry that you had to deal with this alone, without me here to help you."

"That imp wasn't the only thing I saw today," she said as Deacon scooped up the last of the goo. He scraped and wiped and bleached until the hearth was spic and span, a dark wet stain the only evidence of her odd encounter. Finishing up, he dried the hearth with a towel, which she swore to herself that she would never, ever use again. He washed and dried his hands, then returned to sit beside her.

"What else did you see today, Ruth?" he asked, reaching out and palming her cheek. She snuggled into his touch and he pulled her close, burying his face in her hair.

She felt him breathe in deeply, then freeze.

He jerked back from her, his hands gripping her upper arms a little too tightly. "You smell like demon, Ruth. What touched you?"

"K-Kylen," she stuttered. "I saw Kylen today. *He* grabbed me."

Deacon closed his eyes. Even though she couldn't see his aura, Ruth knew he was furious. She couldn't decide whether the anger was directed at her or Kylen. When his eyes opened, he concentrated his stare at Ruth. Loosening his grip on her arms, he started to gently stroke her arms and shoulders.

"Thank God you're okay." He pulled her in close. Ruth was confused. He hugged her so tightly it squeezed the air from her lungs, but this was still much nicer than thirty-seconds-ago Deacon.

Snuggling his face back against her neck, he brushed his lips up and down the veins of her throat, sending goose bumps over her skin. She trembled and felt her body go soft and pliant. He ran his hand up and behind her neck, snaking his other arm around her waist, and crushed her into him. She let out a little moan of pleasure, the green light for him because he was all hands and lips after that.

Easing her back against the couch, he settled over her. She squirmed beneath his weight, luxuriating in the sensation, but wanting more of him. Clutching his back, she slipped her hands beneath his T-shirt to touch his hot, smooth skin. She burned for him to do the same to her.

Rising, he pulled his shirt off over his head, allowing more contact. Her palms slid up and over his chest. She'd wanted to do that ever since she'd caught him sleeping on her couch this morning.

This morning?

She pushed the crazy memories of the day's events out of her brain. She wanted to feel the here and now. Nothing else.

Deacon closed his eyes as she stroked her palms over his ribs, caressing his beautiful chest. Gazing down at her, his dark hair fell softly into his face. She pushed it back, and he turned his cheek into her hand.

As he sat astraddle her, he glided his hands under her shirt and over her bra, cupping her breasts. She arched up into him, begging him for more contact. No one had ever touched her like he was doing. Her body was on autopilot, and she was no longer in control of her faculties or inhibitions.

He pulled the tail of her T-shirt, and she raised herself enough to help him get it over her head. He undid the front hook on her bra, and her breasts sprang free. His hot, smooth palms slid over each one—her nipples were hard as buttons.

When his mouth closed around her nipple, she nearly unhinged. She was still a virgin thanks to her disastrous romantic forays thus far, but she was embarrassed to let him know.

All she could see in Deacon was need and desire— no aura. It was wonderful. Except she wasn't prepared. She wasn't on the pill because she had no need to be, and she had no other protection if things progressed. As Deacon took her breast and nipple into his warm, wet mouth and ran a finger under the waistband of her jean shorts, she really wanted things to advance. Her heart throbbed in her ears as the heat of his hands soaked into her skin.

Not sure how far it was polite to let things go without bringing it up, she was lost between wanting to explain and needing to forge ahead, consequences be damned. Deacon must have felt her hesitate. He cradled her face between his hands and studied her. "What's wrong?"

"Nothing," she lied. "I love it. I want you. I do. So. Much. I've just...never done this before. I'm...not prepared."

"You've never made out on a couch before?" he asked skeptically.

"I've been around all the bases, just not to home," she said, instantly regretting her admission. "Please don't stop."

He considered her for what felt like forever, then settled down on top of her, skin to skin, his face buried in her neck and chest. "Damn," he exhaled.

She didn't know if that was a *good* damn or a *bad* damn. Her heart dropped in her chest, and she was sure she'd killed the moment. His weight crushed her into the couch cushions. She loved it. She felt protected. Safe.

He raised his face to hers. "Your first time isn't going to be on a couch with an imp stain still in sight." Disappointment filled her.

Deacon rose, extending his hand to her, and pulled her to her feet. Hooking her bra back gently, he brushed his hands along the sides of her breasts, and then reached for her shirt. He re-dressed her and drew her against him.

"This isn't finished," he breathed in her ear. "Postponed."

She nodded a yes, but felt too teary to voice it.

"My witch friend will be here in an hour." He inhaled deeply and smiled. "Is that *lasagna* I smell under all of that sulfur and bleach?"

She nodded again. "I'll warm it up for you."

"No, I'll do it. You sit. Talk. Tell me what happened today. All of it. In great detail."

As Deacon puttered around her fridge and kitchen, Ruth somehow managed to get herself back under some semblance of control.

He retrieved the lasagna and set it on the table to cut and serve.

"This isn't a frozen lasagna?" he asked, pointing to the dish with a spatula. "You made this? From scratch?"

"Yeah. I was hungry for some comfort food, not crap."

He looked from the lasagna to Ruth and back.

"Don't you like lasagna?" she asked, unsure of his reaction. "There's no spinach in it or anything. Wait, you like meat, right? You're not a vegetarian or anything? Are you allergic to garlic? Or, you know, repelled by it?" she stammered, getting upset again.

Well, if he doesn't want it, then it will be the last meal he ever eats in this house.

"No, it's not that," he said, staring down at it as if it was a saucy, cheesy piece of heaven. "No one has ever cooked anything for me. Not homemade anyway.

Restaurants don't count."

He cut off two huge chunks and slid them onto the plates and then into the microwave.

"Oh," she said, confused. "You mean...ever? How can that be?"

"The same way you can still be a virgin," he said, with a sly smile. "The opportunity never presented itself, I guess. There aren't many opportunities for home-cooked meals in this line of work...or least there haven't been."

Ruth relayed the account of her day, laying out all the details, including the barbarous butcher, before working up to Kylen and the imp. He listened intently all the while.

"You did a good job with the salt," he said, taking the plates from the microwave. "Perfect. I should have mentioned the chimney. It was an easy rookie mistake to make. Tell me again what Kylen said to you...word for word," he commanded, setting a hot dish before her.

"Nothing really. I think he was just trying to scare me. Which he did... What would he want with me? You said the imp was a demon spy? What about the butcher? And Kylen?"

"How about one question at a time? I'd say that the butcher was probably a boggart. Hard to say which side he's on, so it was a good thing that you got out of there fast. As for Kylen, he probably wanted to distract you so that his imp could climb under your car and lead him to you later."

"You said earlier that they spy for demons... Does that mean that Kylen's a demon?" she asked, her voice a few octaves higher than she'd intended. "What would a demon want with me?"

"Not you. It's me." Deacon brought his plate to the table. "We have history." He sat across from her and sighed in exasperation, giving his lasagna a longing look. "Kylen wasn't always a demon. He was a reaper, but now a demon inhabits his body. I don't know the demon's name—only Kylen would—and the demon can't be cast out unless its name is used in an exorcism ritual. It was his choice. I told you that some choose a darker path, and Kylen is one of those who did."

"Why would he do that? And what does he have against you? Or me?"

"It's complicated," he sighed.

Deacon took a big bite of his lasagna and closed his eyes. She hoped it wasn't in disgust. She hadn't tasted it yet, but it smelled like heaven. She took a bite herself and moaned in delight.

"You're going to have to stop doing that."

"What?" she asked, batting her lashes with mock innocence. "Eating?"

"Moaning," he said, pressing his lips into a tight line. "Or I'm going to clear this table and take you right here, pasta sauce and all."

Ruth quivered, toying with the idea of teasing him further with another moan. She didn't think there would be time for him to carry out his threat before the witch arrived. She sent him her sweetest smile.

Never had she had any sort of power over a man before. She liked it.

"Tell me what Kylen wants," she said, instantly creating a different sort of tension in him.

"Souls," Deacon said. "He's a poacher now. He steals souls when he can. If a reaper is too slow or too busy to get to one soon enough, it leaves an opportunity for him."

"What does he do with them? The souls he poaches?"

"He takes them straight to his master in Hell. Do not pass Go, do not collect two hundred dollars. Each time he bypasses Purgatory, it taints Kylen's soul. It's likely already irreparable. If his soul becomes too damaged, his memories will be eradicated, and he will be lost to the demon who possesses him. Most demons can't ride a body that long, but since Kylen is a reaper, he's a much sturdier host. This one's had Kylen…for a while."

"How long?"

"Nearly a hundred years," Deacon said tightly.

Ruth scooted her food around on her plate. She was still hungry but she couldn't seem to swallow anymore. It made no sense to her why someone would *choose* to do what Kylen had done. He knew the consequences better than most. He wasn't some wannabe dark arts practitioner—he was a freakin' reaper. From what Ruth had seen so far, that was a formidable occupation.

"If he knew the consequences, what could have convinced him to do it?"

"Kylen made a deal for a soul. There was a woman, a valkyrie… Kara. We grew up together, and we were all friends. Kara was exceptional. We knew she was different from the beginning. She was beautiful and fierce and stronger than the both of us. Strong enough to become a valkyrie. Kylen and I had both loved her since we were kids, and we fought over her more than once, but she loved Kylen more. They were together for seventy years, and then she was murdered on a battlefield by a demon poacher. Kylen made a deal for her soul. As soon as he delivered her soul safely to Purgatory, he turned himself over to the demon. Otherwise, the demon would have taken her to Hell, and once your soul has been delivered to the pit, there's no upward advancement. It's the demon who rides him now."

Ruth didn't know what to say to that, but she was worried. Kylen had sent an imp after her today. She wasn't keen on meeting a similar fate as the valkyrie, and she was pretty sure she was nowhere near as fierce.

"The demon is a trickster, Ruth. He likes chaos and turmoil and pain. He thrives on it. He has access to all of Kylen's memories. Every decade or so he shows up to torment me. When he saw the two of us together in Purgatory, he recognized an opportunity to stir things up. He may have even seen a chance to claim a new body. He also knows that the more distracted I am, the more souls he can poach from my territory. That's why I had to leave you today—I had to work, and I hoped that I could draw him away from you at the same time. I'm sorry, Ruth...about all of this."

A chill crept into her chest and squeezed her heart. Being away from Deacon seemed dangerous now, but being with him might be just as bad. She felt as if she had a target painted on her back.

"How did he know where to find me?"

"I don't know. He and I have a bond, so maybe he was somehow able to trace the energy I shared with you. Or it could be that he's accumulated enough spies to cover more territory. Don't worry. After tonight, he won't be able to get to you again. We're going to make sure of it. We were very lucky today. I would have given anything to see the look on his face when you salted him." He chuckled. "I'll bet he wasn't counting on that."

"No, he seemed pretty surprised."

Deacon smiled and scraped his plate clean. "So you have the CliffsNotes history of my life. What about you, Ruth? What's your story?"

Ruth pushed her plate away and sighed. She had no desire to revisit her life story. At least not all the painful little details. But if Deacon could paint with broad strokes, so could she.

"You already know the big things. My father died when I was twelve. That was the breaking point for me and my mother. They'd wanted children very much and tried for years. When nothing happened, and they kept growing older, they finally decided to adopt through the Catholic Church in St. Louis. They got me as an infant."

"Well, that explains the anomaly."

"What do you mean?"

"A reaper's gifts are genetic. At least one of your parents would have needed to pass those traits along to you. After reaping both of them, I knew that neither your father nor your mother had the gifts. Have you ever tried to track down your biological parents?"

"Not seriously. I've thought about it, but my relationship with my mother has been...well, tense...since my father died. I guess I didn't want to make things worse. Now that she's passed and all this is happening? Yeah, I'd love to know. But if they are both reapers, how will I ever find them?"

"That will be a bridge we'll have to cross later. I think we have enough on our plates for now. It's definitely worth pursuing, though." Ruth's mind spun with the possibility of tracking down her biological parents.

As Deacon scooped up a second piece of lasagna onto his plate, headlights bounced down the driveway.

CHAPTER TWELVE

The witch was not at all what Ruth had expected. She'd known he was a man, but she'd been picturing some long-haired, trench-coated 1970s character with amulets around his neck. The man on the other side of her front door was dressed in soft worn jeans and a light gray Affliction shirt, and tribal tattoos covered the surface area of both of his ridiculously muscled biceps. Not that she noticed things like that.

His dark, salon-cut hair was parted at an angle, and a nice near-midnight shadow crossed his jaw. She was pretty sure that the backpack slung over one of his shoulders wouldn't be able to make it across the other without him looking like a turtle with a too-small shell. He was built like a WWE wrestler.

Peering down the driveway, she was relieved to see a Honda parked there instead of a broom with headlights. Sure, that was probably prejudiced, but so far she was learning that all myths had a nugget of truth to them. Back in the day, she was willing to bet that witches had totally rocked the robe and broom scene.

She invited him in.

"Nate, thanks for coming." Deacon reached out to shake his hand. "This is Ruth."

"Ruth, nice to meet you." Nate extended his hand, but she hesitated. He had an aura. Deacon was here, so she felt safe enough, but she still didn't want to get all touchy-feely with strangers who had auras. Still, she was happy to see that he wasn't a reaper or any of the other strange creepy crawlies to which she'd been exposed in the recent past. She didn't lump Deacon into the creepy crawly category even though he didn't have a light and couldn't cross the salt barrier. She decided to grant him special dispensation.

Nate took the hint and backed off.

"Deacon tells me you need the house consecrated. Are you looking to bury some bodies out here, or do you need protection?" Nate asked, getting right to the point.

She glanced at Deacon for help. Hell, she hadn't even learned the secret handshake yet, and she had no clue how "in the know" Nate was. This was more Deacon's rodeo than it was hers.

"Protection," Deacon chimed in. "From evil spirits. It's possible that this place is haunted." Ruth threw a sideways glance at Deacon. She was pretty sure he was just making up a cover story to keep the reality of the situation from Nate.

"Smells like sulfur in here all right," Nate offered. "Something has been here. Today."

"That's why I called you."

"Same ritual as your place, I'm assuming?"

"Yes."

"Okay, then. It's eleven-thirty now. I'm going to cleanse and purify the house first, and then we'll raise the power and cast the circle at midnight."

* * *

Nate lit a bundle of dried herbs, letting them burn for a few moments before blowing out the flames.

As the bundle smoked, the aroma of sage, lavender and thyme filled the small house. Nate walked through the rooms, systematically wafting the smoke up into the corners, across the walls, and over the doors and windows. He concentrated on the scent and visualized cleansing the place of unwelcome spirits. Something supernatural had been here, and recently.

Nate's adoptive parents were a powerful Wiccan couple, and they had taught him everything they knew. But before finding his home with them, he'd spent his first five years in and out of various foster homes.

He wasn't a bad kid, but something strange had happened at each of the dozen families he'd lived with prior to his adoption, frightening his foster parents badly enough to send him back to the system.

He didn't even remember most of these "instances" but a few were crystal clear. The final straw had come when he'd somehow transported himself to a cemetery one night.

Sent to his room as a punishment for refusing to eat some random and disgusting food on his plate, he'd sat on his bed, wishing himself gone. He didn't have anywhere specific in mind because he hadn't been anywhere of note. He just wanted away from the house…and the family.

When he first landed in the cemetery, he'd thought he was in a very vivid dream. He couldn't believe it and had no idea how it had happened…or where he was. Nothing was familiar, and the night was pitch-black with just a shadow of the new moon peeking out. He sat down on the cold ground. Huddling himself into a pile, he scooted back against a headstone, wrapping his arms around his bent knees. His thin pajamas were no relief against the cold October night, and his bare feet dug into the ground as he rocked his body from side to side, wishing again with all he had in him to be back at the house. Back in his room to be exact.

And then...he was.

The whole experience had lasted no more than twenty minutes. Still, his foster mother had already discovered him missing and phoned the police. When he appeared back in his empty room twenty minutes later, the police had just arrived at the house. His foster parents were surprised and embarrassed to find him sitting on his bed when they let the officers into his room to investigate.

Nate had been unable to stop the trembling in his limbs as he rambled incoherently about where he'd been. The police took notice of his dirty feet and disheveled appearance and filled out their reports. Suspecting domestic abuse by the foster parents, they removed him from the home that night, taking him straight to a juvenile facility until he could be placed...again.

The police asked him many questions that night, none of which he could remember now. He'd never mentioned that trip to the cemetery again. To anyone. Why all of this was flooding through his mind as he cleansed the house, he had no idea. Maybe the sage was purging his own bad juju.

That and something was off about Deacon, which made him uneasy. He still hadn't been able to pin down what it was about the guy that made him squirm and trust him at the same time. He was more than a witch, no doubt about it, but Nate couldn't figure out exactly what he *was*. They had more of a "don't ask, don't tell" sort of relationship.

Deacon had called on him over the years to do all manner of spells, but consecration and circumscription spells were the most common. Nate didn't know exactly what they were keeping at bay, but he was happy enough to help out when he could. Deacon paid double for not asking questions. Since he hadn't seen the guy do anything illegal or immoral, he had always been comfortable working with him even though he knew he was only getting information on a need-to-know basis.

This was the first time there had ever been anyone else with the guy, let alone a woman. His curiosity was more than piqued.

* * *

Ruth thought the scent was divine, and if nothing else, Nate's efforts were dampening the smell of bleach and sulfur. He chanted softly as he worked.

It was strange having two men in her house, but somehow she felt more relieved than worried. She thought these two could probably take care of most anything that threatened her. Probably the salt could do the rest until Nate finished his work.

Physically they were both solid and intimidating guys, and she knew from experience that Deacon had more than a couple of tricks up his sleeve. That man had some mad skills, and she was pretty certain she had seen only the beginning of what he had to offer.

While she didn't exactly feel relaxed, she felt safe, and she tried to turn off her worries.

While Nate prepped the house, Deacon stood silently in a corner, gazing out the window at the dark woods. Meanwhile, she was shuffling around the house, continuing in her efforts to get it organized. Pleased that she'd made a good- sized dent in the junk she'd brought home from school, she now had some empty boxes she could use to pack up a few of her mother's things.

It didn't take her long to fill the three small boxes in the living room alone. By the time she was finished,

Nate had also finished his cleansing and purifying ritual.

"It's time," he said, as he moved over to the spot he'd determined to be the exact center of the house. "Stand here with me, both of you. The more energy we raise, the stronger the circle of protection will be."

Ruth didn't know how much help she was going to be. The ten times she'd watched *The Craft* probably didn't count as experience with witchcraft.

"Hold hands," Nate said, reaching for them both. "We need to make a circle."

Ruth took Deacon's hand in hers, and then, after a second of hesitation, Nate's. A blush crept up her neck, which she hoped neither of them noticed. When Deacon gave her hand a squeeze, she looked over at him. He stifled a smile.

Nate took deep breaths, inhaling and exhaling several times in long draws.

"Let's envision a circle with its center here where we're standing. Imagine it extending out about two feet past the exterior of the house. Now turn that circle into a sphere surrounding the house. Both of you hold that image in your minds as we raise the power. Concentrate on it, and don't be distracted. You may feel a pull or warmth, but it won't hurt you. Don't break contact or leave our circle until I say 'Amen.'"

Ruth nodded, as did Deacon. Nate released their hands briefly to light the four candles on the floor in the center of the circle, then took them up again. She tried to clear her head. Already distracted from holding hands with two men—two *hot* men—she tried to push the novelty of the situation away and imagine the sphere. She wanted this to work. Of course she could buy a gun, but there was a pretty good chance that bullets weren't going to kill any supernatural beasties or demons. Closing her eyes, she concentrated on Nate's voice.

As he began to chant, her body started to sway,

becoming lighter and lighter. Nate's chants accelerated to a frenzied pace, and static electricity raised the hairs on her arms and crackled along her skin. She tried to hold herself together and concentrate, but her body betrayed her. If not for being tethered to two men, she feared she might float away like a child's lost parade balloon.

The cool night air brought her to consciousness. Opening her eyes, she looked down on her own physical body as she floated above it and through her roof. Surrounded by the most beautiful silvery blue aura, her house was the first nonhuman aura she had ever seen as she continued to drift away from the house and into the night.

The aura shimmered under her, both beautiful and frightening. Just as she feared she was lost for good, she was jerked back.

The next thing she knew, Deacon was on top of her, both of his hands pinning her shoulders to the floor. He glowed like a campfire.

Trying to raise her hand to touch him, she somehow manipulated the glow around him, and he flew across the living room and into the stone fireplace.

Panic flared in her chest, rolling off her in a wave of visible turquoise light. She cried out, sure that she had somehow killed him. With effort, he got to his feet and shook his head as if he was trying to unring his bell. He made his way cautiously back to her. Nate hung back, a silent but slack-jawed observer as Deacon reached down to pull her to her feet.

"What the hell was that?" Nate asked, clearly rattled.

"I guess Ruth has a lot of energy to offer," Deacon said, smiling.

"Ya think? I've cast a lot of circles, but never one with that much power. It felt…terrifying…and good."

"It's a good circle, Nate. It will hold."

"Yeah," Nate agreed, as he ran a trembling hand through his hair. "Yeah."

"Door?" Deacon asked, his attention still focused on Ruth.

"Right. Ruth, you alone can open or close the circle. You're the key, and you control the door. The only things that can enter, supernaturally speaking, have to be carried or brought in by you. They have to be touching you. Once you are back inside, the circle will close behind you. Imagine it again as a sphere, surrounding your house with light to reinforce it."

"Like a snow globe?" she asked, still shaky on her feet.

"Sure, that's as good an image as any. Visualize it as being complete and impenetrable. If you do that, as strong as your energy is...the circle of protection will be able to withstand a lot."

Deacon led her back to the couch. "When will it need to be reinforced?"

"Each time she passes into it she can reinforce it. After any known attack, you can call me, and I'll patch it up. If it fractures, I can recast it. But it feels strong, maybe the strongest I've ever experienced. You'll be safe against all supernatural trespassers... Now humans are another story. It won't stop your run-of-the-mill human for shit." Nate smiled at her. "But that's what shotguns are for."

Nate handed her a card with his cell phone number in case of a circle emergency. Ruth still wasn't sure which category Nate fell into, human or supernatural, until it came time for him to leave. When he couldn't pass out of her yard, she led him through, his hand on her shoulder. He wouldn't leave until she stepped back inside and the circle closed to his satisfaction.

Now his was a worthwhile and useful talent.

She watched his taillights disappear down the drive

and through the trees. Carrying the card back into the house, she stuck it onto the fridge with a piece of tape. "Well, that was exciting," she said. It was 2:36 a.m., and she was exhausted and wired at the same time.

* * *

Deacon walked the perimeter of the house one last time, pausing to peer out each window and scan the edge of the dark woods. The fat moon shone bright and clear, illuminating the unkempt yard. He could see as far as the edge of the woods...beyond that was anyone's guess what might be lurking. The weeds were so high that they'd be above the sash of the window in another week.

Nate had cast a strong circle, and Ruth's surprising power had fortified it with more strength than he could have imagined. He was still shaken by how she had astrally projected. While raising the power for the circle, her soul had left her body, rising up through the ceiling and beyond. Shocked, he had acted on instinct, making contact with her body before her soul completely ripped free. His interruption had been enough to force it back into her body. Dealing with untethered souls was a tricky and dangerous business. He'd tried to reinhabit a soul once before, and it hadn't worked.

Nate had seemed oblivious to it all, and Deacon hadn't explained the full implications to Ruth. She had been close to dying. Detached from its body, an untethered soul could and would become lost in the ether, an eternal Haunt.

Most people who practiced astral projection took years to master it, learning to tether their soul to their body before projecting, and then reining it in when the time came. Ruth's projection had been accidental, the result of an overload of power coursing through her body. The energy had basically shoved her soul out.

Strong as he was, Deacon couldn't project his soul...and didn't want to. It was dangerous, and it left your body vulnerable and unprotected. Sometimes it left you dead. He could see the advantages of being able to do it, but the dangers were far greater. If Ruth had already awakened such a great gift, what might lie ahead?

Danger.

No, he'd keep her safe. What had happened to Kara would not happen to Ruth. He'd been much younger then, less than a century old. He could and would protect her from any threat...including Kylen. Once his greatest friend, Kylen's choice had turned him into an enemy. Satisfied that nothing lurked in the night, Deacon returned to the kitchen.

* * *

Ruth stared at the fridge, wondering if it would be bad to have a second dinner this late. She settled for a bowl of cereal.

"Would you like some, too?" she asked, pulling out an extra bowl.

"Sure."

Ruth poured cereal and milk into two bowls, and they carried them into the living room, eating in crunchy silence on the couch. Questions coursed through her mind. But at this point, there were too many to prioritize. She pushed them down for another day. She had no idea what had happened while they were raising the power for the circle or how exactly she'd found herself floating above her house, but it both terrified and empowered her. She wondered if it could ever happen again. Or what would have happened if Deacon hadn't been there to snap her back out of it. Would she have floated away into the black night, never to return?

How amazing! How terrifying.

"What was that?" Deacon asked, pointing to the empty bowl in his hands.

"Lucky Charms," she said. She didn't mention that it was one of her guilty pleasures...that and Cookie Crisp. Grown-ups most certainly did not eat Lucky Charms and Cookie Crisp. They ate things like granola and bran and Special K, but she was all about the comfort food.

"Lucky Charms? Huh."

He acted as if it was the first he'd ever heard of Lucky Charms. Was it possible that he was even more out of the loop than she was? Lucky Charms was the breakfast of champions...or something like that. Of course, she had a feeling that his expertise might lie in more important areas than sugary breakfast cereals. In fact, she was beginning to realize that her future might depend upon it.

"We could use some lucky charms." He smiled.

Ruth smiled back. She was pretty sure he'd made a joke. He didn't seem like the joking type, so she appreciated the effort. He had a great smile and she had an almost irresistible urge to brush her palm across his stubble-darkened jaw.

She tightened her grip on her bowl instead, unsure what was and wasn't acceptable behavior. Her personal interactions with men hadn't done much to prepare her for someone like Deacon.

The good stuff she had learned from books, television and movies. Auras didn't show up on the big screen. She was more of a reader than a TV junkie, but over the years, she'd still managed to watch an amazing number of movies. With nothing but time on her hands—no close friends or family or job obligations—she'd filled her time with lots of indoor and solitary pursuits.

It was difficult to know which actresses or characters

to use as role models in any given situation, but she figured it was safer to play it closer to Anne Hathaway as the Princess of Genovia in *The Princess Diaries* than as Glenn Close boiling bunnies in *Fatal Attraction.* Either way, she was screwed, because she had a very limited idea of what she was doing.

She considered the man on her couch from the corner of her eye. He had sprung all manner of frightening and bizarre revelations on her in the past two days, yet she couldn't help but feel herself becoming more and more inclined to curl up onto his lap and let him have his way. And that felt surprisingly good.

Hasty. Stupid. But good.

Deacon looked over at her, studying her as if he was trying to read her mind. Which he had reassured her he could *not* do. She believed him, but she blushed anyway. Why did she have so much sudden and blind trust in this man?

"What?" he asked, his blue-green eyes sparkling.

"Nothing," she lied.

He smiled and set his bowl on the end table, then reached over for her bowl and did the same.

"Come here," he said, his voice a low purr.

She scooted closer to him, and he wound an arm around her, pulling her close. His warm, strong embrace had her heart skipping along at a gallop. He took her hand in his and held it, examining it. She eased her head back against his chest, and wished she could crawl up into his clothes and feel his skin against hers again.

He pressed his lips to the top of her head. She closed her eyes and let herself relax against him. Suddenly being vertical seemed way wrong. Scooping herself up into his lap, she tucked her head in under his chin and snuggled there.

"I saw that you cleared out your mother's room."

"Yes," she whispered.

"Can we go in there?"

Ruth knew he was asking for a lot more.

"Yes," she said to all he implied.

"Are you sure? Because if we go in there, we're not coming out until daylight."

Ruth trembled.

"Yes," she said again.

Yes, yes, yes, yes, yes.

She leaned her cheek against his chest as he rose and carried her the six steps into her new bedroom.

CHAPTER THIRTEEN

Deacon carried Ruth into the master bedroom and laid her gently down on the bed's quilted comforter.

"Don't move," he ordered gruffly.

Lighting two candles, he placed one on each side of the bed on the small oak nightstands. Thunder rumbled in the distance, and Ruth glanced out the bedroom window, where the moon was shining through a covering of clouds above the tree line. It was so late...*or early,* she thought.

Deacon stood at the edge of the bed and pulled his shirt up and over his head before letting it drop to the floor. Ruth stared. Hard. The candlelight reflected off his taut, tanned chest, and the delicate silver cross hanging from the chain around his neck. This man was amazing, no doubt about it. All she had to compare him to were the models and actors in magazines and movies, but real-life flesh and blood was better.

Way, way better.

He undid the top button of his fly and unzipped. Kicking off his shoes, he stepped out of his socks and then his jeans. Her heart raced with possibility, and all he had done was undress…and give her a promise.

We're not coming out until morning.

She wasn't sure what she was supposed to be doing, but couldn't avert her eyes from him, not even for a second, so she watched…and waited. On the one hand, she knew this situation was insane and one hundred percent foolish. On the other, who the hell cared? This was the first and only man she'd ever met who didn't have an aura. If this wasn't fate, then what the hell was it?

"Your turn," he said, crawling onto the bed to lie beside her. The thunder crashed much closer this time, and the first drops of rain hit the metal roof of the house.

Deacon reached for the bottom of her T-shirt and lifted it over her head. She had the giddy feeling of déjà vu, but this time, she was determined to keep her big mouth shut.

He dispatched with her bra, then lay down beside her, propped up on one elbow as he delicately traced a hand across her stomach and breasts, paying careful attention to each new area as he discovered it. She closed her eyes and luxuriated in his touch. Starved for contact, a wispy moan escaped her and tears welled in her eyes.

What was up with all the waterworks lately?

She was full of emotions—they spilled out in an unstoppable flood of need and frustration. She writhed on the bed, her body aching as she tried to will him closer. Faster. More. Placing his warm hand on her waist, he pulled her against his body: he was a human inferno. When their skin touched and her chest brushed his, a warmth let go inside her as she fought the urge to wrap her legs around him.

He leaned in, kissed her lips, and she abandoned herself to him. Any vestige of self-control vanished. She moaned again, and he worked the waistband of her shorts until they were loose. Sliding his hand inside them, over the top of her panties, he cupped her core and smiled down at her.

"You're wet for me," he whispered in her ear, sending a shiver down her spine. "I like that."

"Mmm" was all she managed in reply.

His palm pressed urgently against her and that small pressure alone was almost enough to break her. She wasn't so naive that she'd never experienced release before. Just never with another person.

"Oh, God," she moaned.

So much for not talking!

"If you like that…then you're gonna love this," he said, kissing his way along her stomach to the top of her shorts. "May I?"

"Yes," she said breathily. She had a vague idea of what he had in mind. But no matter what it was, she was on board.

He slid her shorts down and flung them across the room. Ruth see-sawed her legs against the comforter in anticipation and tried to sit up, eager for a better view and for more contact.

"Not yet." He kissed her mouth again until she submitted and lay back against the bed.

Hovering over her, he worked his way down her torso, trailing kisses along her ribs with agonizing precision until she pleaded for relief. Teasing her, he pinched her panties between his fingers and eased them down her legs, flinging them in the general direction of her shorts.

With his tongue, he traced a fire-hot trail beneath her belly button, and goose bumps sprang up across her flesh. His tongue was hot syrup across her skin. He palmed both her thighs and spread her open, brushing his rough cheek against the inside of her legs.

"Beautiful."

Ruth blushed. She was going to have to take his word for that, but she was happy to have his approval. He ran a trail of scorching kisses up and down the inside of both thighs, and she couldn't help but moan and wriggle with each one. Her reaction seemed to encourage him, and he teased and caressed her until she cried out in anguish.

Stroking his thumb over her hard nub, he slid his fingers inside her. Ruth's body took over for her mind as she arched back and drove her body against him.

"Please," she begged, desperate for her needy body to be filled.

He leaned his face down, close to her thighs, and she tried to concentrate on what was happening, but it was all a blur of passion and sensations. Her mind refused to be still. When his hot, slick tongue slid into her core, she lost the ability to think at all. The one coherent thought that stuck with her was the mantra that kept repeating in her mind.

More! More! More!

She clutched at the quilt under her and bunched it up in her fists, pushing herself against his mouth, her body begging him for relief. Grabbing her hips with iron-strong hands, he held her in place as she tried her best to take what she needed from him at a faster pace.

Deacon would not be rushed. He worked at her core slow and methodically, laving her with his mouth and tongue until she was on the edge of insanity. Her heart raced and her inhibitions and embarrassment vanished. The thunder and lightning continued, loud and persistent, punctuating each stroke of his amazing tongue.

Slowing the pace, he licked his way up her torso as she lay panting, desperate to clear her head. It was no use. She was lost.

Consumed.

Ruth knew what she wanted. She reached for him, pulling him down beside her.

She wanted to climb on top of this man. She wanted to rub her body along the length of him and feel him on every inch of her skin, and then she wanted him inside her.

Oh, definitely that!

Lowering herself across him, she kissed his mouth, his face, along his collarbone then down, down, down that beautiful chest. Closing her eyes, she stroked her wet sex over the length of his erection. A shiver raced up her spine, and her heart throbbed at a brisk rate in her ears. It felt so wonderful, and she couldn't stop herself. Inexperienced as she was, she still knew what felt good, and when her core made contact with him, a flame ignited within her. Rubbing her frantic body against his, her pleasure built. Before she could finish what she had started, he flipped her onto her back again and covered her with his entire body, his hard length pressing against her in all the right places.

"Let's do this properly," he said, spreading her legs with his knee.

She had a moment of lucidity as he hovered over her with naked, unflinching desire in his eyes. Her own wide eyes asked the question she couldn't bring herself to voice, desperate not to ruin the moment again.

"Don't worry," he said, stroking between her legs with his shaft. "I can't get you pregnant like this. It takes months of not traveling the consecrated subway for the conditions to be right for pregnancy. I'm clean, and you're safe."

That was all she needed or wanted to hear. Guiding his shaft up against her entrance, she was wet and ready. He pushed the head of his length into her in one slow, all-consuming drive. As he passed her entrance, she felt herself close around him, her muscles clenching in an effort to hold him in. The fullness there was wonderful and overwhelming. She prayed for him not to tease her by withdrawing. Abandonment now would be worse than torture.

"Ohhhh," she gasped.

"Too much?" he asked.

"More!" she demanded.

Deacon pushed into her, past her tight entrance, and then filled her in one long stroke, burying his length inside her warm hold. She wrapped her legs around the backs of his thighs without hesitation, and held him inside her lest he try to leave her body too soon.

He chuckled kindly. "It will be even better if you let me move."

Trusting him, she unclenched her legs. He drew himself away from her and nearly out, and then plunged into her again and again.

Ruth feared she would cease to exist at any moment. Completely consumed, she abandoned her body to the pleasure he was bestowing upon her with every tiny touch and fluctuation. Each stroke brought her closer and closer to the precipice, and when he fondled a thumb over her hard, aching nub, his length still encased deep inside her, she came unhinged.

Crying out, she grasped hold of the quilt and threw back her head. Wave after wave of pleasure cascaded through her, rendering her stiff and immobile save the tiny tremors coursing through her now useless body.

Deacon rode the wave with her, pumping faster and faster into her still-quivering body. His face and neck muscles grew taut as he reached his peak as well, releasing into her in a fiery flood and then collapsing against her. She curled an arm and leg around him possessively, making sure that he'd stay put. Feeling his heart pound wildly against his chest pleased her even more than experiencing her own pleasure. It was real physical evidence that he was as excited and satisfied as she was.

"Thank you," she said, refusing to release her hold on him.

"My pleasure." He kissed her, deep and thoroughly.

Rebirth.

This was the beginning of a whole new life. Even though Deacon had come to her in the strangest possible way and with a whole new world of danger and problems, he'd also brought amazing possibilities and excitement into her once staid life.

Deacon eased out of her. Rolling off the bed, he walked naked into the bathroom. She suppressed an admiring moan as he crossed the room. The man was beautiful.

Returning with a warm, wet washcloth and a towel, he attempted to clean her, but she squirmed and giggled under his ministrations.

When he snuggled up against her back, his arms wrapped around her protectively, it brought a smile to her lips in the darkness. She glanced at the clock: 4:45 a.m. It would be light in an hour. She wasn't sure what the next day would hold. But she wasn't a virgin anymore, and there was a beautiful man lying next to her in her bed who made her feel safe and loved for the first time in...ever. A warmth twined around her heart, and it felt dangerously close to happiness.

She fell asleep listening to the rain tap, tap, tap on the roof and thunder roll on eastward.

CHAPTER FOURTEEN

Deacon barely slept. His skin and nerves felt raw and alive as he held Ruth. Making love to her had been a gift. He'd had many women in his long life, but never had he experienced the tenderness he felt toward Ruth. If he'd been conflicted and distracted by her before they made love, he was utterly consumed by her now. Distracted did not even begin to cover it.

He clung to her in the darkness, making sure as much of his body touched hers as possible. It had surprised him the way she'd taken charge, knowing she was a virgin.

Was.

He had never knowingly deflowered a virgin. So in a way, it was a first for him, as well. He was not disappointed. He already craved her body again. How he would get through an entire day without her touch, without tasting her hourly, he had no idea.

He would have to find a way. He had preparations to make and work to do. Tracking down Kylen was first on that list.

Determined to make sure Ruth was protected before that happened, he decided that it was time for a serious crash-course training routine.

She was stronger than she thought, but she needed more confidence, and she needed to learn how to defend herself. As it was, she wouldn't stand a chance against the demon alone. Deacon would have to make sure she *wasn't* alone. Ever again.

All the demon needed was an opening, and once he got it, he wouldn't hesitate to take it. Deacon didn't want to kill his friend, but he'd tried to find a way to save him for a century. Without the demon's name, it was hopeless. He'd exhausted every avenue, and he'd be doing Kylen a favor by setting him free. Had the circumstances been reversed, Deacon would have expected the same of Kylen. In fact, they'd once made a pact to that effect, but when it had come down to it, Deacon hadn't been able to follow through. Now, he had no other choice.

Losing another love would be intolerable. If he had to kill his best friend to ensure Ruth's safety, he would. Trading love of one sort for another was ironic, but in all of the ways that mattered, Kylen was dead anyway. His body was a tool and mode of transportation for the demon: a suit to be worn. The state of his soul was the one remaining question mark, but there was no way of determining that while the demon inhabited him.

* * *

The morning dawned gray and dreary, but Deacon woke Ruth in the happiest way. She was sore from their earlier pursuits, but it was a pain to which she hoped to become accustomed.

Apparently naked men were more than happy to wake up next to a naked woman in the morning. She would have been pleased to have a repeat performance of their marathon last night, but they ended up enjoying only an appetizer instead. Still hungry for more, she wondered if it was possible to become a sex addict after one night. Maybe sex was like meth or heroin were for some people—one hit and you were hooked.

Deacon patiently explained why they couldn't lie in bed naked all day making love, at least not today. He promised they could soon. She would hold him to that. They showered separately because otherwise they would have just ended up back in bed, and Deacon was intent on giving Ruth her first day of on-the-job training.

Nervous but excited by the prospect of gaining some semblance of control over her life, she was game.

Heck, she would be glad to *have* a life. These past few days had turned her safe little world upside down. She was relieved to finally feel as if she was on a path that led *somewhere* and not on a treadmill passing time.

At last, it appeared, she had a job. Even better perhaps: a purpose.

Deacon finished first, and then Ruth primped in the bathroom. She had never been too concerned with her appearance before, opting for invisibility whenever possible. Often she wore her wild, unkempt hair in a ponytail or under a baseball cap if she had to go out.

Today, she made an effort and left it soft, curly and unbound. First day on the job and all, and she wanted to make a good impression. *Some job.* Was she even going to be paid for this new occupation? She'd have to add that to the mental list of questions for reaper HR.

She wasn't sure whether there was some sort of accepted dress code for reaping, but she figured she'd be safe with casual and black. She'd only ever seen Deacon in scrubs or jeans and a T-shirt. Following his fashion lead, she picked out her own black jeans and black fitted T-shirt. Black seemed appropriate for the occasion...

and besides, she looked good in black.

Deacon sat at the kitchen table shirtless, wearing only his jeans. A big bowl of Lucky Charms sat on the table to his right, along with a glass of milk he'd prepared for her. He was eating a piece of reheated lasagna.

"Morning," she said. "Lasagna for breakfast?"

"Good fuel for a big day. Besides…it's wonderful." He smiled.

"Glad you like it."

He came around and gave Ruth a garlicky morning kiss and said, "I like everything about you."

Ruth blushed. She wasn't used to compliments of any kind unless you counted grades. She gave him an A+ for effort…and great abs.

"If you're going to walk around the kitchen of a newly deflowered virgin without a shirt on, we're going to have to default back to Plan A," she teased.

Deacon laughed and reached for his backpack. He dug through it until he pulled out a tight, dark gray T-shirt. Ruth resisted the urge to help him with it. She had to exercise some sort of self-control, or they would never make it out of the house.

She sat down next to him and tucked into her breakfast, finishing quickly. When she was done, Deacon tossed her a backpack.

"I filled it up with snacks, but you might want to put in a change of clothes, as well. You never know what might happen."

She unzipped the top and peeked inside. It was loaded down, and he'd even stuffed a whole jar of chunky peanut butter into it.

"I'm ready as soon as you are," he said. "It's going to be a long day."

"Okay." She headed back to her bedroom to search for spare clothes. She picked out another T-shirt and a spare pair of jeans, and then added socks and undies.

Lacing up her sneakers, she debated over packing a toothbrush and toothpaste, found an extra of both, and added them to the load. When she left the bedroom, Deacon was standing in the middle of her living room where they'd cast the circle the night before.

"We can leave from here now," he said, admiring her footwear and nodding. "Good choice. I'm glad you wore some reasonable shoes. We'll be traveling a lot by foot today… Come on over here."

Ruth joined him at his side, and he took her hand.

"Ruth, traveling on the consecrated subway is the easy part, and it will get easier and easier the more practice and experience you get. I know it's strange, but you'll love it once you get used to it. I promise."

Ruth wasn't as worried about the traveling part as she probably should have been. She *was* curious about how she would ever learn to control getting from point A to point B.

"Where are we going?"

"It's early. We'll start at the hospital since you're at least somewhat familiar with that location. Before too long, you'll be able to travel all over the place, maybe even across the world one day."

Now that was hard to imagine.

"Think about where you want to be, say the hallway where we ran into each other at the hospital. You'll pop into the consecrated ground that's closest to that location. From there you'll have to hoof it."

"That seems very inconvenient. Why can't you take a bike or car or something with you?"

"You can take with you whatever you can carry, within reason. A car? No. A bike, sure…but then what are you going to do with a bike in the middle of a hospital?" he asked, caressing her arms absently. "You're making it more complicated than it needs to be.

You aren't going to have a problem here. You'll see."

"Won't people be surprised if we appear in the middle of a room somewhere?"

"It will take a few seconds for us to become corporeal again. We'll have enough time to make it to a more crowded location, where we can stay unnoticed."

"So I'm going to be traveling by supernatural subway, and I get to be invisible, too?" she asked, intrigued. She'd been trying to make herself invisible for years, but this seemed a little over the top even in light of her new knowledge about the ways of the universe.

"We're not invisible, but when we need to be—like when we first fade in and when we're about to reap a soul—we're...unnoticeable. People might have a vague notion that someone's in the room or an odd feeling that they're being watched, but nothing concrete. As soon as we are gone, they won't remember us at all."

"Like the stranger who lifts a car off someone and then disappears?" she asked.

"Yes, something like that. Those are Guardian Angels, which also exist, but the idea's similar.

"Here," he said, reaching out to her. "Take my hand and picture the hallway where we met. I'll do the rest. The circle of protection will close behind you, but I can't get in and out of it without you."

"Well, then, I think we can do a lot better than hand holding."

She smiled, circling her arms around his waist and stretching up for a kiss. He pulled her close and deepened the kiss. She almost forgot to concentrate on the hallway at all, but the next thing she knew they were spinning and swirling as her head grew light and swimmy. When she opened her eyes, they were inside the chapel at St. Mary's Hospital.

Deacon grinned down at her. "See, no big deal."

Right, she thought.

Ruth looked around, relieved that there were no chapel visitors. Deacon led her over to a pew, and they both sat.

"That was step one—arriving. Now, when you're ready to go back home, you hold the image of your living room in your mind and concentrate on it…hard. You can't let yourself become distracted until you have a couple hundred flashes under your belt. Otherwise, it's consecrated roulette. Spin the wheel and who knows where you'll end up. If it's working, you'll feel a pull. It might take a few minutes the first time on your own, but you'll get it. Clear your mind, tune out everything around you, and the next thing you know, you'll be home."

"That would have been a useful trick to have known all these years."

"You always had the ability to do it—you just didn't know it. There was no one to teach you. You're lucky it didn't happen by accident. That might have been disastrous."

About a dozen different scenarios flashed through her mind about what *could* have happened if she'd flashed somewhere unexpectedly. Every one of them ended in a total freak-out, so yeah, she was glad that something like that hadn't ever happened. It made her wonder how many other tricks she had to learn. It occurred to her that the newly minted advanced degree she'd earned was going to be next to useless in her new job.

"Now what? Do you have reaping to do here?"

"There always seems to be someone dying in a hospital. But first, we're going to work on your aura reading."

Ruth tensed. Aura reading was about the last thing she wanted to do. She'd tried to avoid people's auras for as long as she could remember, and she didn't think she could suddenly feel okay about inspecting them. Mystical travel? No problem. Looking at the evidence of other people's greed and lust and heartache with wide-open eyes? Problem.

"Don't freak out now," Deacon said. "You've done great with everything so far. Seriously, most people would have imploded already."

Ruth looked at him, surprised.

"I'm kidding," he said. "You're not going to implode. Reapers have the advantage of seeing people's auras clearly. We don't have auras ourselves unless they manifest under extreme circumstances, so we don't have to see them through the lens of our own screwed-up emotions. What you see is what you get. Most supernaturals don't have auras."

"But we have souls, right?"

"Yes, we all have souls. But we are *supernatural*—beyond nature. We can travel in ways humans can't even imagine, to places that surpass their wildest dreams," he said, tucking one of her stray curls behind her ear with his finger. "Ruth, we are vessels. When we carry souls, they fill us up, and it's our responsibility to get them to Purgatory for sorting so that they can move on. You'll reap young and old, good and evil. We don't have to judge them, and we don't choose the time they die. We are conduits. They need us, and most are more than happy to go along for the ride. As your powers grow, you'll be drawn to the places where souls need to be collected. Until then, the easiest way is to go where the dead are. Some souls are more challenging, but they all go unless they get overlooked or left behind."

"How could they be overlooked or left behind? Doesn't God know where they are? You know 'the hairs on your head' and all that?" She thought that the whole gist of God was that he was an omniscient and protective overseer of mankind.

"God gave humans free will, Ruth, and because of that, they're free agents. He wants them to love and worship him, sure. But if they don't, well, they'll face judgment eventually. They all do. If a soul is misplaced or overlooked, which can happen if someone is murdered and left somewhere that's difficult to find or sense, then they'll wait in a suspended state until they're found. You would know them as ghosts. They sometimes try to draw attention to themselves so that they can pass over, and this leads to what some supersensitive people would recognize as a haunting." He continued hesitantly, "That's what happened to your father."

"Because I didn't know to reap him, and no other reaper found him?"

"Yes."

He put an arm around her shoulders and gave her a squeeze.

"You didn't know, Ruth. And you didn't kill him. He's okay now."

"I hope so," she said, filled with self-doubt.

"That's why you have to overcome your fears of the auras so that you can do your job. Do you want to be able to help people, Ruth?"

"Yes," she said. She did. She knew what it was like to be in limbo. She'd been there way too long herself. She knew what that felt like, and she was ready to start living. If making a living out of dying was her calling, then so be it. It was ironic, but it felt right.

"Okay," she said, determined. "I'm ready."

"Good girl." He kissed the top of her head. "Let's go."

CHAPTER FIFTEEN

Deacon took her hand, and they slipped out the back doors of the chapel into the hallway of the hospital. They blended into the daily scene, just two more visitors in the crowd.

Deacon led her down and around several hallways to the E.R. for her first lesson. Ruth couldn't help but avoid eye contact with everyone she passed.

Force of habit.

Hiding her gift had been a matter of self-preservation. Letting go of that habit wasn't going to be easy, but she was willing to give it a try.

"Let's sit for a minute." Deacon led her to an upholstered chair.

They sat in the empty waiting area within view of a nurses' station. Ruth couldn't see into any of the rooms beyond the closed double doors, but the station bustled with staff activity.

"See the nurse in the red-and-black scrubs?" Deacon asked. Ruth nodded. "What is the predominant color of her aura?"

Ruth forced herself to study the nurse. A green glow surrounded the woman, swirling with yellows and blues as she hustled behind the station gathering charts. "Mostly green?" Ruth said.

"Good. Do you know what that color might mean?"

"Green is a restful and healing color, so that makes sense, I suppose."

Deacon nodded his approval. "Yes, good. The colors alone are nothing to fear. Think of them as a facial expression like a smile or even a warning growl from a dog. People express themselves with their energy without even knowing it." He kept his voice low. "Auras don't lie. They're a method of subconscious communication. It will be useful to you in your dealings with people if you understand what the colors mean, but as a reaper, the color you need to pay the most attention to is white."

"The death aura," she said with a shudder. "My father's aura was white right before he died... My mother was afraid of me after that, because I told them what I saw. She thought I killed him. It wasn't too difficult to figure out what white meant after that. My mother's aura was white when I visited her in the hospital."

"Being in the right place at the right time is very important for you in the early stages of your training. Later, you'll begin to feel the pull of the dead and dying, and you'll have a better idea of where to go. The pull is the strongest during and immediately after death, and it starts to fade from that point onward. Your father's soul had no detectable pull since it had been detached so long." He nodded toward another staffer. "Let's practice some more. That transporter there, what color is his aura?"

Ruth looked up at the transporter and tried to isolate the predominant color, but his aura was muddy and mottled. "I can't tell. It's too dark, and it's all mixed up."

"Exactly. We don't know what he's thinking, but we *can* tell he's disturbed and on edge about something. Volatile even. He would be a good person to avoid, say in a bar...or on a blind date."

"I don't think I'm going to have to worry about either of those things anytime soon."

"Practice *noticing* people and their auras. I can translate for you until you get the gist of it or at least confirm or correct your own summations. You've done well to figure out as much as you have without any help. There are so many subtle aura communications you'll never pin them all down, but look for the dominant color, and you'll find the dominant emotion or intent. What else do you know about the colors?"

Ruth sighed, resigned. "A quick checklist might go something like this—purple is spiritual. Blue is balanced, sustaining life. Turquoise is energetic or influential. Green is healing and restful. Yellow is joy, freedom, vitality. Orange is controlling others or exercising power over them. Red is materialistic or physical. Pink is love. And any combination of colors that creates a muddy or dirty aura is trouble. Mustard is anger or pain and white is disease and death."

"You've been a good student already," Deacon teased.

"I might need a raise," she countered.

"You haven't even finished your first day yet."

"Speaking of raises, umm, will I actually be paid?"

Deacon chuckled. "Yes, you'll be compensated. Well and regularly. But let's make it through your first week before we open your 401(k) and start planning your retirement."

* * *

Though Ruth felt as if she stuck out like a sore thumb, particularly given her overstuffed backpack, no one seemed to notice them. Ruth supposed they looked as though they were coming on or getting off a long shift. In a hospital the size of St. Mary's, two new faces were nothing to get excited about.

He led her to the critical-care ward, quizzing her on the auras of the patients in each of the rooms they passed. Ruth felt like an ambulance chaser or a vulture waiting to pick the bones of the dead. In a way, she guessed that's what she was, but she tried to keep the spin positive.

It wasn't long before they found what they were looking for. Right there in 303 was a withered sheath of an old man with a nice, bright white halo around his body. He was full of tubes, and all sorts of wires protruded from his frail body, yet he appeared peaceful. She wondered if maybe he wasn't already dead and didn't realize it.

Deacon walked over to the man's bedside and studied him, and then placed his hand on the man's chest. The white light crackled and sparked all around him, only settling down when Deacon pulled his hand away.

"It won't be long. We'll wait."

Ruth was uncomfortable. She had plenty of questions, but it seemed rude to ask them in front of the man. Besides, she didn't want anyone to hear them talking. Even though they weren't doing anything wrong, she wasn't prepared for a confrontation. And while Deacon had told her they would be unnoticeable while doing their job, she wasn't feeling all that incognito. More like exposed.

Deacon stood beside the bed, and—for the second time that week—Ruth sat in a chair by the window of a hospital room. They waited in silence. She had no idea how long it would take, but she secretly willed the elderly man to get on with it. Feeling guilty, she grew more nervous with every passing instant.

Deacon must have sensed her anxiety because he reached for her, offering his hand. She took it, relaxing as the now familiar orange glow slid through her. Relief was immediate.

Already, he was becoming a habit. An addiction.

He kept hold of her hand, and soon the man in the bed gave out a long last sigh. They watched as his soul left his body through his sternum, and then hovered over his bed. Deacon touched the machinery attached to the man and pushed energy into it, silencing any potential alarms. The patient was beyond resuscitation. His time had come.

They watched as the man's soul settled on the side of the bed, looking down at its former body, and then back to them. At first he seemed confused, but realization settled over his features, smoothing away the tension.

"It's time to go." Deacon said.

The man smiled and nodded, and when Deacon reached out to him, the soul dissolved into a gray stream. Stepping forward into the stream, Deacon consumed him.

Even though she'd seen it once before, it was still disconcerting.

"Okay. Let's go find one for you."

Ruth was pretty sure her mouth gaped open because she was so not ready for one of her own.

Deacon led her into the hallway, and they checked each room on their way out for white halos. She was more than a little relieved when they didn't find one, and she said a little prayer of thanks.

Disaster averted.

Chapter Sixteen

Great, she thought. *More opportunity for disaster.*

They took the elevator down to the basement, and then Deacon led her through the morgue's unsigned double doors. It looked just like morgues did in TV shows and movies—clean, white and sterile with an abundance of stainless steel. Two employees worked at computers at stations on one side of the room, and both of them looked up when Deacon and Ruth walked in.

"Hey," Deacon said. "I'm here to check out the new arrivals for Rothford and Sons Funeral Home."

"Right," one of them replied, returning to his work, which appeared to consist of online poker.

"Sure thing, two and six are the latest. Both came in last night," the other morgue employee said. The first guy continued punching away at his keyboard, uninterested.

Deacon walked over to a stainless-steel door marked Two and pulled out the long tray which held the pale, mottled body of a middle-aged woman. Frowning, he placed a hand on the woman's chest, giving her a shot of orange energy. Ruth didn't see anything happen. No soul, nothing.

He slid the tray closed and moved on to door Six. Sliding out the tray, he cursed—it was a teenage boy, and he was a mess. His limbs mangled and broken, he looked like Frankenstein's monster with the pieces rearranged. Ruth's stomach churned. Despite the cleanliness of the body, it was a horrific sight. Deacon shot him with OJ with the same result: nothing.

"When did these two come in last night?" Deacon asked.

"Both around 4:00 a.m., I guess. I can check the log if you'd like. Car wreck. Both of them died at the scene out on I-64."

"Thanks." Deacon gestured toward the door, and stalked out of it. Ruth hurried to catch up to his heavy and determined steps.

"I can't believe they didn't ask more questions," Ruth said, amazed that they weren't being followed out.

"They won't even remember us by the time we get to the elevator," Deacon said gruffly.

"Why didn't you reap them? Because those guys were there?"

He whipped around to face her. "No, I couldn't care less about those two. There wasn't anything to reap. They were already gone." He dropped his gaze to the floor and pinched the bridge of his nose between his fingers.

"What does that mean?"

"It means that Kylen's demon poached them while we were making love last night. That's what it means. It means that they're both in Hell now because I wasn't on the job." His hands clenched into fists, and he looked as if he was about to punch a hole in the wall.

Ruth didn't know what to say to him because the revelation made her feel queasy, as well.

"You can't work twenty-four hours a day, can you?" she asked in a whisper.

"No. But we have to be more diligent. These are people's souls. Our work is serious. I haven't been this distracted in a long time, and I can't afford to be. *We* can't afford to be. Not now that there are demons …"

"Is there no way to get them back?" She reached for him, but he backed away from her touch.

"Not unless he hasn't taken them through the portal to Hell yet, and I'm sure he has. He wouldn't wait around this long with pirated cargo. He must have been on the scene of the accident within seconds. I didn't even feel them pass."

"What about the soul you hold?"

"I can hold several at a time if it's needed. Carrying them one at a time is actually more exhausting than carrying multiples."

"But you said you were more vulnerable when you carry a soul."

"I can take care of myself," he said, averting his eyes from hers. "I've been doing it for a while now."

His entire mood seemed to have gone dark and edgy, and she was pretty sure that if he'd possessed an aura, it would have been as muddy brown as the transporter's.

She was glad he didn't.

They made their way back to the chapel. When they walked in, Kylen was reclined against the altar.

* * *

Deacon stopped abruptly inside the doorway to the chapel, as the double doors swung shut behind them. Ruth could hear the lock clicking into place, and dread pricked up the hairs on the back of her neck.

Stepping in front of her, Deacon used his body to

block her from Kylen's direct line of vision. His large frame made a pretty good shield, and she appreciated the gesture. She was all for women's lib in general, but there was a time and a place for everything. And now was the time to accept protection. When she placed her hand against Deacon's lower back, she could feel him vibrating with anger.

"What, no greeting? No thank you for pulling up your slack?" the demon sneered.

"Those people didn't need your kind of help."

"Well, I saw no reason for them to go to waste while you were…otherwise engaged," the demon taunted.

Ruth wondered if he really knew what they'd been doing, or if he was just baiting Deacon. The demon casually knocked candelabras and various accoutrements from the altar with a careless swipe as he made his way across the room. Deacon stood his ground.

"So much pomp and pageantry for a God who does so little for his subjects," the demon said, striding closer.

"I suppose you think you have a better deal?"

"Oh, without a doubt. For the truly ambitious, there are countless treasures without any of the limitations of pesky morality," the demon said.

"What are you doing here, Demon? There are no more souls to reap here today."

"Pity. *However,* you carry one now. Correct? How about we barter over that one, eh?" the demon purred, his eyes growing blacker with each step.

"I have no interest in anything you have to offer." Deacon squared his shoulders, readying himself for confrontation.

"Oh, I think you might." The demon carved a long, clawed fingernail down the wooded arm of the pew. Ruth caught glimpses of Kylen from her shelter behind Deacon. She held tight to the back of his shirt, working it into a damp ball in her fist.

"Come out, come out, little one," the demon sang.

"Stay back," Deacon growled.

"What? We aren't friends anymore? Kylen is hurt. He's still in here, you know. Calculating. Plotting. Second-guessing his choices. But of course that's all we are in the end, is it not? A product of our *choices?*" The demon laughed, advancing in slow, methodical steps. "Choices like bedding the woman who cowers behind you like a child, still so soft and fragile. Why, she hasn't even reaped a soul yet, has she, Deacon? A veritable virgin, so to speak. Ripe for the picking. So fresh and new and...*malleable.* There are so many possibilities for her ..." The demon trailed off.

"That's enough."

"Please, you can't possibly be that tied to her already? You reapers are all so weak and predictable. Dear One, I could be a much better mentor for you. I have power, endless resources and a master with a vision like you can't imagine—this reaper is at the end of his usefulness. All I need is a change of scenery, a new body, and then we could have so much fun ..." the demon taunted, edging nearer.

"Stop right there, or you'll see that I'm not used up just yet," Deacon challenged. "I won't repeat Kylen's mistakes."

"But you already have." The demon sighed. "So proud and sure ..." He drew a long, curved knife from the holster on his spine. "We shall see, Reaper."

"Ruth—HOME!" Deacon commanded, as he stepped forward and drew a similarly curved knife of his own from the top of his backpack.

Ruth was confused and conflicted. She couldn't believe that they were about to have a knife fight in the middle of the day in a hospital chapel. She hesitated.

"NOW!" Deacon ordered.

Ruth concentrated on her little living room with all

she had, just as Deacon had instructed her. As her hands and feet began to tingle, her head grew swimmy. Like a giant rubber band stretched too tight, she felt the pull from her sternum. Closing her eyes, she willed herself not to pass out and offered up a silent prayer for Deacon. She let herself snap through the consecrated subway and back to her house.

CHAPTER SEVENTEEN

Ruth landed hard in a crumpled pile, her foot twisted beneath her. She was back in her living room. Alone.

It was a miracle.

She felt the circle close behind her. She worried that Deacon might not be able to flash back to the house with the circle closed, but he would be furious if she left it open. She wasn't afraid of Deacon, but she was afraid of Kylen and whatever other creatures he might send for her.

In an attempt to reinforce the circle, she concentrated on the sphere being a strong silver-blue snow globe of supernatural protection. As energy and light filled her body, her skin tingled, feeling as though it was stretched too tight across her frame. Exhausted, she decided that the circle was good enough. It would have to be—she didn't know what else to do.

A prisoner in her own home now, she realized for the first time in a long time, maybe ever, that she didn't *want* to be alone. For a moment, she thought about calling Nate, but what could or should she tell him? She'd have to wait it out alone.

For the longest while, she sat on the couch, waiting, worrying, and waiting. It was excruciating. She had no idea what was going on back in the chapel, but the fear she felt for Deacon bloomed like a fire in her belly, filling her with dread. Not knowing was worse than being there and watching. She knew that leaving had been the right thing to do. She would only have been a dangerous distraction for Deacon if she had stayed. Still…this was painful.

Hunger and weakness overtook her, and she made her way to the kitchen to warm up some lasagna and fix a peanut butter and jelly sandwich and a frozen burrito and maybe some cereal. The traveling and the stress had burned up her breakfast and then some, and she was starving.

Deacon wasn't kidding about the food part.

If she needed this much fuel after using the consecrated subway, what was going to happen when she actually reaped someone?

She should have felt like puking after having eaten so much. Instead, the pit in her stomach demanded more. Insatiable, she ate an entire box of crackers, half a pound of cheese, some fruit and a bowl of cereal before her hunger abated.

Ruth looked around at all the dirty plates and scraps of food on the table. It looked as if a church potluck dinner had exploded in her kitchen. But instead of an entire congregation eating it, it had only been her.

She puttered around the kitchen to clean up the mess, but she didn't know what to do with herself once she finished. Though she felt compelled to return to the chapel, she worried that with her luck, she'd end up somewhere else entirely…or worse, between the two of them at exactly the wrong moment.

She didn't feel safe enough to venture outside into

her jungle of a yard. For all she knew, some lesser demon, imp or worse was stationed outside, waiting for her on the off chance she'd wander outside.

She was truly trapped. Her seclusion in the past had been self-imposed, but this wasn't. Maybe she was finally getting what she deserved for lying about being agoraphobic.

She looked at the clock hopefully, but it was still only midafternoon. Time seemed to have stopped. She was as nervous as a cat on a freeway.

Pacing the house, she found a few empty boxes and finished unpacking the rest of her stuff. She filled the empty boxes with her mother's things and then set them on the back porch, ready to go to Goodwill.

Hours passed.

Drained of energy and ambition, she lay down on the couch and curled into a ball to wait some more.

* * *

Deacon was in trouble.

One reaper against a demon-possessed poacher was not a fair fight. Arrogant enough to think he could kill Kylen alone, he was further handicapped by the fact that he didn't *want* to kill him.

The demon? Yes. But Kylen? No.

It had been much easier to talk himself into doing the deed before he was faced with the actual opportunity.

Protecting Ruth was his utmost priority. Thank God she'd flashed. He couldn't face the demon and protect her at the same time. If only he knew the demon's name, he could have put an end to this. Even though he possessed neither the magic nor the authority to cast the demon out, Nate could. He'd gone over the possibilities many times with Nate...in the hypothetical terms, of course. Nate was only tangentially involved with the larger supernatural world, but he'd been an invaluable source of information and help more than once in the past ten years.

Facing the demon he'd hated for so long, the demon who had stolen not one but two of his beloved friends, he knew it was only a matter of time before the demon killed again. A demon kill was a double death. Not only did it kill the body, but it damned the soul to eternal suffering, regardless of faith. It stole the free will and future of all it touched.

As Ruth dissolved into the consecrated subway, his relief was large; his determination was larger. He *would* kill Kylen. It had to be done. It was the one way to remove the demon and stop the poaching.

The demon Kylen advanced on Deacon. The time for talk was over. Deacon readied himself and brandished his scythe. It was an impressive weapon. It would slice through a human, no problem, and was the weapon of choice for decapitation. If a supernatural beastie needed to be put down, reapers were the ones who did it. A job perk as it were.

The weapon and the reaper were deadly.

He didn't know if Kylen still held souls, but he instantly regretted the one he carried himself. If the demon was empty, he'd have a powerful advantage on his side.

There was one way to find out.

Deacon summoned an aura of protection around himself and slashed his scythe forward.

* * *

Ruth somehow managed to doze off. She awoke to a dark house and what sounded like lightning sizzling on her roof. Leaping up from the couch, she ran to the front door and peered out. Black shapes hurled themselves against the protective circle. Each time they made contact with it, they sizzled and bounced off, deflected like black moths on a giant bug zapper. It was difficult to make their shapes out for a clear identification, but they looked like imps.

Great.

Now she was even more worried for Deacon. Eleven hours had passed since she'd snapped back home, and she still hadn't heard anything. He could be dead for all she knew. Probably was. And it was her fault. She'd left him there—alone— while he fought to protect her.

She weighed her options. Stay here and hope the magic bug zapper held against the imps, or try snapping back to the chapel to see if he was still there or if there was any sign of him.

She refused to sit and wait any longer. She had to find him. Her heart hurt. Despite the ridiculous meal she had consumed, she had a sneaking feeling it wasn't indigestion. Changing her clothes, she filled her pockets with salt and dropped the rest of the canister into her backpack, along with the silver knife Deacon had given her yesterday.

Just in case.

Considering the weapons both of the men had been wielding before she'd flashed, these small household items seemed lacking. She was afraid, but action was so much better than sitting, hoping and praying. Removing Nate's card from the refrigerator, she tucked it into the back pocket of her jeans. He was the one other person she knew who might not totally freak out in case of an even bigger emergency than she was already in.

Centering herself at the new metaphysical doorway in her living room, she concentrated on the chapel, praying for no mistakes. She checked her watch: 11:30 p.m. Surely no visitors would be there this late. Closing her eyes, she tried to ignore the imps zapping off her shield as she waited for the pull, and then snapped through the consecrated subway.

CHAPTER EIGHTEEN

She crashed into the middle of the dark chapel. Enough light streamed through the stained-glass window inset in the door for her to see that the room was a wreck. Every pew was overturned and most had been reduced to jagged planks and splinters. All of the artwork on the walls was in shreds on the floor, where it sat in a pile like a bizarre indoor bonfire waiting to happen.

Deacon was nowhere to be seen. Kylen, either, she noted with relief. A dark stain marred the floor near the door. Blood. She prayed it wasn't Deacon's.

Wrapping her hand in her T-shirt, she pulled on the door, and then eased it open. She slipped a sliver of the wrecked pew between the doors to keep them from locking in case she needed to return. Sliding under the crime-scene tape stretched across the doors, she exited the room. She'd seen enough detective shows to know that she didn't want her fingerprints showing up anywhere they didn't need to be. As far as she knew, her prints weren't in the system anywhere, but these days, who knew?

She walked down the hallway, trying to look more like a visitor than a desperate supernatural freak on a mission. The one thing she could think to do was to go to the E.R. to see if there were any new patients who might be Kylen or Deacon. It seemed as good a place to start as any. Beyond that, she had no plan.

Making her way through the maze of hallways, she tried to follow the signs to the E.R. She hadn't paid much attention when Deacon had led her through the hospital this morning. Her habit of keeping her head down and avoiding eye contact was hard to break.

Now, she *was* paying attention to the people she passed. It felt good not to be constantly worrying about looking at people or touching them. If she wasn't on such a somber mission, she might have even struck up a conversation with someone.

Okay, probably not, but it was at least a possibility now that she wasn't so afraid of their auras, and of what effect she might have on them.

Finally, after wandering around for several minutes, she found the E.R. reception desk. One staff person sat at the front reception desk on duty. The woman, in her mid-fifties, sat squinting intently at her computer screen. As Ruth got closer, she realized that the woman was playing computer solitaire.

Slow night in the E.R., I guess.

The woman's aura was a nice calm blue-green: relaxing and healing. Ruth thought that was good since there was a high chance the woman had to constantly deal with all sorts of sick and crazy people.

"Excuse me."

The woman looked up from her solitaire game and smiled. Ruth thought she could count on one hand how many smiles she'd seen in the past year, mostly because she hadn't been interested in receiving them. The woman's smile emboldened her. Her name badge read

"Barbara Stevens."

Since Ruth wasn't brave enough to talk her way behind the E.R. doors like Deacon might have, she decided on a more direct approach.

"I'm looking for a man. Late twenties, dark hair? He might have come in with knife or blade injuries?"

Barbara gave Ruth an odd look, and a rush of panic stabbed through her heart. What if the woman pushed a secret buzzer and alerted security?

Paranoia much?

Instead, Barbara punched some keys on her keyboard and nodded. "Yes, we had a John Doe come in earlier today. I can't give you any details on his condition, though, because of HIPAA. Are you a relative?"

Ruth froze.

"Yes, I'm his…fiancée," she lied.

God help me if I get called on it.

Ruth wasn't sure how many bald-faced lies in a row she could muster. She was about to find out.

"You'll have to talk to security before I can release any more information or take you to see him. The police want to talk to him when he wakes up."

Great. This was not going to end well.

"Barbara, can I look in before we go through all of that? I just want to make sure that it's really him …" Ruth begged.

She gave the nurse the best anguished-fiancée look she could muster. The anguish was pretty easy to portray, since she did feel sort of sick knowing that Deacon might be back there somewhere, alone and hurt.

In desperation, she did something she had never done before. Out of her own free will, she reached out and touched the older woman's hand, and then, concentrating all of her energy, she imagined an orange glow, pushing it into Barbara like Deacon had done to her. Unsure exactly how or even *if* it would work, she tried to bend the woman to her will. Her heart beat faster as Barbara looked up at her in surprise. Ruth pushed harder.

Confusion settled over Barbara's features, and then she patted Ruth's hand and she smiled up at her.

"I don't see why we have to get security involved if he's not even your fiancé, honey. Come with me. I'll take you to him, and then we can decide what to do."

Good plan.

Ruth gave Barbara her best smile of gratitude...and relief.

Miraculously, the nurse seemed oblivious to the drumlike sound of Ruth's heart as they walked down the corridor and past several empty E.R. rooms.

Employees in scrubs scurried by on various errands in the otherwise quiet hallway on their night rounds of meds, food and patient care. Barbara led her through a set of doors and down another corridor to the critical-care ward. A yellow sign pinned on the door of the room proclaimed,*Entry of Authorized Medical Personnel Only by Order of Meridian City Police.* Not a good sign.

Barbara pushed open the door and held it for her.

"You go on in, dear, and see if it's him. I'll be at my desk. Come out when you're finished with your visit."

Ruth gripped Barbara's shoulder and sent another shot of OJ through her for good measure. If it were Deacon, she'd need some time. If not, she'd be out before Barbara had a chance for it to wear off. Barbara smiled again—her eyes going soft and unfocused as if she was trying to remember something—and then headed back toward her desk.

Good girl.

Ruth pushed the door closed behind her and flipped the lock for good measure. Crossing to the edge of the bed, she took in a deep breath before looking down at the unconscious man. So many bandages, tubes and lines ran into and out of him that he was almost unrecognizable. But his complete lack of an aura gave him away, and when she leaned in closer and touched his face, she knew without a doubt that it was Deacon.

Suppressing a sob, she swallowed the lump that grew hard in her throat. Her eyes burned. Now was *not* the time to fall apart. Deacon needed help, and he wasn't safe in this room protected by a yellow piece of paper on the door and a generic name. Ruth had no idea what had happened to Kylen or if he was even alive, but she knew one thing: she wasn't going to give him a chance to finish the job if she could help it.

She needed to bring him someplace safe where he could get help. She doubted she could keep her own house safe with the imps attacking it, wearing away at the barrier. Realizing that she didn't even know where Deacon lived, her options were down to one.

The only other person she knew in town who had any inkling of what was going on was Nate. Pulling his card from her pocket, she called him from the bedside phone. She prayed he was home as the phone rang and rang.

CHAPTER NINETEEN

Ruth was ready to hang up sometime after the twentieth ring, so when Nate finally answered, she nearly burst into tears with relief.

"Hello?"

"Nate, this is Ruth Scott. Deacon's friend."

"What's wrong, Ruth?"

"Deacon is hurt, Nate. He's bad. We're at the hospital. It's all a mess. He can't stay here, but I don't know what to do. My house isn't safe. I don't know where he lives. Nate, I don't know how close the two of you are, but you're the only person I know who might be able to help."

"What can I do?"

"This may be a weird question, but is your house consecrated?"

Nate was silent for a little too long. "Yes. Why would you want to know that?"

She didn't have time to explain everything over the phone, and she didn't even know if she could when they got there. But if anyone was going to be accepting of the consecrated subway and all that went along with it, she figured it would be a witch.

"Nate, is the address on your card your home?"

Again a long pause. "Yes."

"I'm bringing Deacon to your place, Nate. Do you have a circle of protection set up like at my house?"

"Of course."

"Open it or this is going to be messy."

Ruth had no idea if this was going to work or if she could even get Deacon back to the chapel, but she wasn't exactly rolling in options. At this point, she didn't see as they had much to lose. Deacon looked terrible, and if he stayed in this hospital room much longer, she was sure Kylen or *something* would be back to finish him.

"How long until you arrive?"

"Ten minutes...*I hope.*"

Ruth hung up the phone and pushed the door to Deacon's room far enough open that she could peer out into the hallway. She searched for the wheelchair she had spotted on the way in, hoping it was still nearby. It was. Looking both ways, she sprinted over to it and maneuvered it back inside Deacon's room, careful not to be seen.

Rolling the wheelchair over to the bed as close as she could, she set the brake. She eased Deacon's legs around before remembering that the tubes were still attached to him. Removing them from the equipment seemed like a better plan than ripping them from Deacon's body. She placed one hand on the monitor, pushed a shot of OJ into it, and tore the tubes and wires free.

She held her breath, waiting for alarms to sound. When none did, she pulled Deacon's legs over the edge of the bed and grabbed him under his arms. Using gravity, she guided him down into the waiting chair.

Deacon was somewhere north of two hundred

pounds of solid muscle; it was no easy task. Luckily for him, he was still unconscious. She wrestled him around like an alligator in a death roll until he was somewhat upright in the chair. He was still dressed in a hospital gown, which she tucked back down and around him, stuffing his arms into his lap in a less haphazard arrangement. He was like a life-size G.I. Joe doll. His head lolled to one side, and she rummaged around the room until she found his clothes in a plastic bag in the closet. Pulling out his belt, she secured it around one of his shoulders and the handle of the wheelchair so that he wouldn't flop over forward.

She lifted his feet onto the flipper foot rests and grabbed one of the thin blankets off his bed to cover him and the myriad of tubes. She didn't think this could possibly work, but she prayed as hard as she could that they wouldn't be questioned or stopped on their way to the chapel.

Poking her head out once more, she assessed the hallway, and was reassured to find it empty. She wheeled him out and down the corridor in the opposite direction of the nurses' station, not prepared to press her luck with Nurse Barbara.

Ruth was relieved to reach a more crowded part of the hospital as she made her way down the maze of corridors and back to the chapel. Another wave of panic coursed through her as she approached the chapel doors, certain that her doorstop hadn't worked after all. But as she drew nearer, she saw that it was still there.

Ruth pushed the door open and rolled Deacon inside.

To her relief, they were back in the chapel. And they were alone.

Her adrenaline abandoned her, and she nearly crumpled to the floor on her shaky legs. *We're not safe yet,* she reminded herself. It had taken much longer than ten minutes to get back to the chapel. She prayed that

Nate's magic door was open. She wasn't sure what would happen if it wasn't, but she didn't want to accidentally pop out blocks or miles away from his house or, worse yet, in the middle of a cemetery somewhere.

She worried that the address alone might not be enough to get them there. She was too new at this to know any, let alone all, of the metaphysical rules and loopholes. Kneeling beside Deacon's chair, she slid one arm over his shoulders and the other under his knees, holding on to as much of him as possible. Repeating Nate's address over and over like a mantra, she began to feel that now familiar pull work its way up and through her body.

Please let this be the right decision.

They flew through the consecrated subway like a fourth-quarter Hail Mary pass.

* * *

"Jesus Christ!" Nate yelled and leaped back from the crumpled heap that had materialized in the middle of his living room.

They landed hard, and Deacon ended up falling on top of Ruth. Her lungs burned, desperate for air as his weight crushed against her. She was pretty sure she also had a broken rib.

"What the hell?" Nate asked.

Ruth was more than willing to try to explain, but he was going to have to free her from Deacon's weight before that could happen. Recognizing her dilemma, Nate managed to get hold of himself long enough to carefully roll Deacon off her.

"Is he dead?"

"Not yet."

Yep, she was Captain Obvious.

"How far is the closet fast-food place?"

Nate looked at her as if she was speaking a foreign language.

"Food. How far?" she asked again.

"Two blocks."

"Go. Now, please. Get three large chocolate milkshakes and one of each number meal on the menu and bring them here. Fast!"

Nate didn't budge—he was clearly confused and maybe in shock, too. It was late and they had popped into the middle of his living room out of thin air, demanding a ridiculous amount of fast food. She could sympathize with his bewilderment, but Deacon needed calories immediately. There was no time for explanations.

"NOW!"

He shook himself out of his stupor and got moving. Sliding into a pair of flip-flops, he grabbed his wallet and keys and was out the door. She didn't bother pointing out to him that he was shirtless and wearing his boxers. Hopefully, he'd use the drive-through.

She tried to make Deacon as comfortable as possible on the floor while they waited. There was no way she was going to be able to move him onto the couch or anywhere else without Nate's help. Finding the bedroom, she grabbed some pillows and dragged Nate's comforter off his bed to wrap it around Deacon.

She rearranged his hospital robe again and tried not to think about how different last night had been from this one. Examining his wounds the best she could, she realized that while they weren't exactly healing, none of them looked life threatening. The E.R. doctors and nurses had treated his wounds and given him fluids, which was all well and good, but she was pretty sure that from what Deacon had told her about reaping—and the fact that his head was still resting on his shoulders—

calories were what he needed…and a lot of them. Much more than that one little IV drip had been pumping into him.

Between the traveling, the reaping and the fighting, she was fairly certain he was in the reaping equivalent of a diabetic coma. She was hopeful that he'd be able to heal himself if they could get some significant calories into him. Ruth was flying by the seat of her pants, but if three triple-thick chocolate shakes couldn't revive him, they were screwed.

Nate burst back through the door fifteen minutes later with two giant bags of fast food. It all smelled decadent and yummy. Her stomach growled, loud and demanding. She realized that she was starving again, too.

Nate helped her raise Deacon into a somewhat seated position, and he also attended to the various tubes and wires attached to him.

"I was afraid to touch them."

"I'm an EMT."

Well, of course he is.

While Nate worked, Ruth tried to force Deacon to drink some of the milkshake. She stroked his throat with her hand, but it wasn't working. She didn't think it would be such a great idea to pour it down him, and she was pretty sure you couldn't administer a milkshake intravenously even if you had the proper equipment.

"Nate, don't freak out."

"Too late for that."

Ruth put her hands on Deacon's chest, closed her eyes and concentrated on pushing some orange juice into him. Her hands grew warm, and they tingled with the glow of a faint orange light. She pushed the small offering into Deacon, hoping it would be enough to kick-start him into at least drinking the milkshake.

"What the hell is that?" Nate asked, his face drained

of color.

"Feed him the milkshake, please."

Nate dipped the straw into the milkshake and tilted Deacon's head back to release the fluid into his mouth. Ruth kept pushing OJ into Deacon all the while, and was relieved when his throat began to work up and down.

Nate filled another straw and repeated the process until Deacon started to suck the now-melted milkshake through the straw on his own.

He drained the first one, and they fed him two more, nearly three thousand calories' worth, before he managed to open his eyes. Ruth was so thankful that tears welled up in her eyes, and she smiled at him. His eyes were icy reaper-gray. The soul from this morning was still inside him.

She wasn't sure if there was an expiration date on souls, but right now that was the least of her worries.

Nate emptied the bags of food and fed one French fry at a time to Deacon, who finally managed a weak smile. He tried to speak, but couldn't seem to get any words out. She leaned in closer. He whispered, "You should have seen the other guy." His breath was warm against her cheek.

Ruth let out a relieved laugh, as did Nate. Deacon tried to sit up a bit straighter, and the other man helped him. Ruth dug through the bag of fast-food carnage for a cheeseburger and tore off bite-size bits to feed to Deacon. It wasn't long before he became visibly stronger and more alert. He reached out to take the rest of the sandwich from her.

"You eat, too."

He didn't have to tell her twice—Ruth was starving. She devoured two entire supersize value meals as Nate watched them, his face painted with disbelief. They were a motley crew sitting in the middle of a witch's house in the wee hours of the morning eating fast food. She was exhausted but relieved.

Content that Deacon was no longer in any immediate danger of dying, she relaxed. She couldn't imagine a safer place for them at the moment than Nate's house. She sent up a little prayer of gratitude to whoever was listening. It had been a long night.

Deacon ate and ate, finishing off the rest of the spread. He was stronger but still shaky and exhausted. Nate offered to sleep on the couch, somehow managing not to ask one question. She thanked him and gave him a little kiss on the cheek. Then she and Nate helped Deacon up, and maneuvered him into the bedroom and onto the bed.

Curling next to Deacon, Ruth drifted off sooner than she'd thought she would. She had no idea what the next day would bring, but she was glad this one was over.

CHAPTER TWENTY

Ruth woke up in Nate's bed, her body wrapped around Deacon's.

My, how my life has changed.

She cuddled up closer and studied Deacon's stubble-covered jaw. He was bruised and beaten, but she was pretty sure he wasn't in any immediate danger of perishing.

His eyes were still closed but a smile found its way across his face, and her heart gave a little leap that had nothing to do with auras or orange juice or fear.

Emotion flooded through her. If she had to put a name on it, she guessed it would be…happiness? It seemed crazy to feel happy in the midst of all this insanity, but she did.

"Thank you," Deacon said, opening his eyes, his gaze somehow heat and ice all at once.

"You're welcome." She stroked his rough cheek.

Taking hold of her hand, he kissed her open palm, and then held it against his heart. She snuggled her face against his chest.

"You saved my life last night."

"I was scared."

"You did great," he said, wrapping his arms around her and pulling her in tighter.

"Nate's going to have a lot of questions. He was the only one I could think of who might be able to help us."

"I'll take care of Nate," he said, stroking her hair. "But there's something else you're going to have to do for me first."

He pulled her face closer and brushed his lips against hers. She forgot to breathe. He was so strong and tender, hard and soft, all at the same time. She lit up inside for him, but she didn't think he looked as if he was up for any sextracurricular activities just yet. Not to mention that Nate had done them enough favors, and it wouldn't exactly be sporting to make use of his bed while he was in the other room.

Deacon broke the kiss and lay back exhausted. He stared at her with serious concern in his ice-gray eyes.

"You're going to have to take this soul to Purgatory, Ruth."

Ruth's eyes grew as big as saucers. That was so not what she'd expected him to ask her. She began to mutter a weak excuse for why that wasn't possible, but Deacon preempted her protest, placing his thumb over her lips and cradling her quivering chin in his hand.

"Ruth, you can do this. It's much safer than what you've already done for me. I can't heal quickly enough with this soul inside me. It's draining. A few more hours and I'll be the flaccid mess you rescued from the hospital yesterday."

Fear bloomed in her stomach and flowed to her chest, gripping her heart. The idea of going back to Purgatory with Deacon was frightening enough, but going alone was unthinkable.

She'd already accomplished things that she would

have deemed not only impossible but too fantastical to even consider just a week ago. Now he wanted her to do more?

"Will you help me again, Ruth? I need you."

Damn.

She melted. She closed her eyes and weighed her fear against her growing feelings for Deacon. No contest. She was less than confident, but she had to try.

"Okay."

"Good girl." He smiled.

Damn you and your smile, too!

"You've already been there, so there's no need to worry about where you'll pop out. Just envision the depot where we landed last time. It will be busy and maybe frightening, but remember that it's a détente there. None of the reapers can hurt you—it's forbidden. They can speak to you and try to engage you in conversation, but they can't harm you. Rashnu would smite them before they drew another breath. There is a zero-tolerance policy for violence in Purgatory. That goes for you, too, Ruth. Don't allow yourself to be taunted into violence of any kind. Rashnu will have no trial or mercy. There are no second chances."

"Great."

She couldn't imagine any scenario in which she'd be punished for being too violent, but still.

"Don't talk to anything or anyone except Rashnu. Don't offer him more information than he asks for, but make sure to answer his questions truthfully and be respectful. As soon as the soul is out of me, I'll begin to heal, and you'll get to complete your first reaping."

She was happy he would heal, but that didn't assuage her growing anxiety. She would have liked a shot of the orange juice herself, but he didn't look up to it.

"Come right back here after you deliver the soul.

We'll be waiting for you."

She flung herself back onto the bed and sighed. So much drama. Yep, she was a drama queen. Deacon smiled at her.

"Let's do this," she said with forced enthusiasm.

Deacon rolled onto her, pressing her into the bed. Her insides went gooey as he looked down at her.

"Breathe it in, Ruth."

He leaned down and gave her a full-on, no-messing-around, openmouthed kiss, and she felt the soul push into her. Ruth gagged and resisted until Deacon shifted and pressed his hard groin up against her core, and her thoughts turned somewhere far south of worry. Deepening the kiss, he added two roaming hands to the process. She gasped and suddenly felt her skin shrink two sizes too small for her body as a current raced through her, and he pushed the soul into her. When she was sure she would burst, Deacon broke off the kiss and collapsed back onto the bed, his eyes closed in exhaustion.

Remembering to breathe, she inhaled sharply and felt a little better. Her body relaxed, but it was still uncomfortably full. The strangest tingle teased at the back of her mind, beyond her conscious thoughts, like the niggling of a task left undone. The soul tested the boundaries inside her and irritated like an itch she couldn't quite reach. It was disconcerting.

She rubbed the back of her neck.

"You'll get used to it. The oddness of the feeling will dissipate with time. It's actually better when there is more than one inside you. They become more muted, not so bright and alive. One demands much more attention than the cacophony of several."

"I can't imagine ever carrying more than one."

"Valkyries can carry hundreds," he said, pulling her close. "In the heat of war or disaster, they have to. There aren't enough reapers."

"Is that why Kara was so easily killed? Was she full of souls?"

"Yes, it was during a great battle in Kosovo during World War One. Men were dying everywhere on both sides. All three of us were there that day. Kara kept collecting and collecting. The demon must have been watching us, biding his time. A dead valkyrie would be a prize kill because he could collect hundreds of souls at one time to take to Hell. They don't say 'War Is Hell' for nothing."

Deacon looked away, and then scrubbed a hand down his face, determined to continue.

"The demon found his opening and struck while we were all occupied. Kara was already weakened when the creature attacked, and she couldn't defend herself. I tried to help, but the demon hit me so hard I lost consciousness. Kylen was carrying the least souls and was the strongest of the three of us. When I woke up he was gone. It wasn't until later that I learned what had happened. After Kara's death, Kylen made the deal with the demon, and then carried Kara's soul to Purgatory, bringing me with him so that I'd be under the protection of the détente. When he went topside, the demon inhabited him. I've been trying to find a way to free him ever since. Now, I'm afraid that the only way to free him may be death."

Her heart ached for Deacon. He had lost two friends that day, and he suffered for it still. And last night, he'd fought with his friend, whose demon was intent on killing him.

Apparently, supernatural relationships were as messy and complicated as human ones. She peered at Deacon. His eyes were a bright blue-green again, a color she realized she was starting to love. She wondered whether the soul had colored her eyes gray.

He took her hand. "Go now, Ruth. The sooner you go, the sooner you can come back to me."

She sat up and pulled her hair back into a rough ponytail as Deacon shuffled gingerly across the bed. He let his feet fall over the side, easing into a sitting position.

She helped him up, letting him lean on her for support as they shuffled out into Nate's living room.

Nate was sitting in his wing chair drinking coffee, which smelled like a piece of heaven in a cup. He was clearly waiting for them, and his aura radiated from him in spicy mustard waves. It didn't take a rocket scientist to guess that he was pissed. She couldn't blame him. She wondered for a moment if he was angry because they'd been making out in his bed, or if the whole strange situation had gotten to him. It didn't take long to find out.

"Deacon."

"Nate," Deacon said as she led him over to the couch. Nate's one-word greeting radiated so much anger. She knew where he was coming from because she was still on the same cruise ship of confusion herself.

The tension stretched taut between the two men for several uncomfortable seconds before Nate conceded.

"What the hell, Deacon? I want it all—the whole story. The *real* story. Don't gloss it over and don't leave anything out. I don't care if the security of the universe depends on you not telling me… I want to know, and I want to know now. I've been doing shit for you on the side, no questions asked, for years. Years, Deacon. I deserve the truth. *All* of it."

He was simmering, and Ruth wasn't too sad that she was about to clear out.

You know it's a bad turn of events when you'd rather go to Purgatory than have a hard conversation.

She shook her head and swallowed down her

laughter. She didn't think Nate would see the irony of the situation.

"Nate, you do deserve the truth," Deacon said. "And I'm going to give it to you—all of it. But first Ruth has to take a trip. You need to open your circle of protection so that she can leave, and keep it open until she comes back. We have to be prepared to defend ourselves while the circle's open. There are enemies hunting us. You're going to have to trust us just one more time, Nate. Have faith. We're the good guys here."

Ruth hoped that was true.

Nate cursed. "Who'll protect Ruth?"

God bless him for thinking of her safety. She was grateful. It was shocking—and wonderful—that he would worry about her after everything she'd put him through. Nate was a good guy, too.

"She'll be safe where she's going. Let's keep it safe here for when she gets back."

Nate cursed again and closed his eyes, considering his options. After a long moment, he nodded and began to mutter an incantation. Ruth felt the air pressure in the room shift, and she knew that the door was open. She couldn't see it, but she could feel it.

Deacon gave her hand a squeeze. "Go, Ruth."

She nodded and looked over at Nate. He really was worried for her, as well as for himself. She couldn't blame him. It was a lot to absorb, and he still knew very little.

Hell, I'm in the same boat.

She envisioned the depot and felt the familiar pull work on her. She closed her eyes, letting herself snap through the consecrated subway all the way back to the belly of the beast.

CHAPTER TWENTY-ONE

When she popped out into the middle of Purgatory, she felt like a groupie sneaking backstage at a rock concert. She looked around, nervous, half expecting a herd of reaper security guards to tackle her and escort her back out...or worse. She didn't belong here, and she certainly didn't know what the heck she was doing.

Talk about trial by fire.

Hoping that she'd attract less attention by moving than by standing around in everyone's way, she started walking. She made her way through the hustle and bustle toward the angel, Rashnu, on the same end of the terminal where Deacon had taken her on their last visit. Wondering if it mattered which end of the terminal the souls were deposited on, she decided to go with the devil she knew. The depot was much more crowded than it had been last time. Reapers of every possible stripe—and species—jostled into her as they hurried by. Horror shimmered through her at each passing touch.

Souls traveled in gray streams, one right after another, against the ceiling, and then down long tunnels on both sides of the depot. Occasionally, one would fly up the main chimney like her father had. She made her way to the back of the queue, trying not to gawk at the diversity of the beings around her. She was definitely in the minority. Although the sex of most of the creature reapers was indeterminate, she seemed to be the only woman among the human reapers.

The line shuffled forward. She felt him before she saw him—a surge of pricking goose bumps crawled up her spine as his hot breath poured down the back of her neck.

"Deacon's pet? Fancy meeting you here... And alone, too? Don't tell me that Deacon has met with some tragic harm."

Kylen.

"Nothing he can't handle," she said, before she remembered the no-talking plan.

"Hmm...last time I saw him he was being carted away on a stretcher. Given the way he tore up that chapel and how badly injured he was, I'm surprised they released him."

The demon Kylen circled her, sucking in a deep breath. While he couldn't touch her with the intent to harm her, intimidation appeared to be acceptable since he hadn't yet been rendered into a pile of ash or anything. He stroked a loose lock of her hair back and tucked it behind her ear. Ruth flinched.

If not for his creepy eyes and talonlike fingernails, he looked human...handsome even. But there was no getting past the eyes and talons. She shuddered as he pushed the bulk of his body up against her.

"First time?" he asked huskily.

Ruth didn't answer—she just shuffled forward, putting space between them. He eased up near her again, pressing against her back with the front of his body. He rubbed himself against her, letting her feel exactly how happy he was to see her.

"The first time is always the hardest, isn't it, love? I could make it so much...more for you," he whispered, his words bringing new prickly bumps to the surface of her skin.

She shrugged him off, trying to ignore him. She really did, but when he persisted, something fierce and unrelenting rose up in her. She reached back and ran her hand across the front of his jeans and over his hard erection. He hissed in surprise. She gripped him hard in her hand and then squeezed, twisting his business with all she had.

He gave out a little choked cough before breaking free and limping off into the crowd. If the salt had surprised him yesterday, this had shocked him even more. He didn't make a scene, and no one appeared the wiser. It was a risky move given Purgatory's no-violence rule, but she couldn't stand having him near her for one more moment. She had gambled on him not wanting to make a scene.

She had gotten lucky. Real lucky. She shuffled forward, sighing in relief when she realized she was next in line. The foul creature in front of her, who resembled some sort of be-winged snake, deposited its cargo and slunk away. Ruth found herself peering up at the angel, who was waiting for her to approach like a child waiting for some sort of perverse Santa visit.

"The orphan! Your training must be going well if you have come alone and are bearing your first soul?"

She nodded, unsure if there had been an actual question in there. She stared down at her sneakers.

"Well, tell me all about it... your first time and all."

Ruth hoped he was asking about the soul because she was so not going into all of the other firsts she had experienced in the past few days.

"It was fine, sir."

Rashnu glared at her. She heard low grumblings from the line behind her, although none of the reapers had the gumption to speak up in protest. She had already taken more time than any of those who had gone before her.

"When I ask for details, child, I expect to get them. Luckily for you, there are dozens of wars and worldwide disasters happening. If I weren't stretched so thin already, I'd make an example of you for your insubordination."

She suppressed a "whatever." She wasn't sure how exactly she was being insubordinate, but she didn't think arguing would win her any brownie points.

"Well? Spit it out."

"Really, sir—it went fine, no problems."

Rashnu's face grew red, and he hissed, "Not your excuses, you imbecile, the soul! Spit. It. Out. Or shall I rip it from you."

The eyes of every reaper on the terminal floor turned to her.

So much for lying low.

Deacon had pushed the soul into her. She had no idea how to reverse the process.

Ruth motioned for Rashnu to lean in closer and whispered, "Then you'll have to take it, because I have no idea how to release it."

"Very well."

He placed a glowing hand on the top of her head and pushed a brilliant bolt of energy through her that filled her sight with tangerine light. A great tearing ripped loose inside of her. Coughing and choking, she felt Rashnu wrench the soul from her. She opened her mouth to scream from the pain, but the soul poured out instead, streaming toward one of the side tunnels in a column of hazy gray smoke.

"Be gone," Rashnu bellowed. His face softened

despite his tone. "Tell Deacon I'll be requesting a private chat with him about this...soon."

Ruth nodded. Hoping that Deacon wasn't going to get in some kind of trouble, she made her way back through the depot toward the stone marker where she had landed. If she was expected to be some big bad reaper, then she was going to need more than half a day of training.

The terminal was dense with reapers, and she edged along the outside stone wall, trying to stay out of the main flow of traffic. Relieved to be free of the soul, her legs were weak and shaky. She'd need to load up on calories again when she got back to Nate's.

As she skirted the edge of a tunnel, so intent on her destination that she wasn't paying attention to the people—and creatures—around her, something suddenly grabbed her arm, ripping her into the dark crevice.

She tried to scream, but her throat was raw from the soul extraction, and the sound that escaped her was inaudible. Dragged farther into the darkness, she was slammed against the wall, her head cracking against it with such violence that her vision blurred. One taloned hand clamped down hard over her mouth. Even in the darkness, it could only be one person: *Kylen.*

He pressed her into the wall, holding her so tightly that she could manage only a cursory struggle. She was unwilling to give up, but her legs betrayed her anyway, and she slid down the wall, scraping her back bloody.

The demon jerked her up straight again, grinding her into the stone, extracting a small cry from her. Screwing up what little resolve she had left, she concentrated hard on pushing him away. She felt the warmth grow inside her until a faint electric-blue glow emanated from her. The glow expanded, sparking and sizzling with power. The demon Kylen hissed but held on to her.

His face contorted in the dim light of her glow. She

hoped it was causing him pain. Concentrating harder, she thrust the energy into him. His face softened ever so slighty and his hold loosened. Confused, he backed away, his eyes searching the walls of the tunnel before settling upon her face. Recognition washed over his features as his eyes lit up. *Normal blue eyes.* He shook her hard.

"Ruth, I don't have long."

She continued to push energy into him, her only defense in the darkness of the tunnel. If she could somehow draw Rashnu's attention, maybe …

"His name is Orithidon! Tell Deacon! Hurry! I can't hold him back much longer. Ruth… run!"

He released her suddenly, and she slid down the wall, crumpling into a spineless heap. The blue light faded out, leaving her feeling drained and hopeless, and for a moment she considered giving up. Then instinct took over and she scrambled to her feet. As Kylen backed away, allowing her to escape, she ran.

Or at least, she wanted to run…her body wasn't cooperating. She pushed herself off the wall, and then shuffled toward what she thought was the entrance, praying she was headed the right way. She didn't want to know what was at the other end of the tunnel.

Terrified, she made her way back into the busy terminal. No one seemed to notice the blood soaking through the back of her shirt from her fresh wounds as she made her way to the stone marker. It was too bad she couldn't just click some ruby slippers. Grabbing hold of the marker with both hands, she envisioned Nate's living room. The pull had started to work its way through her body when a searing pain pierced both of her thighs. She screamed as she spun out of control, the demon's talons holding her fast, penetrating her skin.

CHAPTER TWENTY-TWO

She heard and felt the snap of her leg as Kylen crashed onto her. Consecrated subway travel was obviously not meant to be taken with unintended passengers. They had landed in the middle of a cemetery on the edge of a town that she hoped was Meridian. Somehow Kylen had overridden her intended destination, detouring her here.

Against my will.

She wanted to zap herself back to Nate's without delay, but Kylen had a firm grip on her. He was sneering, obviously quite pleased with his success, but then he got a look at the improbable angle of her injured leg.

Kylen cursed. Or she assumed he cursed. While she didn't understand the language, it generated a lot of spittle and the universal body language of a Class-A curse.

Great, she'd managed to piss off a demon.

He looked down at her leg again in disgust. She wasn't sorry to disappoint him or foil whatever plan he had, but she did wish it could have happened in some less painful way.

"Get up!"

"I can't," she whimpered.

She thought again about trying to snap back through the subway, but she didn't think she was strong enough. She also worried how effective the very human Nate would be against the demon, considering how poorly Deacon had fared. Ruth figured her one hope was to bide her time and wait for a chance to escape.

She had no idea what Kylen had planned to do with her, but her injury had put an obvious wrench in his agenda.

"Fuck!" he growled again. Now that one, she understood.

"Humans are so fucking fragile. Your shell is worthless this way."

She resisted the urge to apologize. Unless he was planning to kill her right off, she was hopeful that he wouldn't be able to watch her or stay attached to her 24/7. A strangled scream escaped her as her vision tunneled down to a thin black line.

God help me.

She was about to pass out in the middle of a cemetery with a demon. And then she did.

* * *

When she awoke, she had no idea what time it was or how long she'd been out. Taking a few moments to assess the situation and her immediate surroundings, she determined she was inside a warehouse of some sort. It was silent—not even traffic noises were filtering in.

Not good.

She lay there for a moment longer, taking inventory, before realizing one more very important thing. She still had her underwear on, but her jeans were missing.

Great.

Opening her eyes hesitantly, she stared down at her naked legs. On the bright side, her broken leg wasn't crooked anymore. It was, however, hot, swollen and tight as a sausage in a casing. It had been reset, but it was still much too painful to move. She couldn't imagine any situation in which she could ever walk again on her own accord.

Lying on her back on an army-style cot, she turned her head from side to side to get a good look at the small, barren room. The one door was closed. A desk with a shadeless lamp sat against the wall to her right, a chair pushed up to it. The single bulb was the only thing illuminating the room. There were no windows and no other furniture. It appeared to be an unused office of some sort. At least she was alone. The demon Kylen was nowhere in sight.

Movement seemed impossible, but she needed to find a way out, and soon. She hoped beyond hope that the place was consecrated. If she had to make it out of here on foot, she wasn't going anywhere. How long before Kylen would return? Or was he outside the door even now?

It's now or never.

Ruth screwed up her courage and braced herself for another hard landing. She concentrated on Nate's place, focusing what little energy she had left on getting herself there. The tingling sensations began to fill her. She felt the pull as the door to the office ripped open, and Kylen crashed into the room. She flashed into Nate's living room alone, and in the nick of time.

* * *

Her escape would have seemed too easy to her except for the landing, which nearly brought her out of her skin. Nate and Deacon immediately descended on her like two mother hens.

Deacon took one look at Ruth, half-naked and in pain, and she didn't have to imagine what was going through his mind. His face said it all. The pain rendered her mute, so an explanation would have to wait. Neither of them tried to move her, for which she would be eternally grateful. She half wished she could pass out again.

Deacon and Nate exchanged a look, and then Nate backed away. Ruth heard him chanting as he fortified the circle of protection.

Ruth could see the glow from Deacon before she felt it. His entire body lit up, and he placed a warm hand over her forehead and another across her stomach. As his hands hovered over her body, a warm gush of green energy flowed through her entire body before settling inside her injured leg.

Deacon's light radiated so bright and clear that it stung her eyes to look at him. A tear slid down her cheek.

In an instant, the pain began to fade. A mantra played through her mind: *Thank God, thank God, thank God.*

Deacon held her in his light energy for what seemed like hours, letting it massage its way through her. It was so blissful and intimate that she didn't want it to end.

Her leg began to itch and cool, and when she opened her eyes and glanced down at it, the swelling had dissipated and the color was back to normal.

Tentatively, she wiggled her toes then moved her ankle in a small circle. She bent her knee a bit and stretched it back out. There was no pain, and it felt just like her other leg. It was a miracle.

Deacon slumped beside her, while Nate watched them in awe from across the room. Ruth could only imagine what he was thinking, but since he wasn't flipping out, she assumed that Deacon must have gotten him up to speed on the whole reaper thing.

"I suppose this means I'm going to have to go on another food run," Nate said, shaking his head. "They're going to think I'm a freak for eating so much."

"Thanks, Nate. We owe you," Deacon said, caressing her leg.

"Yeah, you do… I'll be back."

Nate grabbed his wallet and walked out the door, leaving Deacon and Ruth alone on the floor. She lay motionless, feeling completely and utterly relaxed. The healing energy was much more powerful than anything else she'd experienced from Deacon. Not only had it healed her, it had soothed her down to her very soul.

Deacon stroked her hair in long strokes, grounding her. The green energy had made her nerve endings alight and hyper-sensitive. She could imagine a lot of other good uses for it …

"You scared the shit out of me," he said, pulling her close.

"Well, I wasn't too happy about the situation either."

"What the hell happened to you? You were gone for more than twelve hours. I expected you to be back in an hour tops."

"Things got complicated," she said, snuggling against him. "Kylen grabbed me and followed me out. When my leg was broken in the landing, I guess he abandoned his plan, whatever it was. I don't know why, except that I think I may have become more of a burden for him than he wanted."

"Tell me everything."

"I will, as soon as I can," she promised, her eyelids drooping. She let him hold her tighter, her head on his lap. He leaned down and kissed her sweetly. All Ruth wanted was to curl up next to him like a cat and sleep the rest of her troubles away. This reaper business was exhausting. She'd been on the job an entirety of twenty-four hours, and in that time, more had happened to her than in the rest of her life combined.

How would she get through another day at this rate? She had carried a stranger's soul into Purgatory, been bullied by an angel, and battered and kidnapped by a demon. If this was reaper hazing, they could count her out.

CHAPTER TWENTY-THREE

Deacon filled her in on what had transpired between him and Nate while she was gone, and she did her best to concentrate. While she thought she got the gist of it, she wouldn't be ready for a quiz anytime soon. Her stomach growled, demanding attention. She needed more calories. Many, many more calories.

Not all of her cylinders were firing yet. Deacon dragged her up against his chest, and she relaxed back into him, managing to doze for a few minutes before Nate got back. She felt the shift in the energy of the circle before she even heard his key slide into the lock. Her sensitivity to the flow of energy was already growing stronger.

Nate pushed through the door, loaded down with fast-food bags…again. Deacon had better be right about all this calorie intake business, or she was going to be four hundred pounds by next month. Nate and Deacon both unwrapped burgers and dumped out fries into one big, easily accessible pile. Deacon handed her a milkshake to suck down while they worked at the second impromptu floor picnic in Nate's living room in a day.

Deacon downed a double burger, while Nate did a cursory exam of Ruth, paying special attention to her leg. Having one friend who could fill her with magic healing go-go juice and another who could heal her the old-fashioned way, while spinning magic circles of protection around her, was not a bad deal. Not bad at all.

Nate ran his hands up and down her bare leg, kneading, bending and twisting it to his will. All the while he quizzed her about her pain level. Her answer was unvarying. She was suffering from no pain at all. She had gotten over her embarrassment about the whole pantless thing. Almost. Neither of the men had commented on it.

Smart boys.

After thoroughly examining her leg, Nate stood up and shook his head in amazement.

"There's no way that leg should be ambulatory at all, let alone healed." He stared hard at Ruth, like maybe she was keeping a secret from him.

"Do you want to try to stand on it?" he asked.

"Sure."

He extended his hand and pulled her up, drawing her in against his chest to steady her. He held her for perhaps a second too long. Standing up in a heartbeat, Deacon wrapped his arms around her and drew her out of Nate's embrace.

This is new.

"I've got her," Deacon said, his voice a low rumble.

"Sure." Still, Nate didn't let go.

"I've got her," Deacon repeated. Reluctantly, Nate released her and Deacon pulled her back against him. Ruth felt like some sort of chew toy with a German shepherd on one end and a pit bull on the other.

"How does your leg feel?" Deacon asked, caressing her shoulders possessively.

"Good as new."

Now that the milkshake and burgers were doing their job, she felt almost human again. She chuckled to herself—*almost human.*

"What?" Deacon asked.

"Nothing." She smiled and the two men exchanged a look, raised eyebrows all around. They didn't need to know about every little thing that went on in her head.

A girl has a right to a few private thoughts, right?

Deacon led her over to the couch, and Nate tossed them another sack of burgers and fries before plopping down into his wing chair. Deacon eased down next to Ruth, placing a proprietary arm around her. She wasn't sure what all she had missed, but she really, really wanted to get some pants on.

"I hate to trouble you, Nate, but do you have some shorts or something I could wear?" Somewhere along her adventures that day, she had lost her backpack, as well.

Not too surprising.

Nate jumped up and headed to his bedroom. When he was out of sight, Deacon ran a warm hand up her thigh, giving it a little squeeze as he whispered in her ear.

"Good idea. I wasn't going to be able to ignore this situation much longer."

Nate returned with sweatpants that looked way too huge for her, but they at least had a drawstring in the waist instead of elastic. She slipped them on, cinching the string and knotting it to keep them from falling down. The tension in the room dropped several notches once she was clothed again.

Relaxing into his chair and sighing, Nate exchanged another loaded glance with Deacon. Something was going on between those two. She wasn't sure how much or what it might have to do with her.

"Okay, Ruth, you're up to speed on our end of things, so tell us what happened when you got to Purgatory," Deacon said.

When she looked at Deacon for confirmation that he wanted her to tell the whole story, unedited, he nodded. She spilled out the details to the best of her memory.

Deacon got excited when she mentioned the electric-blue energy she'd generated, the Kylen breakthrough and the whole demon name thing. She knew it was important, and was thankful something potentially useful had come of her horrifying day.

"This is huge! The demon wouldn't have knowingly let Kylen tell you its name. Your light energy may have given Kylen the boost he needed to break through, if only for a moment. And he must have led the demon away from where he was holding you for long enough for you to escape. Otherwise, the demon would never have let you go without a fight."

"Does this mean you can help Kylen now?"

"I can't." Deacon looked over at Nate. "But he can. Like we talked about? Right, Nate?"

Nate nodded. "Theoretically, we should be able to trap the demon for long enough to force him out. I can have the apartment ready by tomorrow night… You just have to get him here."

"No, not here," Deacon said, stroking Ruth's hair. "We need to do this at Ruth's place. There are too many witnesses and potential casualties here."

"Okay, I'll get my stuff gathered up and bring it over. It's going to take a while."

"Have you done this before, Nate?" Ruth asked.

"No. But we can do it."

She admired his confidence. These two men were nothing if not confidence and testosterone embodied. She hoped he was right because she'd witnessed the damage the demon was capable of inflicting. Deacon looked so much better, and the wounds she could see were all healed, but she worried for Nate... And frankly, she worried for herself, as well. Someone needed to be left standing to make a food run if necessary. There was no pizza delivery where she lived.

"So, what now?"

"Now we go clean up some souls and lay a trap for him. We're going to make him an offer he can't refuse."

"Okaaaaay ..." she said. "And how are we going to do that?"

"We'll make sure we're completely caught up, and then tomorrow night, we'll leave him some bait."

"What do you mean? Bait?"

"I'll purge a few souls at a location of our choosing. Demons are nothing if not opportunistic. Between the lure of a few easy souls and the chance to defeat us? He'll come."

It sounded risky all the way around to Ruth, but she didn't have a better plan. If it worked, they had everything to gain, but if it failed? Someone would be reaping *them*. She had no desire to see where the demon would take them.

"Nate, can I borrow your computer?" Deacon asked. After Nate voiced his agreement, Deacon sat down at the neat little desk in the corner of the living room and started jabbing at the keyboard with his index fingers.

"What are you looking for?" Ruth asked, peering over his shoulder.

"Obits, murders and deaths in the area since Tuesday. We're way behind schedule, and there are lots of souls for the picking right now. We need to limit his options."

Ruth watched him peck and find for a good three minutes before it was all she could stand. "Move over," she said, hip-checking him out of the chair. "This is totally my thing."

She pulled up some more suitable search engines, sending a list to the printer in a matter of minutes.

Deacon pulled the list off the printer and smiled. "Damn, now that's a useful talent."

She agreed. At least she had gained something advantageous from her six years of graduate school.

Nate gathered up his supplies as they formed their game plan. Midstrategizing, Deacon looked Ruth up and down and gave her a slow smile.

"You're kind of cute like that."

She didn't feel kind of cute. Her ponytail was a mess, she smelled like a cheeseburger, and it felt as if there were socks on all of her teeth. She was also pretty sure that what little mascara she had put on two days ago was in a raccoonlike circle around her eyes by now. Obviously, he was brain damaged from fighting with the demon.

He leaned in and gave the top of her head a kiss. She snuggled her cheek against his neck, wishing herself back to the night she had spent in his arms.

Nope, I'm still here. Still about to help bait, trap and fight a demon. What the hell?

Nate came back into the living room with two empty duffel bags and another one with a red cross emblazoned upon it.

"What's in that bag?" Ruth pointed to it.

"At the rate you two are going, I think it's a good idea to be prepared for more potential medical catastrophes."

Probably a good point.

"You'll have to open the circle around your house, Ruth, or I'll never be able to get in."

"I don't know if the circle's even there anymore, given how many imps were trying to nosedive their way through it the last time I was home."

"We'll go to the house first to make sure that

everything's clear. We'll leave the door open for you," Deacon said. "Thank you, Nate."

"What else are friends for?"

* * *

Deacon and Ruth landed back in her living room. Even though they'd only been there for a few moments, she was glad to be back home.

"I'm going outside to check the perimeter. Five minutes and we're out of here."

Ruth rolled her eyes at him and headed to her bedroom to pack yet another backpack. She also changed into a pair of jeans that fit her better. The last thing she wanted to do was fight a demon in floppy sweatpants.

Not that I'll do much better in jeans since I still have no idea what the hell I am doing.

She got her things together, stuffed them in the bag and walked back to the kitchen to add a few snacks.

She liked Nate, a lot. But she couldn't figure out what was with all the posturing between him and Deacon.

She shouldered her backpack and left through the back door, where Deacon was ready and waiting. Impatiently.

CHAPTER TWENTY-FOUR

Deacon looked at her. Hard. "That took forever."

"It wasn't that long," she said, making her way to him. "I needed another backpack and pants. I thought it would be best if my pants didn't fall off in the middle of whatever we're about to do."

Softening, Deacon smirked. "Well, I wouldn't go that far."

She wound her arms around his waist. "What's wrong?"

"Nothing." He stood rigid in her arms.

"Well, *something* is going on. What's wrong with you and Nate?"

Deacon shook his head. "He's upset with me for holding out on him all these years. He's been casting circles and consecrating ground for me for a long time without asking questions, which I like about him …"

His face relaxed, and he sighed. "He was pissed to find out how big all of this is so far into the game. I should have told him a long time ago."

Ruth rubbed her hands up and down Deacon's arms,

comforting him. "He's a good guy. I could have trusted him, but I was also trying to protect him. People don't need to know about us...or about all of the real things that go bump in the night. Too much reality is a burden that most people can't handle."

She had to agree with that, as quite enough reality had been dumped onto her as of late. It still felt as if there was a lot more to the story, and then there was that bizarre vibe that she was getting from Nate. Not to mention his befuddled and muddy aura. Even more disconcerting was that his aura was *brightly* muddied. She had no idea what that meant. Was it really just his confused feelings over being left out of the loop, or was it something else? Jealousy, maybe? That part she did not understand at all. It had to be something else, but she had no idea what.

Deacon gave her a squeeze and snatched up his backpack along with the death notices she had printed out. He slipped the pack on and folded the papers, sliding them into his back pocket.

"Let's go. This list is long, and I have a feeling that the demon has already been busy tonight."

He wrapped his arms around her, holding her tight. She felt the pull, and in a few seconds they were in the middle of Meridian National Cemetery.

* * *

The cemetery was situated along two very busy main roads in town. They landed in the middle of the grounds under a gazebo. Deacon pulled out the piece of paper from his pocket. They were looking for George Robert Farr, aged ninety-three. George had passed a few days ago and had been buried today.

It was a big cemetery and there was probably a map somewhere, but George had been buried too recently for his resting place to be on any map. They needed to look for the most recent ground turning and the freshest turf—new earth screamed of fresh death. It was an old cemetery and the newest arrivals were all situated along the periphery, so they headed from the heart of the grounds to the south edge.

Streetlights brightened the otherwise dark cemetery and the luminescent moon made it easier to read the headstones and markers as they made their way across the lot. Since it was the oldest cemetery in town, many of the rock markers were fragile and crumbling.

A variety of headstones were arranged in neat rows, ranging from marble crosses and elaborately engraved granite monstrosities to large box-shaped crypts. Ruth tried to read the dates as they walked through. She was amazed that each time she thought, *This has to be the earliest one,* she'd find another that was even earlier.

Some stones dated back to the early 1800s. Most of the Civil War casualties from the area were buried here along with the more recent fallen service members.

Eighteen hundreds? Ruth did some quick math in her head. If Deacon was 206, he would have been born in the early 1800s?

"Deacon, are you from here? Did you know any of these people?"

He paused, and then took time to look at the stones, studying them. "I grew up near here. I know some of the family surnames."

"How old were you when you first reaped a soul?"

"I was twenty-eight." Deacon walked ahead and Ruth followed close behind him.

"Twenty-eight? So you first started reaping around 1834? How did you even know how to start?"

"Most reapers spend their lives in geographically secluded communal camps where they're mentored by other reapers. It was that way for me. We learned to channel and harness our energy, studied reaper history and trained to fight. We had to reap a hundred souls along with a mentor before graduating to solo expeditions. Even after we graduated, most of us traveled in pairs.

"Contrary to what you've experienced, demon poachers aren't all that common, but they do appear from time to time. They're one of the reasons that reapers carry a scythe. It makes it very handy to decapitate a demon when we come across it. And occasionally, we're called in to dispatch other wayward beasties as reaper bounty hunters."

"Like what sort of beasties?"

"You've seen several representatives already."

The thought of "other beasties" was far more disturbing than the fact that they were walking through a cemetery in the dark of night. She wasn't all that good at dealing with the living, but the dead? Maybe she could learn to appreciate them.

Traffic whizzed by on two of the four sides of the cemetery. National and Sunset were busy thoroughfares, and even though it was nearing 2:00 a.m., there was an uncomfortable amount of activity. Ruth still found it difficult to trust in the whole reapers-repel-normals thing. Deacon didn't seem all that concerned, and she supposed that as long as they weren't digging anyone up with shovels and headlamps, it was pretty unlikely that anyone would notice them even if they *were* normal.

Deacon spotted a potential candidate a few graves ahead, and they made their way over. The headstone had Mr. Farr's name neatly engraved on it next to that of his wife, Olivia Farr.

"Can you...feel him down there?"

"No. It's been too long. He died while I was incapacitated, and his soul detached too many hours ago. Now we get to go old school."

Deacon knelt over the grave, gripping the new turf, and turned on the juice. His hands glowed, and he attempted to summon George's soul from the grave. Deacon pulled and pulled at the grave but the glow dissipated. He rocked back on his heels and stood.

"Nothing. He's already been reaped."

Kylen, 1. Deacon and Ruth, 0.

There were no other unreaped souls at the cemetery. Deacon reached for her, and they spun to their next stop.

* * *

They landed in Maple Park Cemetery next, which was tiny in comparison but much darker. With no visible street traffic, they had about zero chance of being spotted as they made their way through the grounds, which was a relief. The entire cemetery covered a couple of wooded acres. It didn't take long to find the next candidate: Evelyn Opal Carson, aged eighty-seven.

Deacon went through the same machinations and mined the grave for Evelyn's soul. *Nada.*

The demon had been there, done that. Deacon's mood was deteriorating.

"Eighty-seven. I'll bet she saw a thing or two. What about you, Deacon? Have you traveled? You must have made it out of Arkansas at some point."

"I've been around."

"Seriously? That's all you've got? It's going to be a long night at this rate," she prodded.

Deacon sighed in defeat. "Kylen, Kara and I trained together, like I told you. After we'd reaped our quota and graduated, we hung out in Purgatory more than was probably recommended and listened to the reapers share their 'war stories.' Some really were war stories. We chased disasters and wars for about five years, traveling across the world through the consecrated subway, harvesting souls along the way, until our reaper senses began to take over, making things more urgent for us. It's hard to ignore the pull very long when you're stationary."

"Where did you travel? I've never been out of the state."

"In 1834 we went to Western Australia to the Battle of Pinjarra and harvested the souls of the Aborigines killed by British colonists. In '35 an earthquake in Concepción, Chile, killed five thousand. We stayed there for several months after the reapings had been completed, and then came back to the States in '36 in time for the Battle of the Alamo. More than three thousand were killed there. We racked up the reapings and grew stronger and stronger, but we still weren't ready to accept territories of our own. Kara and Kylen grew closer, and we just kept traveling the world as reaping vagabonds until …"

"Until Kara was killed?"

"Yes."

Well, if that wasn't a conversation stopper …

Deacon clammed up after that, and they rode the consecrated subway to three more cemeteries, repeating the process with no luck. Two more possibilities remained on the list for the night. Both were at East Lawn Cemetery.

* * *

At almost eight acres, East Lawn Cemetery was another one of the larger cemeteries in town. To Ruth's relief, though, it was tucked away from the main streets. The downside was that the streetlights were far enough away that the numerous trees made it almost impossible to navigate until their eyes adjusted. One by one, the white headstones appeared out of the darkness like blooming moon flowers.

Ruth's night vision obviously wasn't as good as Deacon's. She could make out shapes but little else as she shivered in the cool evening air. Her discomfort wasn't entirely caused by the temperature. Something was off here.

They were being watched.

They rounded a large crypt with a marble angel perched on top and stepped into the path of some sort of animal scurrying through the cemetery. Ruth jumped and gave a little squeak.

Deacon didn't even flinch as the raccoon raced by— instead he studied the direction from which it had come. Something had frightened it. A dog would likely have been racing along behind it already if it had been the culprit.

Ruth squinted hard into the darkness, trying to make out the shapes and forms around her. Deacon's hand began to glow with white light. He closed his fist, holding it over his head until it radiated like a giant flashlight. Projecting the ball of energy in the direction the raccoon had come from, he watched as it exploded into a camera flash of light upon its impact with the ground.

It was long enough to see the silhouette of a man standing just outside the perimeter of the cemetery grounds. The smell of sulfur wafted across the cemetery.

"You have got to be kidding me." Deacon cursed.

"What?"

"It's *another* fucking demon."

The demon, who most assuredly was *not* Kylen, was standing just outside the perimeter of the cemetery, at least a hundred feet away.

Planning and researching a confrontation in her mind was much different than executing it. A prayer whispered through her head. She didn't want to screw this up.

"Stay here, Ruth. When I tell you to go home, do it. Don't hesitate," Deacon whispered in the darkness.

She nodded, hoping he saw her response. Her throat closed with fear. She wasn't any kind of hero, nor did she feel all that lucky. The one thing she could do was put her trust in Deacon.

* * *

Deacon approached the demon, projecting confidence and determination. Knowing that he was well armed didn't calm the turmoil in his heart. Keeping Ruth safe was first and foremost on his agenda. He'd expected Kylen, not *another* demon. They were multiplying like rabbits. Why did they keep appearing in Meridian? It wasn't that strange for one, maybe two, to "leak" out into a territory from time to time, but this?

He drew his scythe, challenging the demon. No need for a lot of talk. The demon brandished a small knife, and Deacon nearly laughed out loud. At least this time the odds were a little more in his favor. Deacon carried no souls and his weapon was much, much larger. There was no way to know how many souls the demon might have harvested, but considering the quickly deteriorating flesh on its human host, it was safe to assume he was near capacity. The bastard needed an upgraded ride in the worst way.

One thing he did know was that it hadn't gotten its bounty from the cemetery. Demons couldn't cross consecrated ground unless they possessed a reaper or some other holy ride. Hospitals and accident scenes were a different story. It was quickly becoming a game of Whac-A-Mole. Put one demon down, and another popped up.

Could this night get any more fubar?

An added bonus: unlike Deacon, the demon could choose to abandon its body if things went south. It had nothing but a shell to lose. Deacon had a whole hell of a lot more at stake.

Of course, dead was never really dead in the supernatural world. The best he could hope for was that the demon would stream away to the portal to Hell, wherever it was, and disappear like the others. He flicked open his scythe and made his move.

The demon squared off and crouched low, twirling the knife in its right hand as it cocked its head to the side, staring at him with its black eyes. It didn't advance, but it didn't retreat either. It was acting damn strange actually.

It couldn't enter the cemetery but it *could* retreat. *Should* retreat. It was no secret what Deacon was.

Deacon made a wide swipe through the air in a long slashing X pattern, trying to get a rise out of the thing and spur it to some action. Instead, the beast stayed right where it was, as if it were content to let him walk right up and slice its head off.

But as Deacon finally crossed from the consecrated grounds and came within striking distance, everything went haywire. The demon threw the knife toward Deacon's torso like a dagger, and then pulled out another from behind its back. When Deacon dodged to miss the blade, the demon darted along the edge of the cemetery, finally running away.

Right to where Ruth now stood.

* * *

Ruth wasn't even sure what she planned to do until she found herself climbing over the fence, several hundred yards down from where Deacon was confronting the demon. She thought that if she could get behind the thing she might be able to distract it enough for Deacon to finish it off.

And no. It wasn't a great plan. Especially considering the puny weaponry she brandished: a silver kitchen knife and table salt. Terrifying.

The one thing she wasn't going to do was stand by and allow another one of those bastards to hurt Deacon.

She'd just passed over the wrought-iron rail, careful not to puncture her more sensitive areas with the pointy spikes on top, when she looked over to track their progress. The demon was closing in…on her.

A sound she didn't even know she could make escaped her as she fumbled for the little knife and closed her hand around a pocketful of salt grains. It was the equivalent of throwing sand in a bully's face, but it had worked for her once. She just didn't know if she could stand her ground as the hideous thing charged her.

"Ruth, run! Back to the cemetery. Go home!"

She wanted to. She really, really did because the folly of the situation wasn't lost on her as the demon came ever closer, Deacon a few paces behind it. The problem was that she was frozen like an armadillo in headlights, and by the time she decided to move…it was too late.

* * *

Deacon brought his scythe down onto the back of the demon's neck in one powerful stroke, and watched the head fall at Ruth's feet. It was quickly followed by the bastard's body, which tumbled across the lawn, folding into a pile like a train wreck. Seconds later, the black demon streamed out of the open cavity, and Deacon's heart stopped. Instead of flowing away, it headed directly for Ruth.

It wanted a new host.

Demons couldn't enter a reaper without being invited. Apparently, this one hadn't gotten the memo. When Ruth opened her mouth to scream, the abomination silenced her with its filthy essence, trying to force its way into her.

Ruth's eyes were wide with fear, and Deacon all but lost his mind as he began to manifest the most powerful energy he'd ever conjured. He grabbed hold of Ruth's head, one hand on either side of her face, and pushed bright blue energy into her with a force that would have vegetated a human upon impact.

Seeming to understand what was at stake, Ruth somehow managed to summon her own energy, which sparked and crackled against Deacon's, merging into a bright blue orb around them both. The demon backed out but remained trapped within the orb. Its dark black essence grew light gray the longer it was exposed to their light. It filled the space around them until Deacon drew it inside of himself like a reaped soul. It streamed into him and the blue light instantly faded. When he looked back at the body, three souls hovered above it, reformed beside their broken shuttle. Drawn by the force of his energy like a vortex, they streamed into him, as well.

Stunned, Deacon backed away from Ruth, waiting for the beast to overtake him. He wasn't sure what the bastard might make him do. Maybe he'd even make him kill Ruth. He felt so full of both good and evil that he thought he might burst at the seams.

Deacon looked back at Ruth. She wiped tears away with both her palms and started to come toward him.

"No. Stay away from me. You have to go home. Nate can protect you."

"No, I won't leave you again."

"It's only a matter of time before the demon takes

me over. I'm surprised it didn't happen immediately. Go, Ruth. Go before I can't control my actions."

She hesitated, frozen in place once again.

"Now, Ruth!" His harshness was enough to break her out of her shock. "Go while you still can."

"Deacon, no!"

"Do it!"

Ruth blinked at his ferocity but scrambled back over the fence with tears in her eyes. He hated himself already. And he knew the answer to the question that had haunted him for years. How could Kylen have ever let something like this happen? How could he have chosen to become possessed?

Now he knew.

"Go!" he spat at her with as much force as he could muster.

She finally began to shimmer and dissipate before his eyes, leaving him alone in the cemetery to deal with his demons.

And a decapitated body.

Perfect.

CHAPTER TWENTY-FIVE

Deacon crossed back into the cemetery and steadied himself against a large crypt wall, trying to ground himself. Between the demon and the three souls he'd just consumed, his insides felt like a macabre kaleidoscope of swirling colors and emotions. He expected his free will to be overcome at any moment. God help the souls when that happened.

God help him, as well.

He wished he could purge them all, souls included. But there was only one place he could even hope to accomplish that. Maybe if he could make it to Purgatory in time there might still be a chance to rid himself of the fiend.

Then there was the body to contend with. Normally he'd find a place to dispose of it, but he didn't think there was time. Improvising, he carried the corpse and its head back to one of the larger crypts, popped the lock with a blast of orange and threw them inside. He locked the padlock again and memorized the name above the door, hoping the Summerall family didn't have a lot of frequent visitors.

He paced in front of the crypt, wasting even more precious time trying to make up his mind. Now that Ruth was out of his immediate reach and hopefully safe at home, the souls were his most important consideration.

Worst-case scenario: he'd be overcome by the demon in Purgatory, causing him to make a scene, and Rashnu would smite him. Best-case scenario: he didn't hold out much hope for a best-case scenario.

Once again he'd sent Ruth away unprepared and unarmed. Of course, the alternative was no better: frying pan or fire.

He replayed the events over and over in his mind. The demon had appeared to be waiting for him. So where was Kylen?

His head hurt. His *heart* hurt. He wanted the demon inside him destroyed. Good and dead. Since it hadn't made a peep yet, he had no idea of its name, so exorcism was out.

And who knows if Nate can really do what he says he can.

Deacon wasn't equipped to do the job himself, having never successfully captured a demon. Reaping them had never occurred to him as an option...until it was his *only* option. And now? He'd give anything to be rid of the evil force inside him.

Realizing that Rashnu was his only hope was one of the worst parts of the situation. He'd almost rather make a deal with the Devil than that pompous asshole angel, but Deacon was confident that Rashnu would know how to destroy the demon permanently, or that he could at least lead him to someone who could.

He needed permanent. For all their sakes. Because *two* demon-possessed reapers on the loose would not end well for anyone.

He willed himself to the one place he might seek

refuge.

* * *

Landing in Purgatory, Deacon strode toward Rashnu, his rage increasing with each step as the demon pulsated within him. He hoped he had enough time left to state his case.

The reaper hoards parted in front of him as he stalked across the depot. Surrounded by a glowing bright white light, which—he realized with surprise—was his own aura manifesting, electric-blue sparks danced from his fingertips as he made his way.

He was death incarnate. And Death was pissed.

* * *

Rashnu raised his eyes to the spectacle approaching his platform. Looking down at his doppelgänger at the other end of the depot, he gave a silent signal. The queue before him turned in unison to face Rashnu's alter-self, making their way to the other end of the platform, well out of the wake of the approaching storm.

Through all the many millennia Rashnu had been the soul sorter in Purgatory, he had known only one other Potentate that had risen the ranks. It took a special combination of lineage, skills, talent and motivation to create such an entity. The stars had to be aligned just so. Grim had been the strongest, the most powerful, and until recently, the *only* Potentate.

But Grim had ascended and there was a vacancy to be filled. As Rashnu watched the light and dark energy emanating from Deacon, he was all but certain there was a new sheriff in town.

* * *

Deacon grimaced as the reapers parted, giving him a wide berth on his way to Rashnu. It occurred to him he felt…good. Really good.

Pissed, but good.

Traveling through the consecrated subway had somehow revitalized him, making him feel more powerful and electrified than he'd felt in the cemetery. He was certain that this feeling and the new aura were signs that the demon's tentacles were digging in and preparing to overtake him. His nerves were tight as springs, ready to snap into action. Still, whatever the reason, he felt energized. Alive. And all but crackling with power.

Rashnu descended from the pedestal to meet him, staying well out of reach, he noticed.

"Deacon, I see you have urgent business. Let's retire to more private accommodations, shall we?"

Deacon rolled his neck and heard his vertebrae crackle. "Not until these souls are deposited. Then we do indeed have other business."

"Of course, let us do that in private as well, shall we? Many eyes are watching, and we have much to discuss. More than I think you are aware."

Deacon looked warily at Rashnu. He knew that he'd probably never return if he went into the inner sanctum. But if it meant keeping Ruth safe and saving himself from a life like Kylen's, it would be worth it. Still, a warning nagged at the back of his mind.

On the other hand, he felt as if he could wrestle rhinos right now if necessary. The energy he contained seemed to be getting stronger with every passing minute. He realized with growing terror that he was a hazard. Trying to calm himself, he assessed Rashnu. The angel, of course, had no aura. The bastards were the master manipulators of auras. Wrote the book on them.

Deacon felt an almost uncontrollable urge to reach out and touch Rashnu.

Not a good idea, man. Keep it together!

He was coming undone.

Rashnu motioned to a doorway in the far corner of the depot. The door swung open, illuminating a hallway filled with bright white mist. Mesmerized by the light, Deacon followed as the angel disappeared into the white cloud ahead of him.

Down, down, down they walked, until the mist parted, and they passed through yet another door into a brightly lit chamber. What he saw in front of him was nearly indescribable.

At the very end of the corridor, a figure in a white flowing robe was standing on a platform. Part human in appearance, it was clearly *more* than human. Its face was something between a man's and a child's, and it seemed to be fluid and changing. Three sets of great wings extended from the entity, stretching out behind it, and it appeared to be floating on the platform, its feet not quite touching the stone floor. The creature's essence was so bright it hurt to look at it. Even so, Deacon couldn't pull his gaze away.

Seraph.

The souls inside of Deacon stirred and swirled, beating against his corporal form, demanding release. Never had a soul he carried struggled so much to be discharged.

They were drawn to this being by a force he could no longer contain. The demon, on the other hand, was cowering in some metaphysical corner.

Deacon fell to his knees before the creature and threw back his head. His mouth opened in a yowl, and the souls spewed forth in a thrum of power, screeching and tearing themselves from his body. The demon latched on inside him with invisible claws, grappling for purchase.

Deacon held fast against it.

Rashnu nodded toward the creature, giving it a slight bow. "Deacon, meet Grim. You two seem to have some things in common."

Deacon locked eyes with the being as the souls that had fled his body swirled around it in adoration. Just when he'd thought things couldn't get any stranger.

What the hell? Grim—as in THE Grim Reaper—was a Seraph?

Rising to his feet, Deacon looked over at Rashnu for...*guidance?* He didn't know what he expected from the angel.

"Go," Grim commanded, sweeping his hand toward the souls. Hesitantly, they began to stream away. They vanished up through a chimney in the center of the stone room, drawn to their destination by an unseen force. Deacon's retinas felt as if they were burning. The glow coming off the creature before him was sharp and painful.

"Sorry for the glare, it's an occupational hazard, I'm afraid. With great power, comes great light. I'm sure you're feeling a bit of that right about now, as well. Power, that is," Grim said, his feet settling against the floor.

Yeah, power. That was what he was feeling all right. That and a whole lot of *what the hell.* The demon thrummed inside him.

"Approach," Grim commanded.

Deacon hesitated a second before approaching the being.

"You have a gift, Deacon. Capturing a demon is no easy task. Few survive it. I suppose that you'd like to find some depository for it other than yourself? Yes?" Grim asked, folding all of his wings, which disappeared behind him, and settling down into a large chaise on the platform.

A depository? Yes, that is definitely what he wanted.

Wait, no, not a depository.

He wanted it destroyed.

"No, destroyed. Permanently," Deacon managed to say, his hands trembling.

"Well, that is a whole other thing entirely. A demon can be destroyed. Everything that is born can perish. Demons are born of death and evil, so they can only die in the purest white fire. You have the bare demon's essence inside you for sure, but the question remains: Do you have the fire in your belly to follow through? Because, you see, if you consume it and destroy it completely, there's no going back. To *consume* the darkness and remain living yourself brings great power. You'll be endowed with new strength if you succeed. After that, things will become…more interesting."

Deacon had no idea what the Seraph was talking about, but he wanted this thing gone, and if it was within his power to destroy it, he was all in.

In for a penny, in for a pound.

Grim continued. "If you succeed, you'll be elevated to the Potentates: *The Powers.* You'll be recognized as an angel of the Sixth Choir—a warrior, as I once was—expected to be completely loyal to God. You'll guard the border between the realms, protecting human souls from the very demons who inhabit your friend and, for the moment, you. You may choose this path, or you may relinquish the demon, and we shall send it back to Hell. Of course, that would be temporary. The demon may return at any time to continue its quest for souls. And it will. What is *your* choice, Deacon? Choose wisely."

Deacon's mind reeled. *Powers?* He tried to remember the hierarchy of angels, learned long ago in his reaper history lessons: Angels, Archangels, Principalities, Powers, Virtues, Dominions, Thrones,

Cherubim, Seraphim?

Yes, that seemed correct.

It appeared he would be skipping a few steps. If having your mind blown was a side effect of ascension, then he was already halfway there.

And as for choices? Deacon didn't think there was one. He'd do anything it took to survive this and return to Ruth. And though he'd spent half his life trying to avoid the spotlight, the power that suffused him made him feel that there was only one path left. Forward.

"Let's do this."

"Very well. Summon your new power and purge the spirit that cowers inside you. Allow your light to consume it."

"How is it that the demon hasn't overcome me like Kylen's did him? What happens to me? Can I go back up top? What changes?"

"You, dear boy, didn't invite the demon in. You reaped it. For now, you should continue on with business as usual. There will be many changes, but you'll continue to inhabit your corporal form. You'll no longer be limited to the consecrated paths, and you'll be able to move between the planes and heavens freely. Other gifts will develop with time. And, of course, there will be many challenges. It's not all ice cream and rainbows."

"And Ruth? Kylen?"

"Oh, yes…the orphan and the traitor. No path is clear or predetermined, Deacon. We all make our own choices, and then must live with them. They may soon face some hard choices, as well."

"What's going on with all these demons? Why have so many of them been showing up topside?"

"There has been discord since the beginning, Deacon. The faces change, but the battle remains the same. Someone always wants what someone else has. In what is perhaps the oldest battle, Lucifer continues to toy with God's greatest and most pleasing creation: humanity. He wishes to find purchase on the earth and establish dominion over what is not his to dominate. It's our job to fight against him and his minions. The demons' increased activity is a sign that a new battle is coming...so is the fact that your powers have been awakened. The Powers are only activated when they are needed."

"Are you going to stand here chitchatting all day, or are we going to get on with this?" Rashnu asked impatiently. "Sir," he corrected.

Deacon didn't know which was more disconcerting, discovering that his hero and now mentor Grim had ascended to Seraph, and they were all about to be on the frontline of an epic battle, or having Rashnu call him "sir." Both were troubling.

Deacon closed his eyes and attempted to summon his power from its real source: The One True Light. Almost immediately, energy began to pour through his body. He imagined the energy as a bright white fire forming around him. His body on turbo charge, the power exuding from him was more intense than anything he had ever experienced. Opening his eyes, he was blinded by his own spectacle.

The demon twisted inside him, trying to retain purchase with its invisible talons. It was a losing battle. The thing streamed through Deacon's sternum, a wild frenzy of black smoke that became trapped within the walls of the circle he held.

Flattening his palms against the barrier of light, Deacon sent electric-blue fire coursing through it until the demon dissolved into dust. Deacon's white fire consumed the ashes, drawing them back into his sternum like an errant soul, until nothing was left of the demon. He collapsed into a heap, exhausted. It was done.

"Good work, Deacon." Grim rose and motioned

toward the door. "Now, let us walk and discuss some *other* matters."

Deacon stretched inside his skin, happy beyond measure to be free of the invader. Now, if he could only do the same for Kylen.

Chapter Twenty-Six

Ruth landed upright for the first time, on her own, in her living room. Closing the circle immediately, she was relieved to hear a whole lot of nothing but the tapping of rain on her metal roof.

She was exhausted. And Deacon was God knows where facing God knows what…and there was nothing she could do but wait. Again. She had a feeling that more things would continue to go wrong.

Tears threatened to spill down her face, but she blinked them back with stoic resolve, refusing to let them come. Because if they started…she'd be lost.

Padding across her living room, she made her way to the master bathroom. She turned the water as hot as she could stand it and stepped into the shower. Letting the water rush over her, she willed it to take her worry and uncertainty down the drain with it. Walking out into the steamy bathroom, she towel dried her hair, picking it out until the rats were gone.

Nightgown on and her hair blown dry, she crawled into bed at 5:00 a.m. She felt like hell. As she pulled the covers up around herself, she prayed for peace. Prayed for Deacon. Prayed for them all. As she began to drift off to sleep, she remembered at least part of the reason why she was so spent...she hadn't eaten. She'd expended more energy than she'd taken in as fuel maybe ten times over. At this point, she was too exhausted to do anything about it but sleep. There was no delivery out here and no one around to send for groceries. And although she couldn't completely rule it out after all she'd seen lately, she wasn't going to count on fairies bringing her a nice plate of heated lasagna.

Had she remembered to reinforce the circle? Suddenly she was sure that she hadn't, and she definitely needed to do that ... She did the only thing she was capable of achieving at that moment.

She closed her eyes and let sleep pull her under.

* * *

The phone was ringing. *Where was the damn phone?*

Ruth wanted to answer it, but apparently twelve hours of sleep wasn't going to be enough to get her body to cooperate with the orders her brain was issuing.

And then she remembered that she hadn't eaten. Anything. Deacon had warned her of what might happen if she let herself get too depleted, and she was feeling the effects of it now ...

Still with the ringing?

She managed to fling her arm toward the phone on the nightstand, making an awkward, fumbling connection with the receiver. She plunked it down in the general vicinity of her ear and mouth. If this was a solicitation, she was going to ask the caller to dial 911, because she was pretty sure this effort was the last one she'd be able to make without help...and a Big Mac.

"Hello," she managed to squeak out.

"Ruth?" Nate asked, concern apparent in his voice.

"Yeah."

"Ruth, what's wrong with you? You sound terrible. Is Deacon there? Are you okay?"

"No and no."

"Are you in danger? Are you under attack?"

"No…food."

"You haven't eaten? You need food? Can you get it?"

"No," she said, letting the phone fall from her hand and crash down to the floor. Faintly, she could hear Nate still talking, but she began to slide past consciousness, and she wasn't sure she'd ever be able to find her way back up.

Moments later, she was swimming through a dark lake filled with white and bloated floating corpses. Some were facedown, others faceup. A woman's hair fanned across the surface of the black water as Ruth bobbed up and down, riding the waves, trying to push her way toward the shore. She was far away from it.

She tried, without success, not to touch the corpses. But she couldn't keep them from bumping up against her and poking at her with their inanimate limbs. They bobbed along the surface for as far as she could see. The entire landscape was colored in shades of gray, and none of them had auras. They were good and dead.

In the distance, there was a faint glow on the shore: a tiny beacon. She concentrated on getting to that light. After swimming for a while, though, she was too exhausted to do anything more than float and let the water slowly push her toward the lights. She wondered if she could stay afloat until she got there. It seemed as though she'd been bobbing along endlessly. Hours already. It would be so much easier to stop trying and let herself sink down to the bottom and be done with it.

So easy to give up.

If only she could stop and be still, she could rest. But that damn light was calling to her like Daisy's green dock light in *The Great Gatsby*. Sink or swim to the light? One choice was so easy, and the other insurmountable.

She swam. Hard. If she didn't make it, there would always be the opportunity to quit the fight and let the water take her. But if she did make it …

She flailed and kicked, struggling through the corpses, pushing them aside. Relenting, she dragged herself up onto one of them, using its body like a kickboard so she could have a momentary reprieve. She was sickened by her mode of transportation, but it was getting her closer to the shore.

Her feet made brief contact with the sandy bottom, and after riding a few more waves, she finally found purchase on the sand. She made stepping motions toward the shore, feeling like a moonwalker given the ups and downs of the waves. Eventually, the water receded to just under her breasts, then her waist, and finally her knees. Her body grew heavy without the water to hold her up, and the bodies pushed against her, throwing off her balance.

Her knees buckled and her head and face went under the water. On instinct she inhaled and a big gulp of water filled her lungs. She marveled at the irony of making it to shore only to drown on the beach.

Coughing and sputtering, she managed to turn her face upward and twist her body to follow. The waves pushed her further and further up onto the shore with each surge until she finally reached dry land. She turned her head back toward the light. This close, it was bright and blinding.

She blinked repeatedly, trying to clear her vision. Startled awake, she thrashed for purchase once again, until she realized she was in bed. Not a sea of corpses.

And Nate was holding her eye open, shining a bright pen light into it.

* * *

She slowly took in the details of the world around her. It was dark outside, and she had an IV in each arm. Bags of fluids hung on a hook over her bed.

"Welcome back." Nate smiled, hovering over her, his face close to hers.

She was so weak that she wasn't sure if she could even talk. Her head was still swimming, and it seemed as though her vertical hold was defective. Nate's face rolled by in frames, as the happy juice slowly dripped into her depleted body.

Ruth tried to puzzle out how she'd come to be in this situation, but she couldn't remember. It seemed important …

Nate crossed to the other side of the bed and turned off the drip leading to her left arm, removing the needle, as well. It was instant relief. She hated needles. He crossed back to the other side and pulled one of her kitchen chairs closer to the bed and sat and waited.

Ruth tried hard to keep her eyes open. She didn't want to be back in that sea of the dead anytime soon. The minutes ticked by. The clock on the opposite wall said 11:00 p.m. Once again, she had no idea what day it was. She was going to have to get a smartphone, if only for that reason.

Nate watched her, obviously relieved she was at least sort of conscious. Slowly his image stopped rolling past her eyes every time she blinked. He reached over and took her cold hand in his warm and steady one.

Thankfully, her head did seem as if it was beginning to clear. The fuzziness was lifting. She took a deep breath and let it out in a sigh. Nate squeezed her hand.

"Thank you."

"You're welcome." He smiled at her. He really did have a great smile. "The IV is for nutrition. I didn't think I'd be able to get a milkshake down you until you were a little more coherent." He removed the IV needle from her other hand. "I don't have the magic touch that you and Deacon have."

Deacon. That was what was so important to remember. Deacon. The demon. The souls. Where was he?

"Where is he, Nate?"

"I don't know. He hasn't been back. I left the circle open for him, but I haven't seen a sign of him."

"Kylen?"

"I don't know the guy, but you haven't had any demonic visitors. I called your house to see if you two needed anything before I headed your way, and I realized you were in trouble. Ruth, I'm pretty sure you would have died if I hadn't shown up."

"Not died, but close. Thank you." She was beginning to feel much more coherent, and she suddenly realized that she had to pee like crazy.

"Uh, Nate? Can you help me to the bathroom?"

Nate nodded and reached under her shoulders and knees, lifting her into his arms. He carried her into the cramped bathroom and sat her on the edge of the tub. She really hoped she could take it from there.

Nate stood in the doorway facing the bedroom while she fumbled with her nightgown, trying to get herself situated. She wiggled her panties down and scooted herself the exhausting ten inches to the toilet. *Sweet, sweet relief.* One more water-related dream, and she would have wet the bed.

She took care of business, but then couldn't get her clothes arranged correctly, let alone stand up.

"Nate?"

He turned, saw her struggle and came to help. When he pulled her upright, her gown fell down to cover her body. With one strong arm around her, he held her upright, while the other hand reached down to pull her panties back up into place.

It was awkward but not sexual. At least not on her part. Nate's aura was so mixed up and bright that she had no idea what he was thinking, but his face was hot and red. He seemed confused.

Good, that made two of them.

He held her against him and shuffled out of the narrow bathroom. Scooping her into his arms, he made his way over to the bed and set her down carefully, pulling the covers over her.

"I don't think you need another IV, but you could probably use some real food. Man, I'm going to have to start buying these supplies in bulk for you two."

A few minutes later, Nate walked back in with a tray full of food. He was becoming quite the housewife. It was still mostly fast food that he'd bought on his way over, but he'd also reheated some lasagna for her. Nate handed Ruth a plate.

"You eat, too. You look terrible," Ruth said, diving in.

Nate shrugged and pulled out a sandwich from one of the bags.

"What's going on with you, Ruth? What happened out there? Did Kylen show?"

"Not exactly. Another demon found us. They fought. I got in the way trying to help and was attacked. Deacon took in the demon." She choked up with emotion and the burger sat like an anchor in her belly.

"You mean he's like Kylen now? There are two of them loose?"

"I don't know. He was surprised that the effects weren't immediate. He sent me away because he was afraid he might hurt me. I didn't want to leave him again, but he was so…terrifying. Nate, if you hadn't come …"

"You should have called someone for help, Ruth. Your family?"

"There's no one to call anymore. I'm all alone."

"No one?"

"My mother just died. That's how I met Deacon. He came to reap her, and things went crazy after that. My father died years ago."

"Siblings? Aunts? Uncles? Cousins?" Nate stuffed a man-size hunk of burger into his mouth.

"Well, my parents do have relatives, but they all live out of state, Florida mostly. I was adopted, and my mother and I were estranged for the past…forever. It's complicated."

His eyebrows raised, and he swallowed the barely chewed chunk of meat. "Yeah? I was adopted, too. How old were you when you got your family?"

"I was a baby. You?"

"Not so lucky. Five."

"And where are they?"

"There's a coven nearby. They're still very active, and they live on a property the families own together."

"Huh."

"What?" Nate asked.

"Sounds a lot like the story Deacon told me about reapers, how most of them live together in groups. It must have been nice, going from no family to tons of family." She smiled at him.

He nodded. "It beat foster homes."

A ruckus in the living room had Nate upright and alert in seconds. Ruth struggled to untangle herself from the blankets and food carnage.

Then Deacon walked into the bedroom.

* * *

Even though nothing had happened, Nate looked startled and guilty, and he moved away from the bed. Ruth wasn't sure how to read that. While she was thankful for Nate, and she liked him a lot, she only had eyes for Deacon. She hoped that she hadn't somehow sent him different vibes out of naïveté.

"What's going on here?" Deacon asked, crossing the room in two long paces and placing himself between the two of them. Nate took another step back.

"Nothing. I was just looking after her. She's weak. She was in an exhaustive coma when I found her. That seems to be par for the course with you two."

Deacon frowned as he eased himself onto the edge of her bed, stroking her hair.

"What is all of this?" he asked, pointing to the IV bags still hanging above the bed.

"I had to get some electrolytes into her before I could feed her. I also gave her a sedative so that she could rest and heal. The other is IV nutrition. She just came around. It's been twenty-four hours."

Deacon shook his head and sighed. "Did you bring this food, too?"

"Yes, what's left is in the fridge. She was too weak to eat until now. The IV at least got her kick-started. I'll go warm something up for you, too." Nate left for the kitchen, seemingly in a hurry.

Deacon buried his face against Ruth's neck. "I'm sorry," he said, kissing her collarbone.

"It's okay."

"No, it's not. Every time I have to leave you, something bad happens." Deacon reached for her hand. She gave it to him and peered into his eyes searchingly.

"And are you...*you?*" she said after a long moment.

Deacon pulled away from her briefly, and then

pressed his lips to hers with such tenderness it was all the answer she needed.

"A miracle?"

"Something like that. Ruth, if Nate hadn't been here...you could have died."

"You said we were hard to kill." She smiled, trying to defuse his anxiety.

"But not impossible. I didn't expect you to test the boundaries so soon. You aren't fully a reaper yet. Until you reap a soul, *really* reap a soul, you are mostly human. If your life force gets low enough, you might not be able to be revived with conventional means. Human doctors would think you were dead and pronounce you so. It only gets worse from there." Deacon stroked her hand and arm. She wanted to pull him into the bed next to her, but she didn't have the energy.

"Nate did the right thing for you...again. We need him around."

As if he'd been summoned by Deacon's words, Nate returned with more food.

"Thanks. Not only for the food. Thank you for taking care of Ruth. She needed someone, and you were there for her." Deacon reached out his hand. "It's good to know that someone has our backs."

Nate shook hands with him. "Eat."

Smiling, Deacon forked a piece of lasagna the size of his head. "Are the preparations ready for Kylen?"

"Not yet, I've been otherwise occupied." He nodded over at Ruth. "But I can be ready in a few hours."

"Why was Ruth's circle down?"

"I didn't have time to repair it. When I got here, she was in rough shape, and it was wide open. Her energy was so low that the circle would have been worthless even if she'd been able to close it."

Deacon fed Ruth a big bite of lasagna. "We can't take any more chances. From now on, let's assume that there's always a chance of danger. We have to protect ourselves at all times. Especially Ruth."

Nate handed her a melted milkshake. It was glorious.

"Now that I know what's really going on and what specifically you need kept out, I can tweak the circle so that the three of us can enter and leave at will while still repelling intruders. Supernatural intruders anyway. If you had told me the truth in the first place, we would have been better protected," Nate said, setting the plate aside.

"And would you have believed me, Nate? Besides, I was trying to protect you."

"*Seeing* is believing," Nate said. "I'm a believer now."

Ruth smiled. She wanted them to get along. They needed each other; all three of them did, but in different ways. Nate needed validation for his magic and a cause to fight for. Deacon needed companionship, and Ruth needed someone to teach her how to survive in this new life.

"What about Kylen?" Ruth asked.

"We'll make our move when you're back to a hundred percent. In the meantime, you're staying home. Nate can get things set up, and we'll all try to rejuvenate so that we're at full strength when we confront him. We're going to need it."

"Where is home, Deacon?" Ruth asked, trying to sit up.

"It feels like it's here, if you're willing." He took her hand in his, and Ruth felt her heart grow tight as her eyes filled with tears.

Stupid girl tears.

The thought of Deacon staying here long-term made her very happy.

Deacon turned to Nate. "Will you help us care for Kylen if we're successful? You have the expertise, and he's going to need more help than Ruth and I can give him. And Ruth's going to need help staying healthy while she learns to cope with her new abilities and this life."

Nate ran a hand through his hair and let out a sigh. "I already have a fulltime job."

"You'll be well compensated. Think it over, Nate. Your medical skills and hospital connections have already come in handy, not to mention your skills with magic."

"Seems to me that you both have a lot more power than I can summon," Nate said, picking at the plate before him. "I don't know Kylen, but I have to assume that he's equally well endowed."

Deacon smiled. "Well, I don't know about that, but yeah, he's powerful. What do you think, Ruth? Don't you agree that Nate would be an asset to the team?"

Even though she was still a few Quarter Pounders short of logical thinking, this decision was a no-brainer.

"Yes. Let's keep him."

CHAPTER TWENTY-SEVEN

Deacon somehow seemed more alive since returning from Purgatory. Maybe Ruth was still groggy from too many sedatives and too little food, but she knew something was different. Everything had happened so fast and was such a blur that at this point it was easier to accept things and move forward than to try and understand them all... Still, questions lingered.

"What?" Deacon asked, walking over to close the door while Nate prepped in the living room.

"What happened after I left, Deacon? How were you able to come back to me instead of ending up like Kylen?"

"I knew my only chance was with Rashnu. I went to Purgatory, hoping he could either save me or kill me. Something *did* happen to me, but certainly not what I expected. I managed to destroy the demon, and then somehow got a promotion. I've ascended to an order of angels called the *Powers,* and I'll be in charge of protecting humans from demons. I'll be a demon border guard essentially."

"Deacon, that's wonderful! And an angel? But what does it mean? You look the same."

"Good question. For now, we'll keep on doing our work like usual, but a battle is coming. The *Powers* aren't activated unless they're needed. If a demon border guard has been activated, then you can bet there is or *will be* a need for it. Grim seems to think that this cadre of demons that's been popping up is the test group. The calm before the storm. All the more reason to save Kylen so that he can fight for us instead of against us."

"And you think you can do that? Save him?"

"Yes. With Nate's help and the demon's name, I think we really have a chance."

He leaned in to kiss her again but she pulled away. "Morning breath," she said. "I think I need a shower and definitely a toothbrush before any more kisses. But then? I'm totally game."

Deacon laughed and scooped her up out of bed. "I think both of those things can be arranged."

He carried her to the bathroom, and while she brushed her teeth, Deacon started the shower. The bathroom steamed up almost immediately. He walked up behind her and burrowed his face under her hair and against the back of her neck.

"I don't know...you smell pretty good to me already."

She leaned into him and felt him reach for the hem of her nightgown, and then draw it up and over her head, leaving her bare against him. He cupped her breasts and pushed up against her, closing the distance between them.

"Too many clothes," she said, turning in his arms.

Leaning down to kiss her, he unfastened his jeans and Ruth pushed them to the floor so that he could step out of them. She pulled his shirt up his torso and over his head, breaking off the kiss. Palming his chest, she glided her hands over his smooth, hard muscles as his breathing got hard and frantic.

He reached over and opened the shower door, and then pulled her in with him. She leaned her head back under the water, letting it wash everything away from her.

As the water soaked her long hair and plastered it against her back, she tried to push all of her worries away and relax.

He snugged up against her under the hot stream of water, pulling her to him in an embrace and pushing his erection between her legs. After a long moment, he sat on the shower bench, pulling her astraddle him. Reaching behind her, he grabbed the bottle of shampoo, squirting some into his palm. He smoothed it over her hair and massaged in through her tangled locks, the smell of strawberries filling the shower.

"You smell good enough to eat," he whispered against her neck, brushing his lips across her skin.

She leaned her head back into the water and let the soap rinse down her body. He stood, and pulled her up, gently angling her so that she faced the back of the shower. He raised her hands above her head and held them pressed against the shower wall. The water beat down her back as he washed her with shower gel, his hands sliding up and down her body in long, slow strokes.

Her legs trembled, weak and shaky, as he slid his hand down and parted her thighs, washing her gently. His erection slid between her legs from behind as he leaned into her. One arm snaked around her stomach and held her upright, as he nuzzled her neck. His hot, electric tongue licked up the side of her throat, sending a shiver down her spine.

Her legs shook with anticipation, causing her to

tremble beneath his touch. Pulling her back out of the direct stream of the shower, he eased her back onto the corner bench again, going to his knees in front of her. She leaned against the shower wall, thankful for the support. Caressing the top of her thighs, he slid his hands behind her buttocks and pulled her to the edge of the seat as he licked the water rivulets from the inside of her thighs.

Her heart beat briskly, and she hitched in a breath as he slid his white-hot tongue into her core. She grasped his head and pulled him into her, trying to impale herself on his tongue. He laved at her core and sucked at her nub, now painful for release.

"Mmm, see, I knew you were good enough to eat. Let's move this to the bedroom."

He turned off the water and grabbed a towel from the little cabinet. Pulling her to her feet, he toweled her off gently, kissing her while he fisted the towel around her hair, absorbing most of the water. Grabbing a dry towel, he wrapped it around her body. She wanted to return the favor, but he lifted her onto the counter to wait as he dried himself.

He was a miracle in motion, and she loved watching him. His muscles rippled as he bent to dry the water from his smooth, taut legs. She would much rather have licked all the water from him with her tongue, and if her legs had worked correctly, she would have done it.

Scooping her up into his arms once again, he carried her back to the bed and gently set her down, the towel falling loose around her. He pulled the damp towel from under her and tossed it aside. The bedroom was chilly after the steaminess of the shower, and her skin prickled once again. He lowered himself down and covered her with his big, warm body—the best comforter ever.

He held her face in his hands and lowered his warm, wet mouth to hers. She released a moan into his kiss.

Her nails raked his back as their kisses became more frantic, and he spread her thighs with his knee, readjusting himself so that his erection lined up between her legs. Reaching down, he pushed her legs together again so that he could pump down into the space between her thighs and still rub against her nub.

The friction was exquisite, but she couldn't keep her thighs pressed together for him. They parted of their own accord in invitation. He growled a moan and slid back down her body to taste her once again.

"So damned good," he said, rubbing his stubble-covered cheek against her thighs. "Turn over."

She rolled over onto her stomach, and he pushed her long, damp hair aside, nibbling at the back of her neck as he snaked an arm under her stomach and pulled her hips up off the bed. Reaching down with one hand, he worked her nub as he slid two fingers into her core.

"Deacon!" she cried out.

"Mmm."

"Please!" she begged.

He pulled her hips higher off the bed and brought her onto her knees, his hands gripping her thighs as she felt the head of his erection push against her opening.

"Yes!" she pleaded.

He thrust into her in one long, wet stroke, and stars exploded behind her eyes as the air huffed out of her. It felt so good. He retreated and repositioned himself to thrust again. She arched back into him, wanting to take all he had into her body. He pounded into her over and over, until a green light began to glow around them both, and she heard herself begging him for more. He accommodated her obediently. His rhythm grew hard and fast, not like the first time but better, so much more. The light increased with each thrust, growing brighter and sharper around them.

He reached around and brushed her nub again as he

thrust into her. She exploded in wave after wave of pleasure. Pausing, he thrust one last time before releasing into her, filling her with his energy. Collapsing onto her, he pinned her to the bed with his spent body, pushing the air out of her lungs. Finally, he rolled them both over onto their sides, spooning her into his body so that his erection didn't have to leave her.

Flipping the comforter up to cover them both, he wrapped his arms around her, kissing the back of her neck as he cupped a breast in each hand.

Ruth couldn't speak. She was so satiated, and her already trembling limbs had somehow been rendered even more useless. She couldn't imagine feeling any more loved than she did at this moment.

* * *

An hour or so later Ruth woke Deacon with a kiss.

"I'm not complaining, but I'm not sure we have time for this," he teased. "You're supposed to be resting. Why do I have the feeling that this foreplay will lead to hours and hours of sex?"

"Past experience?" she asked, flipping the covers off him. "Hmm, looks like you're up for it." She reached between his legs to cup his balls and stroke her hand up his shaft.

"I guess I can't fool you. I'll have to make sure I live up to your expectations."

"I don't think that's going to be a problem." She giggled as Deacon rolled onto her, lowering his mouth to her breast and tracing his tongue around her taut nipple.

Ruth pulled him into her and sunlight streamed through her bedroom window, illuminating Deacon. She gasped. He looked like an angel. The sunlight cast a soft yellowish-white glow around his entire body. His skin began to grow warmer under her touch, which told her that something else was happening... It almost looked like a halo.

Something was *wrong*. She could see it in his eyes, but he couldn't seem to talk. His eyes closed for a split second, and when they opened again, they were the icy gray of a soul carrier. Deacon fisted the comforter on either side of her head and tried to speak. His jaws clenched as his body tensed and strained. Ruth watched in horror as he faded away before her eyes. One minute her hands were on his magnificent hips, and the next, he was gone.

She screamed.

* * *

Nate ran through the house, nearly breaking down the door to get to Ruth. If Deacon had hurt her, so help him, Nate would tear him limb from limb—friend or not.

Ruth lay naked on the bed. She scrambled for the comforter to cover herself, but not before Nate got an eyeful.

He was momentarily flummoxed as he tried to figure out what had happened. She didn't appear injured. Nothing was broken. No one was in the room with her.

No one was in the room? He looked around and peered into the bathroom.

"Where's Deacon?" he asked, glancing inside the closet, and then out the closed windows.

"He vanished. We were about to make love. He was in my arms, and then an angelic glow appeared around him, and he...faded away. Just disappeared."

"You mean he flashed?"

"No, he didn't want to leave. I think that's why it took so long for him to vanish. He was trying to stay here. I think someone took him!"

"What the hell? Can they do that? Can they yank

you out of your life like that?"

"All I know is that one minute he was here, and the next he was gone, against his will."

"Fuck."

"Sadly, no."

"Jesus."

"Maybe that's closer."

CHAPTER TWENTY-EIGHT

Ruth had no idea where Deacon had been taken, but after their conversation about his promotion, she thought she knew someone who might: Rashnu. He was the best place to start. The problem was that she couldn't get into Purgatory alone to search for him without a reaped soul to carry. As Deacon had explained, even Kylen needed to be carrying a reaped soul to visit Purgatory. She was fairly certain the same rules applied to her. She needed to talk to Rashnu. And she couldn't talk to Rashnu without getting into Purgatory. She'd been once with Deacon and once alone, but she'd had a soul then, one Deacon had spoon-fed to her. She still hadn't harvested one herself.

The prospect was terrifying.

But leaving Deacon to whatever fate awaited him on the other end of that cosmic pull was even more terrifying. She'd failed him twice now. She wouldn't do it again. Collecting herself, she wrapped the comforter around her body and walked over to the dresser to grab some clothes.

"What are you doing?" Nate asked.

"I'm going after Deacon."

"How do you plan to do that? You don't even know where he is."

"No, but I know where to start. And I only have to do the impossible to get there."

"What do you mean? *Where* are you going?"

Ruth hip-checked him out of the way and opened a drawer, gathering jeans, a T-shirt, underwear and socks before stomping off to the bathroom. This was not how she'd planned to spend the day. She'd have to fill her pack with snacks and hope she wasn't too depleted to finish what she was about to start.

"Ruth, answer me! Where are you going?" Nate asked, grabbing her elbow as she passed.

"Purgatory."

"I'm going with you."

"Nate, we don't even know if you *can* go, or if you're able to travel through the consecrated subway. Have you? Ever? Besides, you can't go to Purgatory unless you're with another reaper carrying a soul or are carrying a soul yourself. I don't even know how I'm going to accomplish this, let alone try to take you with me."

Nate tightened his grip to the point of pain. Ruth cried out, "Nate!"

"I'm sorry. I'm sorry. Jesus, I hate this. Every time we all split up, more bad things happen. Ruth, I'm going."

"I don't think it will work."

"We're going to try. If you go… I go." Ruth studied him hard for a silent moment.

"Well at least imps aren't pinging off the circle of protection," she finally said.

"Yet," he said, releasing her arm.

Ruth continued to the bathroom and closed the door

to change. She leaned back against it, shutting her eyes. An hour past sunrise and this day was already shit.

* * *

Ruth headed to the kitchen to stock her backpack. Food, salt, more food. She noticed Deacon's backpack leaning up against the end of the couch where he'd left it.

On second thought, she took the provisions out of her pack and stuffed them into his instead.

After she was finished, she ran her hand over the scabbard at the back of the pack, and pulled out the scythe. It was heavier than it looked. As she gripped the ornately engraved steel handle, the metal warmed in her hand. She gave the scythe a hard swift flick with her wrist and elbow and jumped when it opened up into a deadly weapon capable of beheading man or beast. Holding it felt good.

Nate walked in as she was admiring it. Unamused, he reached forward to take it from her.

"No," Ruth said, stepping out of his reach.

"You're going to get hurt. If you want a weapon, take your mace or stop and buy yourself a Taser or something. That thing isn't going to lead to anything good."

"I think that's the point of a deadly weapon, don't you? We're not facing puppies here, Nate."

"We don't know what we're facing. Maybe he's not even in trouble, Ruth. Maybe he wanted some time away."

"Really?" she asked incredulously as she folded the blade closed and slid it into its scabbard. "Naked? You think he'd flash himself away somewhere *naked?*"

Nate turned his back to her and walked over to the kitchen window, obviously trying to process the whole strange situation.

"Probably not, but what if you run off half-cocked, and he comes right back? Then we'll have to find you and save you, and... Jesus, it's never going to end. It's going to be one emergency after another."

"Good that you know a thing or two about emergencies, then. I'm going after him, Nate. You're not going to stop me."

Nate bowed his head, defeated. "At least fuel up this time."

"I intend to."

Nate followed her into the kitchen and began pulling food from the fridge and cabinets. They already needed to make another grocery run. Ruth didn't have time to worry about it now. She ate six Hot Pockets turnovers, a box of Toaster Strudel pastries, three cans of soup, and drank a boxful of Capri Sun juices.

She didn't own a scale, but she knew from the gap in the waistband of her jeans that she had lost weight. It made her think of that Stephen King book *Thinner* where the main character had been cursed to lose weight until he died. Maybe King knew a thing or two about this crazy world she'd been thrown into.

When she couldn't stuff in one more bite, she slipped on her shoes and hoisted the backpack. She realized with a frown that she didn't even know where to start. No way was she going back to the hospital. Even though it was unlikely that she'd be questioned, she didn't feel like pressing her luck without Deacon to back her up. And for all she knew having Nate along for the ride might mess with her reaper mojo.

Then there was the whole waiting for someone to die thing. Ideally, she would find someone who was already dead...and alone. She cursed herself again for not getting the internet hooked up. Now she was going to have to fly blind.

At least she and Deacon had been to several cemeteries yesterday—*It was yesterday, right?*—so she knew where to look. Panther Valley would be the most secluded, but it was also a long shot. Hundreds of local founding family members were buried there, but these days there wasn't much action there. She would have to go systematically from cemetery to cemetery looking for a fresh grave and hoping for the best. It was a terrible plan. It was the only plan she had.

She decided to try Maple Park Cemetery first. It was tiny, but it offered more cover with all its giant oak trees, and it was in a much quieter part of town. Broad daylight might not have been the ideal time for what she was attempting, but her options were limited.

She told Nate her plan, such as it was, and he shouldered a backpack of his own. He had tucked what looked like a butcher knife just under his belt loop, and it was lying flat against his hip with a piece of cloth bundled around the blade in a homemade sheath.

"Are you sure you want to come, Nate?"

"I'm not letting you do it alone."

"Suit yourself. Ready?"

"I hope so. Promise me you won't pull that scythe out in public."

"Only if absolutely necessary."

"So how does this work? Or not."

"Deacon said that reapers can take things or people with them if we're strong enough and if the passenger has enough supernatural ability."

"And if I don't?" Nate asked, skeptical. Ruth didn't blame him for being concerned. She wasn't exactly a pro at any of this.

"You'll stay here. Don't worry. You're not going to get cut in half or anything. You can either travel or you can't. It's that easy." She parroted Deacon's teachings with false confidence.

Nate muttered something under his breath, but all she could make out was "easy" as he moved to the center of the living room. Ruth held out her hand to him. He took it reluctantly, and she slid her arm around his waist, snugging herself up against him. Ruth was pretty sure that Deacon had been serious about the not getting cut in half thing, but just in case, she thought it was a good idea to have some full contact going on. She didn't want to have to deal with a severed hand or something worse when they landed.

She tightened her grip around him and concentrated on Maple Park. Her skin tingled, and in no time, she was squinting her eyes into the bright sun filtering through the hundred-year-old oaks in the middle of the cemetery. She congratulated herself on landing on her feet. And further congratulated herself when the worst thing to happen to Nate was that he projectile-vomited from motion sickness.

Yep, been there. Done that.

Glancing around to make sure that no one was gaping at their sudden appearance, she was relieved to find that they were alone. Completely and utterly alone.

"Jesus Christ!" It seemed as though Nate had once again found his religion.

While he got himself back together, figuratively speaking, Ruth made an assessment of their situation.

No cars on the streets. Good. She made a quick scan searching for any freshly turned earth in close proximity to them. *Nope.* She was going to have to canvas the grounds and hope that she found a fresh grave that Deacon hadn't already visited.

She walked through the cemetery, Nate trailing behind her, clearly not quite recovered from his first five-ticket ride through the subway.

Rookie.

In the far back section, she found what she was

looking for. The turf was raised a good six inches on top of the freshly turned ground. She noted the headstone,

Earnest Bradley Stone 1931–2013. Eighty-two. Good. No way was she ready for a young one. She glanced around again, making sure that no one was watching her.

Kneeling at the edge of the grave, she placed her open palms on the soft turf, pressing down into the ground. Summoning what energy she could, she pushed it down as she had seen Deacon do. *Nothing.* She closed her eyes and tried again. Imagining the orange glow surrounding her and flowing down into the grave through her hands, she reached for Earnest. Imploring him to come forth.

She was startled when she felt a sharp tug, like a fish on a line, and she let out a little gasp of surprise when Earnest's soul came streaming up through the soil.

Jumping to her feet, she found the spirit staring at her. His misty gray form hovered before her, her heart beating so hard it was painful.

"Hey, Earnest," she said softly, wiping her dusty palms on her jeans while the elderly man's spirit hovered, looking thoroughly confused. "I guess there's no need for a long conversation here. Just so you know, I'm a reaper, and you're my first soul. So, give me a break if you can."

"You have one? A soul? Already?" Nate asked, his eyes the size of softballs.

"Apparently. Do you see him?"

"No."

Interesting. She had no idea what that meant. There really should be a handbook for all of this.

Ruth stepped forward and reached out to Earnest. She imagined the orange glow again and let it envelope both of them as she opened her mouth and inhaled deeply, willing him to enter her.

Oh please, oh please, oh please, she pleaded as Earnest began to shimmer and quiver in the bright sunlight. Sure enough, he stretched long and thin, and then streamed down her throat and into her body. She didn't know whether to be excited or disgusted. She felt like throwing up.

Instead, she swallowed hard and took some deep breaths, wondering what would happen to Earnest if she hurled. It was a toss-up as to who was more surprised by her success: her or Earnest. Nate remained clueless.

"It's done."

"And I missed the whole thing?"

"What can I say? Some of us got it. Some of us don't."

Ruth couldn't believe she'd gotten so lucky. Thank God Kylen—and whatever other demons might be lingering around—had missed this one. There were probably other souls that needed to be reaped, but she wasn't about to press her good luck. She walked over to a large walk-in crypt, which could offer her some protection from prying eyes.

Deacon had assured her that once she was carrying a soul, she would be completely unnoticeable. Still, she felt naked and anxious without the cover of darkness... But the thought of doing this alone at night was terrifying, too. She was going to have to get a whole lot tougher, and quick.

Even though she didn't feel like it, she pulled the cheesy crackers from her backpack and a can of protein shake, gagging them both down.

"So the soul is in you? Right now? You don't look any different." Nate was watching her as if she might sprout another head at any moment.

"What about my eyes? What color are they?"

Nate leaned in, then startled backward. "They've changed. They're gray."

"That's the soul."

"That's the most incredible thing I've ever *not* seen."

"Oh, it gets better. Next stop… Purgatory."

Ruth stuffed the empty can and wrapper back into her pack and offered a silent prayer. Considering what Deacon had told her about Grim becoming a Seraph and his own heavenly promotion, her prayers suddenly felt much more personal. A few short weeks ago all of this would have seemed like a fanciful fairy tale to her. *Now?* She had a soul inside her *that wasn't her own,* and she was headed to Purgatory…again.

"Let's go." She wrapped her arms around Nate's waist and closed her eyes, letting herself swirl through the consecrated subway to Purgatory.

CHAPTER TWENTY-NINE

Ruth landed in Purgatory.

Alone.

For whatever reason, Nate had been allowed through the consecrated subway, but he was apparently *not* allowed into Purgatory. She briefly considered flashing back and trying to take him home again, but she was probably already pushing her limits.

Ruth took quick inventory of her surroundings. It seemed as though everything in the Great Beyond's clearinghouse was business as usual. She snorted to herself.

It was ridiculous to even think that *anything* could be usual about Purgatory. This routine had already becoming way too...routine.

Rashnu resided on his usual perch—both of them. She walked toward him, exuding a confidence she didn't have. He was not going to intimidate her this time. She was on a mission. She was a reaper. And by God, he was going to help her get the answers she demanded or...or something.

She wasn't sure what she could use to blackmail an angel into helping her, but she was hoping for some creative ideas to spring forth once she got rolling. And that was the extent of her plan. Bend Rashnu to her will. Find Deacon. Take him home.

Flawless.

There were two other reapers in front of her. She studied them carefully this time. She was done avoiding eye contact. She wanted to know exactly what she was up against, and what sort of creatures she could expect to meet in the course of her work, no matter how slimy and disgusting they were. And geez, but they *were* slimy and disgusting. She was thankful that the initial nausea she'd experienced after consuming Earnest's soul had passed and the snacks had given her a second wind, or she would so be tossing some cookies right now.

Rashnu caught her eye and gave her a startled nod of his head.

That's right, you'd better acknowledge me, you winged freak.

She approached and managed to keep her sassy comments inside her head...for the moment anyway.

"We meet again, my dear. Sadly, there is never enough time to get more properly acquainted." He readjusted his robe, casting his eyes about the rambling crowd of reapers. "I assume that Deacon must have instructed you well for you to be here again so soon, alone?"

"It was more trial and error. And Deacon was taken."

Rashnu lasered his sharp stare at her. "Taken where? By whom?"

"That's what I was hoping you could help me to figure out."

"Indeed," he said, as he stepped down from his platform. He raised his gaze to the other end of the depot, sending the rest of the reapers in line in an about-face toward his alter self.

"Well, my dear, it seems that get-to-know-you meeting will happen after all. Come with me."

Ruth followed Rashnu as he led her through the crowd to a tunnel in the center of the back wall of the terminal. The stone tunnel was dimly lit, but the lights brightened when Rashnu crossed the threshold. Ruth looked around to determine the source of the light, discovering it was Rashnu himself casting a bright white glow before him. Darkness closed behind them, and Ruth's heart fluttered with a flash of panic.

One trip down a dark tunnel in Purgatory had been quite enough for her. Maybe she was in over her head after all. No one would find her down here if Rashnu chose not to release her. Could she get trapped in Purgatory?

They continued down the corridor for many long minutes before they came to a large, ornately carved wooden door. Rashnu placed his palm on it, sending a warm orange glow into it, which swung it open.

The room was huge and lavish, filled with velvet-upholstered couches dotted with richly colored pillows. Satin curtains hung over nonexistent windows and sparkling gold accoutrements bedazzled every surface. A spectacular glittering chandelier hung from the center of the room, and she was pretty sure that the jewels that were dangling from the arms of the fixture were obscenely large diamonds. She could see no obvious source of the light coming from the chandelier, but the light reflected off the stones in prisms of color along the white-washed walls of the room.

Rashnu motioned to a couch. "Sit."

He walked over to a mirrored bar that lined one wall and poured two drinks, presenting one of them to her.

"Tell me what happened. Leave nothing out."

Ruth took the drink. She wasn't a big drinker, but she was willing to give it a try. However, she did worry about what it might do to Earnest.

"Do you mind if we do something about the soul I'm carrying first?" she asked, clasping the drink in her hands.

"Ah, yes, details. Well, out with it."

"Uh, again, not so sure about the extraction part. I got lucky on the consumption side of things."

"Deacon has still taught you nothing?" He downed his drink in one quick gulp and looked longingly at the bottom of the empty glass before setting it on the table before him.

"Well, it's simple enough. You must expel the soul the same way you drew it in, only in reverse. Summon your light energy, and let it fill your solar plexus chakra, and then use that energy to push the soul from your body through your throat chakra. Later you may allow them to exit through any or all of your chakras, but for now that will be the easiest. See, it's simple. Much better than having it ripped out, don't you think?"

Ruth had studied chakras a bit when she'd researched aura colors long ago, but she'd never thought she would do anything substantial with that knowledge. She wouldn't have even believed in it at all if not for her own strange and unexplained ability.

"Well, what are you waiting for?"

Ruth didn't like being pressured, but at least there wasn't a huge audience this time. She closed her eyes and imagined her energy growing. As it began to build, she felt a warm tingle in her chest, which she allowed to grow until it threatened to burst out. She opened her mouth and threw back her head, pushing Earnest forth. He flowed out in a gray mist and hovered above her head, unsure.

Rashnu pushed an orange ball of light at him, and he

streamed out through the closed door, on his way to God only knew where.

"Much better," Rashnu said, turning his attention back to Ruth. "Now, where were we?"

Ruth struggled to regain her composure. "Deacon is gone, taken. I thought you might know where… Actually, I thought *you* might have taken him," Ruth said, bringing the glass to her lips.

"How was he 'taken' exactly?"

"He began to flicker as if he were about to flash, but he didn't go willingly. He was trying to *keep* from flashing."

"Was there anything else? Anything unusual?"

"The morning light was streaming through the window and for a minute there, he was surrounded by it. He almost looked like …"

"An angel?" Rashnu finished for her.

She downed the contents of the glass in one gulp, choking as the warm liquid slid down her esophagus like hot broken glass, settling above her heart. It burned like fire.

"What the hell was that?" she gasped.

"I like to call it Daddy's Little Helper." He smirked.

"More like Daddy's Little Killer." She coughed.

"Yes, well, I find it helpful in stressful situations. You might, as well."

She doubted that. "So where is Deacon…exactly?"

"Powers can only be summoned by the Chief of Powers. Unfortunately, the current chief, Camael, has fallen and is otherwise engaged in Hell, commanding his legions. Grim will be the new Chief, but until that officially happens, Camael retains the power and the right to summon his charges."

Ruth swallowed hard, rubbing her chest, trying to ease the lingering burn of the liquid. "What would he want with Deacon? How do we get him back?"

Rashnu snorted. "There will be no 'we.' It's not possible to go marching into Hell and back. Not even for a reaper. It's generally a one-way trip unless you're a demon. You aren't part demon, are you?"

"I don't think so, no. Why did he summon Deacon? What's happening to him?"

"Nothing pleasant, I am sure. It's Hell. Camael is not to be trusted. His fall was a great defection, and even after all these millennia, he is constantly trying to corrupt those on our side."

"What about Grim—can't he rescue Deacon? Isn't he the one who promoted him in the first place?"

"Until Grim is installed as the new Chief, I'm afraid not. The reactivation of the Powers was…unexpected. It will take some time, but be assured we shall rush to make it happen. Deacon is invaluable now. We should have perhaps foreseen this possibility. Regrettably, there have been many distractions and disasters as of late." Rashnu crossed to the bar and refilled his glass. He tipped the bottle toward Ruth. "More?"

"No thank you," she choked out. Any more of that stuff and she'd be coughing up a lung…or worse. "Well, there must be some way to get to him sooner rather than later."

"Dear, even *I* cannot just *go* to Hell, no matter how much you might wish that I could. The portals are ever changing, and even if you managed to find one, you would be lost in the endless labyrinth of Hell's circles for the rest of your existence. Trust me. It's not a pleasant way to go. The only way into Hell is with a guide. Someone who has been there. Someone who knows how to find a portal. Someone who knows how to get around once you arrive. Unless you have a demon friend in your pocket, I know of no other way. Let me suggest that you return topside and continue with your…*work* until you are instructed otherwise. Camael is nothing if not persistent, so I would not expect to hear from Deacon anytime soon. But once Grim is appointed, we will make arrangements for his retrieval."

Ruth stood before him, defiant. "If you won't help me, I'll find a way without you. I won't leave Deacon to hang."

"You are perhaps stronger than you appear, dear one. God bless. In the meantime, I'll send a replacement reaper to cover Deacon's territory while he is indisposed. Now, let us go. We both have work to do, yes? The dead are ever dying."

Ruth followed Rashnu back through the tunnel and into the depot. Reapers went about their work, oblivious to her troubles. She was not bestowing BFF status upon Rashnu for his complete lack of help. She would find another way. She would. Even now, Deacon could be suffering. She knew that if she was the one who was missing, he would scour Heaven and Earth to find her.

All she had to do for him was go to Hell.

CHAPTER THIRTY

Deacon was in Hell. Literally. In all his two hundred and six years, he'd never actually been to Hell. As he sat naked in a stone cell, listening to the screams and moans that emanated from every direction, he decided he didn't want a tour. On the upside, it was stifling hot in his cell, so at least he wasn't cold. On the downside, he was still naked…*and in Hell.*

He'd yet to meet the one who had summoned him. Shit, he didn't even know he *could be* summoned. One minute he'd been about to make love to Ruth and the next he'd started to flash…against his will. He'd tried to fight it, but the pull had proven too strong.

Ruth must have freaked.

He squatted with his back against the wall, facing the cell door, ready for whatever approached him. What he thought he was going to do—naked and with no weapon other than his body—he had no idea, but he didn't plan to stay here one minute longer than necessary. Of course he'd tried to flash nearly fifty times, but his efforts had only succeeded in exhausting him more. He needed sleep, but he didn't dare take the chance of making himself any more vulnerable than he already was. Which was plenty. Besides, who could sleep with all that infernal noise?

No wonder they called it Hell. This was torture.

His head bobbed on his neck despite his determination to stay awake. He was damned for sure. Leaning his head back against the wall, he closed his eyes. Just for a second.

* * *

Nate paced the cemetery on shaky legs. He had no idea how long Ruth would be gone, or if she would even come back for him. Surely, she'd come back for him. Right? If she was as weak as she'd been when he found her at her home, he had no idea what he'd do. He'd have to call 911, but how would he explain himself or her? He just prayed that she'd materialize soon and everything could go back to normal.

His gut told him Normal was a town he'd never see again.

He thought about the last time he'd found himself unexpectedly alone in a cemetery. At least this time it was still daylight.

The world seemed like a much more dangerous place now. He'd grown up working with the supernatural, but he'd never experienced anything like this before.

Given the enormity of the forces they were dealing with, something could happen to him, something bad.

Even though his adoptive parents lived nearby and he retained active ties with the coven, he didn't visit very often. If he went missing, it would be months before any of them went searching for him. At least his lack of regular contact made them less of a potential target. Hopefully it would keep them away from whatever danger he was attracting to himself through his involvement with Deacon and Ruth.

As far as he could see, danger and death were the main ingredients of this life. He was a healer. Not a warrior. Not a reaper.

* * *

Ruth made her way to the portal out of Purgatory, her mind churning. Rashnu had mentioned something about portals to Hell. That was the one piece of useful information he had imparted. Otherwise, all she'd gotten from him was a headache from that stupid drink.

Her number one goal was finding Deacon and getting him home. Come hell or high water. She was pretty sure which one of those two catastrophes it would be.

That's when it occurred to her.

She knew one person who might have some insight into portals to Hell.

Kylen.

She placed her hand on the portal and zoomed back to Maple Park, where Nate would hopefully be waiting for her.

* * *

Ruth landed just feet away from Nate, startling him into a near cardiac arrest. Damn but it was a convenient way of traveling. Better even than the jet packs that scientists had promised decades ago.

He didn't think he'd ever get used to popping in and out of places at will. It was unnatural. He had done it twice himself now, and it still freaked him out. Give him the Honda any day.

"I was worried sick."

Ruth slid the backpack off her shoulders and dropped it by the crypt.

"I know. I'm sorry. We didn't know if you could go to Purgatory, and I guess we just got our answer." She rummaged through the pack, setting out the bizarre array of food. He was glad that she'd come prepared this time. "We've got some problems, Nate. Big ones. I met with the angel, and he was less than helpful. But I think I know how we can find Deacon."

"Why do I feel a big *but* coming on?" Nate removed food from his own pack and added it to her stash.

"*But*…there is one tiny thing we need for this plan to work. Deacon is in Hell. He's been summoned by the Grand Poobah in charge or some stupidity. And if that's not bad enough, you can only get there via special portals that change regularly. Oh, and it helps if you're a demon. We are going to need Kylen to take us there. He's our only way in."

"Shit."

"Yeah," she said, popping a peanut-butter-covered cracker into her mouth.

Seriously? Nate thought. *Hell?*

He looked at Ruth, worried that she'd lost her ever-loving mind. And how did she think Kylen was going to get them there when he was still possessed by a demon?

Oh, Hell and no.

Without Deacon, there was no way they could capture him, exorcise his demon and get him travel-worthy. And those were only the most obvious flaws in her plan.

"So what do you propose?" Nate asked, leveling a glare at her.

"We're going to save him first."

* * *

Deacon awoke to a low growl emanating from nearby. His muscles tightened, preparing him to spring before he even opened his eyes and locked on to the source of the sound. Outside his cell, a leopard paced back and forth in front of the entrance, its haunches rising and falling with each step. Deacon eased up from the floor slowly as the leopard sat back on its haunches and stared at him.

He'd encountered many creatures in his travels, but this was a first. What he wouldn't have given for his scythe…and pants, come to think of it.

That was what he was angriest about, that he'd been snatched away as naked as a newborn. It just wasn't right. He was thanking his lucky stars for the bars of the cell between him and the leopard when they melted away. Deacon tensed. He was somewhat confident that the brute couldn't actually kill him, but he didn't exactly feel like spending a long and miserable time healing from a mauling.

As he stared the animal down, the beast began to shimmer, slowly morphing into a humanlike figure.

Not a man, though… It's something else.

Deacon balled his hands into fists, ready to fight. He could do some damage to a man, even a supernatural one. At least it would be a fairer fight.

"Down, boy, you are not under attack."

Deacon stayed at the ready. No reason to trust his captor. Now or ever.

"Why am I being held?"

"You cut right to the point. I like that about you. And no whimpering…yet, anyway. Admirable."

Deacon glared, silently considering various ways to disembowel the beast and escape.

That's probably what Ruth thought when I appeared in her *house.*

Ruth. He was worried for her. Had the same assholes come for her? And Nate? Were they being held in similar chambers? He had no idea what was going on. It was time for some answers.

"Again, why am I being held?"

"My friend, I only want the opportunity for a candid conversation with you. And since I couldn't easily go to you, I summoned you *here,* as is my right as the Chief of Powers. I am Camael. Your boss."

The name meant nothing to Deacon. He had never paid attention to the hierarchy or bureaucracy of Heaven and Hell. Perhaps he should have taken more of an interest. He was pretty sure the name was meant to spark respect and fear in him. Instead, it sparked more anger. He hated feeling powerless and until recently, that had been the status quo.

"Grim is my boss. I'm afraid I'm unfamiliar with your name, and I still don't understand why you summoned me here…naked."

"Well, the naked part was unfortunate, but the summoning was necessary since you were about to embark upon a mission that is in direct conflict to my own."

"What mission would that be?"

"The demon controlling Kylen is one of my finest apprentices. I can't have you mucking up the works by killing his strong host or *removing* my minion from it. Besides, I wanted to make you an offer. Before you start working with Grim, you should experience the full spectrum of possibilities before you. And since you dispatched one of my scout demons so thoroughly, I've become, let us say, more motivated to ensure that we work together."

"That demon was poaching souls. He had it coming."

"I'm not surprised that you would see it that way

given your previous occupation, but there's more at stake here."

"Isn't there always?" Deacon sneered, shifting his weight and assuming a more combative stance.

"So defensive. Perhaps some clothes would put you more at ease?" Camael waved his hand at Deacon, and he was immediately clothed in jeans and a T-shirt. He even had on some boots. Definitely better, but he was far from grateful to the beast.

"I'm sure we can arrange for some more comfortable accommodations, as well. It's always so dreary down here in holding. I suppose we should do something about that at some point. Oh well, it is Hell, you know. Might as well get the souls used to things right off. Don't want them getting too warm and fuzzy. You, on the other hand, are a guest, not an inmate. Come," he said, smiling warmly at Deacon.

Camael turned, leaving his back vulnerable to Deacon. He briefly considered an ambush attack, but he didn't know what lay beyond the door. Better to case out the surroundings before planning his escape. He warily followed the creature out of the cell.

"No need to travel the hard way," Camael said, facing Deacon once more. He began to shimmer, and Deacon felt the pull as they both dematerialized from the holding area.

CHAPTER THIRTY-ONE

"Did you get everything ready at home for when we bring Kylen back?"

Nate hesitated, his mind racing as he tried to think of an alternate plan. "Yes, but I really think we're in over our heads here, Ruth. Not to be a buzz kill, but what makes you think we can even find him?"

Ruth held a slab of beef jerky between her teeth as she stuffed the food debris back into her pack, and then hoisted it over her shoulder. She snatched the jerky out of her mouth. "I'm pretty sure he'll find us, actually. All we need to do is spend time in a location where he *can* track us down. He's already attacked me twice. Third time's a charm, right? What better place than a cemetery?"

"So you plan to camp out here all night in hopes that he shows?"

"Not here. Good Springs. It's closer to home, it's really secluded, I'm fairly sure he's been using it to get closer to the house and spy on Deacon...or me."

Nate considered her deductions. Was he ready to put

everything on the line for Deacon? For Ruth?

His brain said no. But his heart said yes.

"Shit."

"Sounds like a yes to me." Ruth smiled and wrapped her arms around him. "Ready to fly?"

Before he could answer, they were swirling through the consecrated subway.

* * *

Deacon reappeared alone in an extravagantly appointed suite somewhere in the depths of Hell. It seemed like an oxymoron, but if Hell could be considered lavish, this was. Somewhere between a penthouse at Caesars Palace in Las Vegas and the real thing, the suite had every accoutrement of comfort including an elaborately dressed four-poster bed the size of a small bedroom. A bar and kitchen area took up one side of the suite while a grand bath jutted out onto a balcony which was swathed in an expanse of red light. Steam rose from the octagonal bath as bubbles percolated from an unknown source. It was decadent and inviting. But the best part was the silence. It was blissful after all of the anguished screams in the holding cell.

Deacon should have been disgusted, but he eyed the bed with something akin to lust. What he wouldn't give for a good night's sleep. He felt his will to fight ebbing. He was clothed, the room was warm and comfortable, and there was no obvious threat for the moment. He strode out onto the balcony and looked out. Nothing but a red-orange fog for as far as the eye could see. Unsettling. He wondered what lay beneath the fog. He had a feeling that he would find out soon enough.

For shits and giggles, he tried to flash again. Nothing. Whatever bound him here was still in effect. Before he got too comfortable, he needed to fashion a weapon of some sort that he could hide for later use. He had a pretty good idea he'd need one if he was going to make his way out of here.

He longed for his scythe, but that was not going to happen. He found an ornate mirror along one wall and carefully removed it from the hook. Placing the toe of his boot in the center of the mirror, he applied pressure until he heard the crack of breaking glass. Instead of shattering into tiny splinters, the mirror broke into larger more usable pieces, perfect for his purposes. He removed an eight-inch, blade-shaped piece and went about forming it into a shiv. It was crude but effective.

Better than nothing.

He made a makeshift scabbard and secured the weapon around his chest, its blade resting vertically along his spine. He eyed the bed again. Even an hour of sleep would go a long way toward restoring his strength. With sleep *and* a weapon, he was confident that he could find some way to escape. He lay on the bed carefully— the blade was wrapped, but he didn't need a sliced spinal cord on top of everything else. He closed his eyes.

* * *

Ruth didn't know how long they would have to wait. But she was prepared to spend the entire night in the cemetery if necessary. They'd watched the sun set, eaten everything left in both backpacks and rehashed their game plan over and over ad nauseam.

The night was warm and dry and the full moon gave them just enough light to take the creepy edge off. Mostly.

"So what did you think about traveling the consecrated subway for the first time?" Ruth asked, breaking their long run of silence.

Nate maintained his quiet in the darkness. Thinking

that the silence *was* his answer, Ruth gave up on small talk and resigned herself to waiting silently.

"It wasn't my first time."

Ruth couldn't have been any more shocked if he'd admitted to being some new supernatural beastie. "What do you mean?"

"I think I traveled through it once before...when I was five."

"And you didn't see this as pertinent information until now?"

Nate bent forward and cradled his head in his hands. "At one of the foster homes where I lived as a kid, my foster parents sent me to my room during a horrible argument. When I got there, I wished and wished I could be anywhere else. The next thing I knew I was in the middle of a cemetery. I was in my pajamas. It was cold and dark, and I was terrified. I don't know how long I was gone, but I prayed and prayed to be back home, and suddenly I was. The police came to my bedroom door because my foster parents thought I'd run away. They took me out of the home, and I never went back. I don't know how that happened."

Ruth was speechless.

"You *flashed* from your *bedroom?* What, did you live in a monastery?"

"No."

"How is that possible? Deacon said it has to happen from consecrated ground."

"I have no idea."

While they pondered that little tidbit, she kept her eyes on the perimeter of the cemetery. It gave her some comfort to know that imps or demons couldn't reach them within the confines of the consecrated grounds. Not that they'd seen any imps or demons. Still. She'd learned her lesson about climbing over cemetery fences.

Nate had finally stopped trying to talk her out of

their course of action. She knew it would work, because it *needed* to work. They certainly couldn't leave Deacon in Hell for however long it took for the powers that be to get their bureaucratic ducks in a row and crown the king or whatever nonsense was going on. She needed to take action.

Okay, so there wasn't currently a lot of action going on unless you counted the skunk with whom they'd nearly had a close encounter of the stinky kind, but she was confident that things would start rolling once Kylen showed.

And just as that thought was scrolling through her mind, who should appear at the gates of Good Spring?

Kylen.

Ruth was on her feet instantly. Nate stood slightly in front of her and to her side. How he planned to protect her against Kylen she had no idea, but she appreciated the noble gesture all the same. The best weapon on their side was the complete randomness of what they were about to do. Even if Kylen or his demon were prescient, neither of them would see this coming.

"Ready?" Ruth whispered to Nate.

He nodded and let her pass him as she approached the demon.

"Kylen," Ruth said, holding him with her gaze as she made her way closer to him.

"Ruth." He looked around nervously. She didn't blame him. It was odd. He had probably expected to find her cowering in fear. Just as she had every other time they'd met. "What's this? And who is this? And while we're doing the twenty questions thing, where is Deacon?" He drew his scythe from the scabbard on his back and let it dangle by his side, unopened but at the ready.

"Deacon...is on a mission. A very important mission. And we are on our way home. The real question is what are you doing here?"

"Stay where you are, Ruth."

"What are you talking about? You aren't afraid of a rookie reaper and a human...are you?" She was less than six feet from him now. All she had to do was make contact and maintain it for a few moments.

"Stop, Ruth. You don't want to get hurt here." He flicked open the blade.

"You're suddenly concerned for my health? You didn't seem to care when you ruined my leg on the way out of Purgatory. I thought you wanted a new ride."

"You're...offering?"

"Absolutely. I don't think I'm cut out for this reaper business. I've seen where the real power lies."

"And him?"

"An offering. A starter soul."

"An off ..."

Close enough.

Ruth grabbed hold of Kylen's shirt and launched herself against him, knocking him to the ground. The look on his face was almost worth it even if she was about to go down in flames and scorched flesh within the next few moments.

Her hands lit up like orange spotlights, and she pushed a bolt of orange energy into him, startling him into place as Nate piled on, trapping Kylen's scythe arm to the ground.

The glow encompassed them all. Their combined emotions fed the light energy, and she drew from Nate's aura, powering the light more and more. Anger, fear and hatred from Kylen and his demon mingled with her own energy until she thought that all three of them might ignite into a bonfire in the middle of the cemetery.

What sort of power had she tapped into? Twisting her hands around both of their shirts, she pulled them in toward her until all three of them were touching. She looked into Kylen's shocked eyes and screamed, "Home!"

Instead of the slow pull to which she was accustomed, they were ripped through the consecrated tunnels, a tangle of bodies, blades and backpacks. For a moment she feared they might all be ripped to shreds.

CHAPTER THIRTY-TWO

They landed in the middle of her living room in a pile of scrambling arms, legs and loose blades. Below them, engraved into the wood floor, was a six-foot circle of burned symbols. Both men were instantly on their feet and facing off, leaving Ruth to gather herself and her senses. Nate swiftly stepped out of the circle, and then grasped her legs, dragging her out, as well.

The demon slashed out with his scythe but hit a whole lot of invisible demon trap.

Realizing he was caged inside the engraved circle, the demon howled, cursing and spitting. If ever there were a time to believe in the power of magic, now was the moment. The fact the demon couldn't escape the circle to act on his obviously murderous thoughts was a miracle. Ruth wanted to kiss Nate for his ingenious trap, but wrong place, wrong time was an understatement.

Nate was all business, and he began chanting in Latin while the demon spewed insults, taunts and threats at them.

"You think this is the end? This body will be useless

if I leave it. I'm scrambling his brain right now. He'll be ruined. And his soul …" The demon laughed and tore at its clothes, his claws ripping into Kylen's body.

"Ex is vir everto, Orithidon, solvo is humanus vacuus vulnero physical vel mental, ex is vir nunquam ut reverto ut alius victus res a vomica super vos ut nunquam iterum reperio refugium in terra plagiaries." Nate repeated the chant over and over.

The temperature in the room plunged, and Ruth shivered as goose bumps crawled over her arms and legs. The wind picked up outside, roaring through the trees like a tsunami wave. She concentrated on reinforcing the circle, making it an impenetrable shield around her house. She felt it fortify and not a moment too soon.

Nate continued to chant. The demon thrashed Kylen's body around the small space, bloodying his flesh in crisscrossing slashes. His clothes dripped with his own blood. The shield outside sizzled, and she assumed that more of the demon's imps were crashing into the circle, bouncing off like fried June bugs.

It was a very satisfying sound. The demon continued to summon aid as he did his best to destroy his host's body with his claws. "Hurry, Nate."

Kylen was losing a lot of blood. The demon thrashed and slashed, cursing as Nate picked up the pace. The protective shield sizzled like bacon in a cast-iron pan as more and more of the imps hit it in their attempt to obey their master. You had to admire their loyalty, however misguided.

The demon halted in the center of the circle, making eye contact with Ruth. Smiling, he plunged one long talon into Kylen's jugular, blood jetting out of his neck in rhythm with Kylen's rapidly beating heart. The demon was abandoning its host.

"Now!" Ruth cried.

Nate struck a match and lit the edge of the engraved ring on fire. The flames flared up, and then raced in a whoosh as they made their way around, kindling each symbol. The demon wailed, plunging both clawed hands into Kylen's chest, laying open skin and exposing ribs. He dragged his claws down the entire front of Kylen's body.

Kylen's head snapped back, and the demon rolled out of his chest in a stream of black sulfurous smoke. Ruth watched as the stream of black smoke congregated, and then rose up to her ceiling and into a wooden box fixed in place above it. The smoke filled the box, condensing inside its walls. Nate leaped onto the hearth and reached up, slamming the box shut. He wrenched it from the ceiling, bringing a good-sized chunk of the plaster with it. Kylen's body crumbled into a bloody heap in the center of the circle, his head hitting the floor with a sickening crack. The flames snuffed out.

Nate chanted over the box and lowered it into a small iron safe covered in glyphs and symbols similar to the ones that had been burned into Ruth's floor. He closed the safe by sliding the open door down onto some notched grooves on the other side. As soon as it was in place, the edges of the opening merged together to form a solid cube. There was no key or combination lock. It appeared to be one solid and continuous piece of iron. If she hadn't seen it open to begin with, she would never have guessed that it *could be* opened or that there was anything inside of it. Nate placed the box on the hearth and turned his attention to Kylen.

Ruth was already tending to the bleeding reaper, trying desperately to put pressure on his gushing jugular wound. A large pool of blood spread across the floor as the color drained from Kylen's face.

They were a long way from a hospital.

"Keep the pressure on his neck wound, or he's going

to bleed out," Nate said, pulling equipment and bandages from his bag. "I can't fix him here. I'm an EMT, not a surgeon. He's never going to survive an ambulance ride."

Ruth leaned over Kylen and placed her hands on his exposed chest, near his heart, pushing healing green energy into him. It wasn't enough. His injuries were too great, and she wasn't strong enough to heal him alone.

"We have to get him to St. Mary's, Nate."

Nate nodded and Ruth wrapped her arms around Nate and Kylen, summoning what energy she had left. She felt the pull, but without any help from Nate or Kylen, it took forever before they began to leave. Finally, she felt the three of them being drawn toward their destination. She prayed that they weren't too late.

CHAPTER THIRTY-THREE

They landed in the chapel, Ruth still holding pressure on Kylen's neck wound.

"Nate, you have to leave the chapel. Get out, and then come back with the others when I call for help. It'll look too suspicious if they know you're here with me. As soon as he's stable, we'll bring him back home."

Nate hesitated.

"Go!"

"Shit." Nate ran to the door, peered into the hallway and then vanished down the corridor. Ruth gave him a good forty-five seconds before she started screaming for help.

Covered in Kylen's blood, she must have looked more like the patient than the rescuer when the first three nurses arrived and jumped into action. A code blue was called over the intercom and Nate and the E.R. team arrived with a gurney and a crash cart. Their medical parade clattered down the hallway in a rattling and clanging procession through the chapel doors. A large puddle of bright red blood had pooled across the floor between Kylen and Nate, and Ruth felt sick to her stomach. She wasn't sure how much more he could have in him to lose. Sure, Deacon had told her that the only sure way to kill a reaper was beheading, but still …

Nate fell into EMT mode. "He's down at least four units, maybe more from the looks of the chapel floor. Puncture wound to the jugular. Multiple lacerations over his neck and chest, exposed ribs." They grasped Kylen and lifted him onto the gurney.

Nate gently pushed Ruth aside, holding the pressure on Kylen's neck wound in her stead. The techs and Nate raced back to the E.R. suite and into a room. A nurse hoisted a bag of O-negative blood onto a hook while another fished around Kylen's inner elbow for a vein to tap into. They had trouble finding an un-mutilated area to administer the blood. Finally, the E.R. doc came into the room and the techs got him up to speed on Kylen's condition.

"You can take your hand off the wound," the E.R. doc told Nate. Nate pulled back and the blood erupted from the wound once again. Ruth's stomach churned as she stood against the wall, trying to become invisible. She wanted to know what was going on, but she also didn't want to answer too many questions. This was one situation in which she'd be more than happy to benefit from reaper anonymity. She had no idea what she was supposed to say about how they'd come to be in the chapel, but she wanted to keep Nate as uninvolved as possible. There was a lot of potential danger in this situation, legal and mortal.

She didn't want to leave Nate hanging, but these were his people, and if anyone's presence here was going to be interpreted as suspicious, it was hers. At least Nate was an EMT at this hospital. Making eye contact with him, she made a silent plea. He gave her a subtle nod in the midst of all of the chaos, and she slipped out of the E.R. room, making her way out into the labyrinth of the hospital before anyone could talk to her.

They hadn't considered this turn of events, but Kylen was in good hands, and Nate was fully capable of handling himself. He'd figure something out. Now, she had to do the same.

But where should she go?

She couldn't go back to the chapel. The police were already there by now. Working her way toward the exit, she walked out into the predawn summer morning.

The cicadas buzzed in the few trees around the hospital. The air was thick and palpable—a storm was brewing.

Her hair curled up tighter and clung to her neck from the humidity as she walked down the sidewalk.

At any moment, she expected hospital security to come bursting out after her, but no one came. She kept walking.

As she made her way down the street, away from the hospital, she became aware of just how many cemeteries, funeral homes and churches there were along her path.

While doing the research for where she and Deacon might find some loose souls, she'd discovered that in Meridian alone, there were a dozen funeral homes, twenty-eight cemeteries and two hundred and sixty-five officially recognized churches with brick-and-mortar buildings. That was a whole lot of consecrated ground, which in turn meant a whole lot of entrances to the consecrated subway.

She'd also found out that there were more religious institutions per capita and acreage in Meridian than in any other city its size in the world. Banks and Chinese restaurants were second and third on the list. The people of Meridian loved their God, their money and their

Cashew Chicken.

She walked nearly eight blocks before it began to sprinkle down a light rain. Spotting St. Agnes Cathedral, she headed that way. It was a Catholic church, and it was most likely locked up tight at this time of the night, but she had to give it a try. She was ready to go home. They'd done all they could for Kylen at this point. Right now, his care was beyond their abilities. He needed his physical injuries to be tended to by professionals, and then they could bring him back home and help him recover more quickly. The quicker the better.

Nate would call her when he could, and they'd make a plan to retrieve Kylen.

The church was well lit. Not wanting to draw any attention, she didn't linger out front. Steady traffic cruised by, and she prayed that no one would take notice of her.

Peeking through the glass doors, she wondered how much of the property was actually consecrated. Inside the building? The whole block and grounds? She found herself wishing again for an instruction manual for reapers.

She walked around to the back of the church and down a side alley until she reached an interior courtyard in the center of the church complex. A beautiful little garden with a fountain sat behind a locked iron gate. Several spotlights illuminated the grotto in a buttery yellow light. Unfortunately, spotlights likely also meant surveillance cameras.

Since she wasn't planning on vandalizing anything, she prayed there would be no reason for anyone to review those recordings.

She climbed up and over the gate, holding her breath in anticipation of setting off a motion alarm. She landed on the other side and let out a deep sigh of relief. No alarm.

Calming herself, she concentrated on home and slid through the consecrated subway, alone again.

* * *

Deacon woke to the unwanted ministrations of a woman who was attempting to unbutton his jeans with her teeth. He jerked awake to realize that there was another woman behind him. Both were beautiful, one with long, flowing red hair and the other a natural blonde. Yeah, they were both naked.

Shrugging them off, he scurried off the bed and reached for his blade. After Camael's transformation, he didn't trust anything down here to be as it appeared. No telling what these two really were.

"Come back to bed, lover," the redhead cooed, writhing against the blonde.

"Tempting," he said, putting some more space between them.

"Isn't that the point?" the blonde purred.

"Look, we brought you sustenance." The redhead pointed to the table.

"Of all kinds," continued the blonde, sliding her long legs off the bed in one fluid motion and prowling toward him. He didn't want to have to kill them, but if they got much closer... He didn't trust their intentions. At all.

Puzzled by how they had gotten into the room, he ignored them and explored the walls again, looking for an entrance. Camael must have flashed them in. Otherwise, the only way in or out appeared to be the red fog surrounding the balcony. He wasn't quite that desperate yet. He pondered how he could possibly learn the secret to flashing here. Maybe all he had to do was give up his soul.

The women fawned and rubbed up against one

another before him, entreating him to join them. Deacon stood his ground, his body not even bothering to betray him.

When it was clear to them that he couldn't be enticed, the women pouted and began to thrash about, pulling their hair in frustration. Their skin began to discolor and their beautiful faces melted away, revealing the raw white bones beneath.

They were hideous and fearsome and yet pitiful at the same time. As they wailed, begging him to come to them, Deacon stayed just out of their reach. At last they began to dissolve, disappearing in a flurry of strangled cries and screams. He was alone again, but he was hardly relieved by that knowledge.

He cringed, wondering what would come next. Gazing at the repast that lay on the table, his mouth watered, but the last thing he wanted to do was partake of anything that might make his situation more than temporary. Camael had said he wanted him to know what he had to offer. Well, if this was any indication, he'd have to do a whole lot better.

Deacon only had eyes for Ruth.

CHAPTER THIRTY-FOUR

Once again, Ruth found herself waiting at home while drama played out elsewhere. Deacon was in Hell. Kylen was in critical condition in the E.R., and Nate was at the hospital looking after him. She did the only things she could manage while she waited to hear from Nate: she ate, she slept and she cleaned. And then she ate some more.

She was not going to be a victim of reaper depletion again. There was too much at stake.

Even though she only managed a few hours of sleep, she felt much, much better than she had in the past few days. If not for the constant gnawing in her gut urging her to speed things along, and the fact that the two people she cared about most in the world were in great distress, everything would be swell.

She grabbed a box and headed to the junk room to start cleaning and sorting.

* * *

The junk room closet was more updated than she'd expected, with a wire storage system instead of the typical rod and shelf. While it was mostly empty, the uppermost shelf was stuffed to the ceiling with old bank boxes and other flotsam and jetsam. Obviously, this was a place to stow the things that had no other home.

She dragged over a chair, climbed on and reached up to pull down the boxes to sort through them. As she removed the last one from the shelf, the rotten bottom fell out of it, and the contents scattered across the floor. Cursing, she grabbed the empty box from the futon and sifted through the documents as she tossed them into it.

A thick binder caught her eye. It was from a law office in Meridian. She pulled the binder out of the pile. Her heart clenched in her chest as she read the cover. "Herrling, Gratz and Saltzman, Attorneys At Law.

Adoption & Child Placement. Mary and Charles Scott. 1985."

Her palms started sweating. The dustiness of the box made her feel confident that no one had been through it for a long, long time.

Clutching the binder, she walked over to the futon and sat down. There was no telling how this information might complicate her already complicated situation, but she couldn't resist the pull. She'd never pursued knowledge of her birth parents. She and her mother had already had so many problems… But now?

She flipped open the first page and spent the next hour consuming and memorizing the contents. The four words that made the biggest impression on her?

Elaina Carter, Birth Mother.

She wrote it on a sticky note and stuck it to the front of the folder.

* * *

Nate waited in Kylen's hospital room. Monitors and machines buzzed, wheezed and beeped. He had managed to arrange for a private room for the reaper, which helped. Quick and skillful, Nate checked all of Kylen's stats. While he had been pronounced stable, he looked terrible. He'd survived the surgery to patch him up and had received multiple transfusions. He still looked like hell. Despite his muscled mass, he wasn't healing like Ruth and Deacon had.

Covered with a thin blanket, he was still an intimidating man, his fierceness only slightly diminished by all the gauze and bandages covering him.

Nate checked the IV. One of the reasons Kylen hadn't regained consciousness was undoubtedly the inadequate nutrition he'd been receiving. From his limited experience, an injured reaper needed more than ten times what the doctors had ordered for their patient. Kylen was in a state of suspended animation. Without some serious reaper healing mojo and, oh, about ten thousand calories, he could stay in a coma indefinitely.

The hospital was already making arrangements to transfer Kylen to St. Louis, so they had to act soon. Nate picked up the bedside phone and called Ruth's house.

"Hello."

"Ruth, it's Nate. Listen, they're going to transfer Kylen tomorrow. We need to get him out of here tonight if you want to try to heal him. They've done all they can for him here, but if he gets transferred, I don't foresee him improving anytime soon."

"Stay put. I'll get there as soon as I can."

"Bring my car, Ruth. We're going to need some things."

Nate hung up the phone, realizing that he was about to kiss his job goodbye and likely become a felon in the process. If they were going to heal Kylen, he'd need to steal supplies from the hospital.

* * *

Ruth parked in the lot at St. Mary's and made her way to Kylen's room. Mercifully, no one stopped her, and she didn't have to answer any questions. She didn't know if her reaper repellent was working or if everyone was just busy. Either way, she wasn't going to look a gift horse in the mouth.

Nate was waiting for her when she walked through the door.

They quickly hatched a plan to divide and conquer. Nate would spend the next hour or so gathering and appropriating the necessary hospital equipment to care for Kylen at Ruth's house. Then he'd drive home, calling Ruth when he was ready for her to flash with Kylen.

Ruth planned to juice him up as much as she could once they got back. But she didn't dare waste her energy here, where it would be so easy for them to get into trouble. She didn't know how fast she could heal Kylen, but she was going to give it her all.

Kylen's injuries were vast even for a reaper, and his physical injuries were the tip of the iceberg. Being possessed by a demon for so long must have poisoned more than just his body. Neither of them knew what the condition of Kylen's mind would be, or even more importantly, his soul. With a corrupt soul, all the medical care in the world could be for nothing.

* * *

Nate unloaded the last of the supplies from his Honda and carried them into the house. He'd appropriated the junk room, setting it up as the makeshift hospital room. It was full. It was amazing how much stolen hospital equipment he'd been able to jam into the Honda.

The only things missing were paper gowns and the smell of cafeteria food. It was nearly 5:00 a.m. and would be light in an hour. He called Ruth.

"How did it go?" she asked.

"I don't hear any sirens or see any flashing lights, so I'm basically hoping for the best."

"That is good news. Wish me the same from my end. Are you ready for us?"

"As ready as I'm ever going to be."

* * *

Ruth deactivated the machines and monitors connected to Kylen with a jolt of OJ, and then removed the lines, including the IVs, just like Nate had shown her earlier. No telling what the staff would think when they came in for rounds and their second John Doe in a week had vanished. Ruth was grateful she wasn't the one who would have to try to explain it to them. It would probably become hospital legend.

Nate had surreptitiously managed to consecrate the room, which was a small miracle in and of itself. That man was amazing.

She slid her arms under Kylen's shoulders and knees and snugged up as close to him as she could without reopening his wounds. Then she began to pull them home.

They landed in a pile on Ruth's living room floor. Of course. Rookie landings were the worst. Landings with unconscious passengers? Impossible. Nate scrambled to Kylen's side.

He was pale and seizing on the floor, going into shock.

"Help me get him to the bed," Nate cried out,

grabbing his shoulders. Ruth lifted his feet, and they maneuvered his herky-jerky body onto the futon bed.

"Get more blankets. Now!"

Ruth scrambled to follow his instructions.

"You're going to have to calm him down so that I can get and *keep* an IV in him, or he's not going to make it."

Ruth's hands sparked with pale green light. It wasn't the strongest energy she'd ever manifested, likely the result of carrying a passenger through the consecrated subway, but it was still visible. Placing her hands on Kylen's shoulders, she held him down against the bed.

The pale green light flowed down into the reaper's arms and across his ruined chest. Soon his entire body radiated with light green luminosity. His seizure calmed, and he lay motionless, breathing shallowly.

Nate inserted the nutrition IV into his right arm and taped his left around the bedpost in case he began thrashing again. Ruth dropped to her knees beside him.

"You need to eat, Ruth," Nate said softly. "Kylen's going to need a whole lot more of that green energy as soon as possible. This IV will help, but not like that green stuff."

Ruth got to her feet and went into the kitchen. She nearly cried in relief when she saw the groceries that Nate had brought home.

* * *

Once Kylen was sedated, his seizures stopped. Nate scrambled around to get him reconnected to the various monitors he'd set up in a semicircle around the head of the bed. He adjusted the drip and sat on the chair beside Kylen's bed. The first rays of the morning sun broke through the window as Ruth finished yet another meal.

"Let's get some rest. Then you can give Kylen some

serious attention."

"I will, but you need to eat and get some sleep, too. Flashing will probably affect you the same as it does us."

Nate nodded and Ruth went to her room.

* * *

Ruth awoke with further delusions of grandeur.

"Nate, I think we need to try to re-create what we did the night you cast the circle. It won't be the same without Deacon, but I'm betting we can do a pretty good job by ourselves. Can you do that? Can you raise that kind of power?" she asked, placing a palm over Kylen's forehead to check his temperature.

"Sure, the problem is containing and directing the energy. We had a receptacle for it last time, a purpose."

"And we will this time, too. Me. I want you to cast it into me. I'll use it to focus as much green healing energy as I can muster into Kylen. I can't imagine that it would hurt him. Maybe, just maybe, it will be enough to wake him and help him heal more rapidly. Rapid would be good. Can you do it?"

Nate's shoulders slumped. It was a terrible idea. They had raised a lot of power last time. More than he was sure *could* be contained. Deacon had been able to pull Ruth back from the brink the last time she had been glutted with too much power. Could *he* pull her back from the abyss? Could they even *raise* that much power again? Nate wanted to help Deacon. Hell, he wanted to help Kylen if they could, but was it worth taking a chance with Ruth's life?

He hadn't known Ruth for long, but one thing he did know was that she was stubborn and persistent. If he didn't help her, she'd find a way without him, and that might put her in even more danger.

"I can do it," he said. "My stuff is in the closet."

* * *

Ruth knew she was dabbling with things she hadn't even begun to understand, but desperate times called for desperate action. She watched as Nate set up candles at the foot of Kylen's bed and lit them. Next he started to cleanse the room with a smoking bundle of herbs. Once again the smell of sage, thyme and lavender filled the small space as Nate softly chanted. Ruth waited by Kylen's side, stroking his forehead and whispering words of encouragement to him. After several moments, Nate joined her and wafted the smoke above Kylen's entire body and then Ruth's.

He cleansed himself last.

When he was finished, he placed the smoldering bundle in a stainless-steel bowl beside the bed, allowing the smoke to surround them.

Satisfied, he reached out over Kylen's body to Ruth. "Take my hands."

She did and Nate began to recite a soft incantation. As he chanted, Ruth felt the energy build between them. He continued until the air around them grew thick and heavy with power. Her hands warmed and her body began to radiate heat, as if she was lying on a sun-warmed rock on a summer day.

Sliding into relaxation, she experienced a slight tingling in her hands and arm, which began to fill her entire body. As she grew warmer and warmer, Nate removed his hands from hers. She placed her palms together over Kylen, as if in silent prayer, until she could keep them together no longer. The energy building inside her threatened to explode from her very pores. Her hair stood on end, and her skin prickled into gooseflesh.

"Ruth?" Nate asked, more of a warning than a question.

It was now or never. Ruth placed her hands over the worst of the injuries on Kylen's chest, her palms hovering over his flesh. Concentrating on capturing the energy and pushing it into Kylen, she filled the voids inside him, knitting together his wounds with the green glow.

Nate continued to chant, his cadence increasing faster and faster as Ruth kept channeling energy into Kylen. No room for doubt. No room for questions. Only energy. And it felt…good. Powerful. Addictive.

She pushed and pushed the green light into Kylen, wringing it out of her own body and into his. Kylen's back arched, and his upper body lifted from the bed, as though he were reaching out for the source of the light. Her body hummed with power, and a green glow radiated from Kylen until Ruth's own light began to fade, becoming dimmer and dimmer. She faltered. Nate stopped chanting and hurried around to her side, sweeping her off her feet and breaking the connection.

As he stood there with her in his arms, Kylen's eyes opened. They glowed with green light.

Ruth passed out.

CHAPTER THIRTY-FIVE

Deacon didn't have to wait long for Camael's next temptation. The women, the food...neither had even remotely tempted him, but what now walked into his room from the balcony could be his undoing.

"Kara?" Deacon's voice faltered. As he crossed the room in long strides and embraced her, his mind flooded with memories.

"Deacon. Deacon." She caressed his hair, raining kisses over his face.

"How? Why? Where have you been?" he asked, not sure he wanted the answers. What he wanted was the feel of her warm and alive in his arms. What Kylen would give for this moment... Reality slammed into Deacon, and he jerked back, unsure if she was real, or if this was another trick. This was one way to get to him. Camael would know it. He could think of nothing crueler or more tempting.

Kara smiled sweetly. Proof positive that it *was* a trick. Kara wasn't sweet; she was fierce. A valkyrie. Her long white-blond hair was like satin, shiny and slick. She was pale and breathtaking and exactly like he remembered her. It just wasn't her. Not really. It couldn't be. Her features were right, but her demeanor was off.

"Deacon, what is it? Aren't you pleased to see me? I've come so far. I miss you. I miss Kylen. Tell me about Kylen," she said, reaching for him again.

Deacon stepped back, putting space between them. He longed to keep holding her, but the more she spoke, the more he became convinced that she was an impostor. An animated doppelgänger. He also knew that he couldn't bring himself to kill her if it came down to it. Not with her looking so much like Kara. He prayed she wasn't an assassin.

She took a step toward him, trying to engage him. "Please, Deacon, hold me. I miss your touch, your kindness, your friendship. I miss you so much." She dipped her head and looked up at him through dewy lashes. Her eyes sparkled, and he reached for her in spite of himself. Then her familiar eyes morphed for a second, the pupils turning to vertical slits. She blinked once, and they were back to normal. But he'd seen it. For a split second.

Demon.

He backed away. Maybe he could kill her after all. If he had the proper weapons, of course. His homemade shiv was not going to easily dispatch a demon, and no demon exited a host of its own free will. None that he'd ever met anyway. He was a long way from help now. The demon advanced toward him.

He felt the shiv press against his spine. If he had the right opportunity, he'd have to try.

Smiling, then reaching for him, she closed the distance with unnatural speed. When she stroked his cheek and leaned in for a kiss, Deacon snaked one hand around her waist and pulled her tight up against him as he withdrew the shiv from its hidden sheath. He plunged it through her back and into her heart, ripping the blade up through her body. His stomach turned as he watched the surprise on her face—Kara's face—but he plunged the knife in again, determined to force the demon from its shell.

Could he consume it as he had the last demon? He was a Power after all. That had to be good for something. The demon struggled to stay inside of the host body, but with no life force, there was nothing to keep it tethered. It streamed out and off to the balcony. Hovering in a formless black mist over the railing, it seemed hesitant to go any further into the red fog. There were worse things than death.

Cornered, the demon waited for the inevitable. Deacon closed the distance. There was a fine line between possession and consumption, but he was willing to take the risk. Deacon was pleased to see he could still manifest a bright circle of energy around the demon and himself, trapping it inside the sphere. At least all of his mojo wasn't gone. Opening his mouth, he drew in a deep breath and willed the demon into him.

As the demon dissipated to nothingness inside him, Deacon felt confident that his path was clear and no amount of trickery would deter him from his work.

He felt good. Strong even. Though he needed sleep, he felt fortified from dispatching the demon and its burst of energy. He walked over and looked down at the body that lay before him. It was only a husk now, not Kara, not anything human. Revulsion filled him. He wanted it gone.

Kicking at it with the toe of his boot, he pushed it onto a nearby rug, which he rolled up with the remains encased inside like a giant stuffed sausage. Scooping it up, he carried it to the balcony and stared down into the red fog below. As he tossed the macabre bundle into the abyss, he hoped it hit something important on the way down.

Nothing happened. No fireworks, no wailing or gnashing of teeth, no alarms. All it did was tumble silently through the gloom until it disappeared from sight. He never heard it hit. It may have fallen for an eternity as far as he knew. He was startled by the sound of someone clapping behind him.

"Nicely done," Camael praised, leaning over the edge of the balcony to look below. "I never liked that one much anyway. Always trouble. A real bleeding heart." Camael turned and walked back into the living area. "Did you like her shell, though? I made it special for you. I do aim to please—let it never be said otherwise."

He lowered himself onto the couch and kicked his heels up onto the coffee table. "I am a little upset about the rug, however. It really pulled the room together," he said, laughing fiendishly.

Deacon wasn't in a laughing mood. At all. "How much longer can I expect to be held here?"

"Oh, that's entirely up to you, my friend. You are free to go as soon as I feel that you are firmly devoted to my cause. Free will is such a bitch. It would be so much easier if I could *make* you want to work with me, but of course it has to be your choice. That was the biggest mistake he ever made. Trust me, I've reminded him more than once."

Deacon wondered what would happen if he plunged his shiv into the fallen angel. He had a pretty good idea that he'd be the next one to fly off the balcony if he tried, but the idea was so...tempting. He shook his head. Was this another temptation? Killing or not killing Camael? He had no idea what was even real anymore. The thought niggled at him as Camael rambled on about wars, legions, battles and choosing sides.

"Are you even listening to me, or am I wasting my breath here? I have things to do, souls to plunder and torture. In fact, you could assist me with some of that. Be my right-hand man as it were. Get out of here for a while and see the sights. Yes?" he asked, dusting couch lint off the legs of his black pants. "A trial run?"

"No, thanks." Deacon balled his hands into fists and fought the urge to catapult his body across the coffee table and bury his knife into Camael. He was pretty sure that any attempt against him would only piss him off. Deacon held his ground and tried to hold his tongue, as well. Less talking usually meant less trouble.

"Really? Not even a day trip? You know, I could flash you there like I did here. But I have a feeling you would only be a burden to me. I see that you're going to need more motivation. Perhaps a few more days of solitary confinement will do the trick? Enjoy."

And Camael was gone. No slow fade, just gone. The slight smell of sulfur lingered near the couch where he'd been sitting. Solitary confinement was fine by Deacon. He didn't want or need any more visitors. What he needed was time to think and to build up his strength. The demon slaying had left him feeling strong, but with a few hours of sleep and some peace and quiet, he would be a new man.

And then the screaming began.

* * *

As Ruth slowly regained her senses, she opened her eyes and puzzled at the unfamiliar jawline that was so not Deacon's. It took her brain several clicks to catch up—she was in *Nate's* arms—and then she immediately looked over at Kylen. She gasped. His eyes were open, and they were glowing with the green healing energy she had forced into him.

Nate let her feet ease to the floor. Her knees nearly buckled, but his firm hold around her waist kept her upright. She reached for Kylen, whose eyes were wide and wild with confusion. Nate pulled a chair under Ruth, and she sat, keeping her own eyes glued to the reaper with the glowing green eyes. When Nate reached for Kylen's chest bandages, Kylen flinched.

Raising his palms in a gesture of submission, Nate said, "I'm not going to hurt you, man. I need to take a look."

"Kylen, Nate has been caring for you. We both have. You're safe here. We are protected."

Kylen looked from Ruth to Nate, studying them for a long moment, and then gave the slightest nod of consent. Nate reached for the bandage again and peeled it off. The edges of Kylen's skin, where the tape had adhered, looked angry and raw, but the wound itself had knitted itself back together. A jagged pink scar that cut down his body from stem to stern was all that was left.

"Jesus." Nate removed the rest of the bandages that covered Kylen's chest and neck and torso. All of the wounds had healed to scars. He was obviously shocked by what he saw, and his eyes went even larger as the tape irritations vanished in front of them.

Ruth beamed. She knew that they could do it. Together their powers were so much stronger than they were individually. Maybe Nate wouldn't doubt their abilities anymore.

If Kylen was still *Kylen,* whoever he had been before his possession, maybe they'd have a snowball's chance of finding Deacon.

* * *

Kylen raised a tentative hand to his chest and searched the rutted scar with his fingers and eyes, surveying the damage that had rendered him comatose. He reached to his neck and ran his smooth palm down his ragged throat. Healed? How could it be?

He wasn't sure how long he'd been out. He recognized the woman as Deacon's woman, Ruth, but the man? A complete stranger. He didn't even have a guess.

He could feel a circle of protection humming with power around the house, and he could sense that the house was consecrated. For a brief moment, he considered flashing away, but where to? He had no idea what awaited him outside this house. Was the demon biding his time, waiting to claim him again? Cold terror filled him at the thought. He'd die before he'd let it take him again. At least then, perhaps, he could be with Kara.

His mind was full to bursting with questions, but unless these two attempted to do him harm, he'd stay put. He felt...good, actually, but he had no delusions about how he would fare in a fight...naked and without weapons. He was helpless.

The thin blanket that covered him was not enough of a barrier between him and these two strangers. He looked from one of them to the other, and back again. The concern on their faces seemed sincere, but he couldn't imagine how it could be considering the fact that he meant nothing to them. They couldn't even know what he was, or had been, could they? His stomach growled long and low.

Ruth giggled. "Sounds like he's a lot better if he's that hungry. Nate, can you remove those IVs so that we can get him some real food?"

Nate nodded and went to work on the IVs while the woman hurried off to the kitchen with more than a skip in her step. Kylen didn't resist Nate's attentions. He was more than happy to have the wretched needles out of his body. The skin healed over as the needles were withdrawn. Nate gathered up the remaining bandages, flipping off the monitors.

Kylen tried to form words three times before his voice obeyed him. "Clothes?"

"Sure, I can get you some clothes," Nate said, walking over to a backpack. He pulled out a pair of jeans and a black T-shirt and held them out for him. "You can borrow my stuff until you get some of your own."

Nate stood nervously, waiting to see if he needed help.

"Privacy?"

"Sure, holler out if you need help," Nate said and left the room.

Kylen closed his eyes, taking inventory of his body and his overall condition. He didn't feel bad, all things considered. Of course, he hadn't tried to walk yet, but he was reasonably sure he remembered how. He wasn't going to be reaping souls anytime soon, but he was hopeful he could at least get some clothes on.

Small victories.

He couldn't even remember the last time he had achieved a personal victory, large or small. Being free of the demon, of Orithidon, was of course a huge victory. He couldn't wait to discover how that had come to pass. A hundred years with that piece of shit. But he'd do it all over again to save Kara's soul.

He'd wanted so badly to visit her, but the demon was bound to Hell and Earth. Purgatory was the closest he had ever gotten. Even now, free of the demon, he would never get past where Kara lived. His soul was a black stain that could never be healed, no matter how much magic these strangers poured into him.

Gingerly, he eased over onto his shoulder and pushed himself into a sitting position. His head swam and his focus failed him. He gripped the edge of the bed until his knuckles were white, but he managed to keep his eyes open. He did *not* want to pass out.

The wave of nausea dissipated, and he tested his legs one at a time, stretching them out to the floor. He let his weight slide off the edge of the bed and lowered himself down.

So far, so good.

He stretched up to his full height, letting the blanket slide to the floor. He pushed his shoulders back and felt his back stretch. It felt good.

His head cleared somewhat, and with a growing confidence in his limbs, he managed to find his balance and pull the jeans on one leg at a time. They were a little big on him, and he realized how much weight he'd lost while he'd been incapacitated.

He remembered himself as being the size of the man who had been tending to him. Looking down at his protruding hip bones, he ran his hand over them one at a time. A few more days of energy starvation, and they'd have buried him somewhere. If he'd ever woken up again, it would have been in a coffin. That was the worst *death* for a reaper. Death by demon was the shits, but to waste away so much that humans thought you were dead? That was worse.

Slipping the shirt over his head, he pulled it down his torso. Considering his diminished physique, he was going to have to pack in the calories and work out to get himself back into shape. That damn demon had let his body go. Still, he felt his strength returning with each passing minute. Hell, he really did feel good enough to flash. They'd never be able to find him. He could regroup and figure out his next move. But where to go?

* * *

Ruth finished making the peanut butter and jelly sandwiches and piled them eight-high on the plate. She carried another plate full of cut fruit and veggies. Nate had gathered several bags of chips and various snack cakes, as well.

"Do you think this is enough?" Ruth asked. "We're getting low on food. One of us might have to make a run into town tonight. Seriously, we should move into a grocery store. Or maybe we should have holed up at your place. At least you have delivery!" Ruth said as they headed to Kylen's room.

"Oh, yeah, my neighbors would love having imps and God knows what else bouncing off my apartment all the livelong day and night."

Ruth pushed open the door with her hip and looked over at the bed. The blanket lay in a pile on the floor, and Kylen was gone.

"Oh, no!" She set the plates down on the bed and ran to the window, peering out into the woods. She couldn't see three feet in front of her into the moonless night.

Nate left his load of food on the bed, too. The clothes he gave Kylen were gone. The reaper must have dressed and flashed. He should have anticipated this happening. It was way too easy for these...reapers to disappear. He couldn't even bring himself to believe they were reapers. Even after all he'd seen with his own eyes.

Ungrateful bastard.

He was pretty sure that whatever small chance Ruth's plan had of working was now toast.

* * *

Kylen walked out of the tiny bathroom. They both stared at him as if he was on fire.

"What?" he asked.

The woman's face filled with relief. "Oh, thank God," she said. "We thought you'd...flashed."

She rushed over to him, throwing her arms around him in a hug. He tried to fend her off at first, but he finally settled into the hug. With surprise, he realized that she had no aura. None at all.

He looked over at the man. His aura was a greenish-brown color, mottled and dirty but not dangerous. More conflicted. Kylen knew exactly how he felt.

"Look," Ruth said, finally pulling away and leading him by the hand toward the bed, which was now covered with a lavish spread of food. "We're running a bit low, but this will be a good start. Maybe we can fill you in a bit while you eat?"

She pulled the chair around for him, and Nate settled himself on the edge of the bed. Ruth deposited herself on the floor between the two men.

Kylen took one of the sandwiches and pulled up the top piece of bread to peer inside. He crammed half of it in his mouth before clamping down, chewing in obscene bliss. He devoured all eight of the sandwiches in a matter of minutes. Ruth forgot to ask him any questions as he consumed the food. She gaped at him in awkward silence as he ate.

"What was that?" he asked, wiping his mouth with the back of his hand.

"Uh, peanut butter and jelly," she said, barely containing her amusement. By the time he moved on to the fruit, she seemed to have collected herself.

"Kylen, what do you remember? Do you know what's happened to you? Were you aware when the demon was possessing you?" she asked, peering up at him through long black lashes.

Kylen looked at both of them before speaking. "Of course. I remember everything. Everything except for him." He pointed at Nate. "This guy, I have never seen before."

"That's Nate. He's our friend."

"So, you're a reaper after all?" He pointed over at Nate again. "And you? What are you?"

Nate hesitated. "That's a good question, my friend."

"He's a witch," Ruth said proudly, "and we are learning every day that he has many other useful and amazing skills."

"Witch?" After finishing up the fruit, Kylen moved on to a bag of chips.

Ruth cast a look at Nate and then sat up a little straighter. "Kylen, do you remember Deacon?"

"Of course," he said. "Where is he?"

"Deacon captured a demon, took it to Purgatory, and instead of disposing of it in some demon prison, he consumed it. They promoted him to Powers for his success. Are you familiar with that group?" she asked.

Kylen swallowed. He'd heard stories of the Powers. Legends created to keep demons in line. They weren't his memories, he suddenly realized, but his demon's.

"Apparently that's the only way to ensure it's good and dead. Forever dead if you know what I mean."

He did.

With Deacon as a Powers, what had happened to Grim? As the number of reapers grew, Grim had been promoted to Chief of Purgatory over his minions. His power was made all the more fearsome by the fact that few had seen him in the flesh. He was both a ghost story and a superhero for young reapers everywhere. But when demons began escaping from Hell or were *released* to wreak havoc, The One True Light decided that there needed to be a border guard to patrol the realms and keep them in check.

Grim became the first Powers angel, and the only one…until now. Kylen couldn't wrap his mind around it. *Deacon? Powers?* His first thought was of Kara. If Deacon was now an angel of the Powers, he could travel between the realms. Hell, he could even call souls back if he wanted. Could he call Kara back? *Would* he call back Kara? His mind raced, his stomach clenching at the thought. He set down the bag of chips. He was done eating.

"So you know of the Powers?" Ruth asked, her eyes fixed on his face.

"Yes. Where is Deacon? Take me to him." He hesitated, then added, "Please."

"Actually," she said, reaching for his hand, "we were hoping *you* could take us to him."

CHAPTER THIRTY-SIX

Ruth laid out the scenario for Kylen, telling him the story from the very beginning, when she and Deacon had first met. She glossed over the rougher patches.

She told him what Deacon had told her about his promotion, and how he'd disappeared from this very house, summoned by Camael. Finally, she recounted Rashnu's unhelpful response, telling him why they needed his help to find Deacon.

Nate listened from his perch on the futon, some of the story apparently new to him, too.

Kylen stayed silent throughout her monologue, not asking any questions. He did indeed know where a portal was. He'd been awake and aware the entire time the demon had possessed him. It was only his most recent memories that were fuzzy.

Why? He had no idea unless it was the trauma of his injuries. Surely those memories, too, would return with time. Taking them both to Hell was beyond dangerous. Getting in would be easy enough. Finding Deacon and extracting him against the Chief of the Order would be suicide.

He'd been to hell with Orithidon several times a month since his ordeal began. He hadn't enjoyed any of those trips. Orithidon was a lesser demon, but he held the respect of many of the hordes of Hell for the sheer number of souls he'd claimed for the Dark One. Much to Orithidon's dismay and Kylen's relief, even after all this time, an invitation hadn't been proffered to meet the Dark One in the flesh.

He had no idea what reception might await him if he were to return. Word of Orithidon's capture would have made the rounds. Then again, the Dark One was a busy beast. Maybe one demon wasn't that much of a concern for him. Kylen didn't know why he was even bothering with all the self-debate—he would go for Deacon. And if these two wanted to commit suicide along with him, the more the merrier.

"So that's the whole story," Ruth said, stretching her long legs out across the floor. "Can you help us? Can you lead us to Deacon?"

"There's a portal in the city that we can use. Darkness will help hide us from curious eyes. Once we're inside, though ..." He trailed off and shook his head. "If he was summoned by the Chief of the Order there's no telling where he's being kept. There are cells and cages of all kinds down there. It's oppressive, the smell is nauseating and the sounds...the sounds alone are enough to drive you mad. He could even be in the palace for all we know."

"There's a palace in Hell?" Nate chimed in. "You mean like one of Saddam's palaces? Seriously."

"Once we're inside, we'll find him. I know it. You get us there, Kylen, and everything else will fall into place," Ruth promised.

"You're more confident than I am," he said, picking at his food.

"Let's try to get some sleep. It's almost dawn. If we sleep for a few hours, we'll all be stronger. At least we'll have that on our side. Then we'll pack our equipment and weapons and bring him home."

"Sounds good to me," Nate said, rising and walking toward the door.

Ruth caught up to him, grabbed his arm and pulled him down toward her, kissing his cheek. "Good night, Nate."

Nate grunted.

Obviously, the guy wasn't too keen on Ruth's plan.

Smart man.

* * *

Kylen's dreams were filled not with images of the souls he'd stolen under Orithidon's command, but of Kara.

Beautiful, fierce Kara.

He hadn't let himself think of her, much less dream of her, since the day he was possessed. He hadn't wanted that bastard demon to have the pleasure of even one memory to hold over him. To taunt him.

At first light, he awoke and stared out the window. Lying alone in his body, aware and alive for the first time in so long, Kylen no longer feared death. He'd *lived* his death already. The true and final death would be a relief at this point. If Deacon could by some miracle bring Kara back with his new promotion then...maybe ...

If not, he had nothing to live for, not really. Once Deacon was safe, again, he would make his request. If he was refused, he saw no reason to continue on. He'd ask to be reaped. Maybe Deacon would do it for him this time.

Deacon owed him that. And more.

They had been like brothers once. Deacon had made a solemn bond to kill him if he was ever overtaken, but had he? Of course not. Kylen had hoped to free Kara's soul, keep Deacon safe and then await his end. But the wait had lasted forever, and the end had never come. Orithidon had kept him far away from Deacon and anyone who was even remotely family. Until the demon had decided to make sport of Kylen's misery, bringing him back again and again through the years.

He closed his eyes and almost allowed himself to pray, but quickly stifled the urge. Kylen looked at the clock on the wall. He'd slept nearly seven hours. That was more than enough.

He rolled off the bed in the only clothes he had and went off to explore the house.

* * *

Ruth woke to the smell of food cooking again.
Deacon?

She leaped out of bed and raced to the kitchen to find… Kylen. He stood at the stove as Nate buttered toast, hot out of the toaster. She couldn't hide her disappointment. She plopped down in a chair at the kitchen table, her unbrushed curls bouncing into her eyes.

Ruth knew Nate wasn't keen on her plan, but she also knew that he would help. She prayed that they could trust Kylen. He hadn't given them any reason not to yet, and he had stuck around when he could have flashed at will. Ruth was determined that Deacon would be home by the next sunrise. Back in her life and back in her bed…where he belonged.

Both men were dressed and ready for what the night had to offer. She needed coffee. Lots of it. Some of the bravado and confidence of last night had faded, and she was beginning to doubt her own plan. Her own skills.

What if she got them all killed? It would be her fault. She'd lived in fear for so long, and she was only now realizing that she'd been afraid of all the wrong things. She hadn't needed to fear the auras. She should have feared what she couldn't see, not what she could. Now her eyes were wide open. She needed a shot of encouragement.

Kylen sat a hot mug of coffee before her and gave her a tentative smile, the first she'd seen from him without his creepy demon eyes. He looked so much better that it would have been unbelievable that he was the same person if she hadn't witnessed the transformation herself.

Ruth's heart melted. He might be a big, bad, recently demon-possessed reaper, but his humanity was at least somewhat intact.

Thank God, she thought.

With Nate's magic and whatever was inside her, they had managed the impossible. And the impossible had just handed her a mug of coffee. She felt a little like Frankenstein must have after he'd animated his monster. She hoped her story ended better.

Kylen joined her at the table, setting a plate of bacon, eggs and toast before her.

"I might have an idea for finding Deacon once we get through the portal," Nate said, picking at his food.

"You do?" she asked, excited. Anyone's plan had to be better than hers.

"I looked up a location spell. I've got everything I need except a few of the herbs. I'll have to stop by my apartment and pick them up. Once we're past the portal, we'll have to find a place to hide for long enough to perform it."

"Oh, Nate! Have you done one before? How can I help?"

"I haven't, but I've seen others do them...for lost pets. I'm pretty sure if you give me a drop of your blood since you...since the two of you...know each other so well, it should be a little easier to find him."

Oh, if only it could be that easy to find him. Nate had never trapped a demon before Kylen, and a location spell had to be easier than that. Hope filled her heart again.

The atmosphere at the table was tense, but her confidence was renewed. Kylen was still here, Nate had half a plan to help, and the day was bright and shiny, for a few more hours at least. Then the real challenge would be upon them, but the only way past adversity was through it. And she planned to blow it to pieces.

They all finished their breakfasts. Another crazy thing about this new life was that her internal clock was totally screwed. It seemed like one day bled into the next. She hadn't picked up her mail from the P.O. box in days. Her life had never been normal, but this was impossible. There was going to have to be some serious domestic restructuring when all the chicks came home to roost.

She picked up all of their plates and set them in the sink. "I'm going to pack my backpack, and then I'll be ready to go."

They nodded, and she headed back to her room.

Ten minutes later, they all three stood in the center of her living room. Nate gave Kylen a backpack, and they were loaded for bear.

"I guess my apartment is the first stop."

"Lead the way," Ruth said, taking his hand and reaching for Kylen's.

"What?" Nate asked.

"You've traveled through the pathways now. You yourself said that you've even done it alone before. What if I'm not with you sometime, and you need to get back? You can do it. I'll give you a little boost so that we can spread out our energy, but that's all."

"Are you insane? I can't do this alone."

"You can *try*. What is there to lose? Just imagine where you want to be and hold it in your mind. You can do this, Nate."

Kylen shook his head in disgust. "Now would be good."

Ruth laughed and Nate fumed. He closed his eyes, and in moments all three of them faded into the consecrated subway.

* * *

Somehow, they all managed to land upright in Nate's apartment. Definitely an improvement. Nate was shocked to have succeeded. And even though he was visibly shaken, he rushed about his apartment, quickly collecting the supplies he needed.

"You're up, Kylen. This is your rodeo now," Ruth said, squeezing his hand and reaching for Nate's.

"More like a circus," Kylen said, staring her in the eyes as they began to swirl through the subway again.

* * *

They landed at St. Agnes Cathedral. The same church Ruth had managed to flash from after leaving the hospital. Kylen walked straight to the prayer garden. The gate unlocked when he touched it.

"This is the portal to Hell? The prayer garden at a church?" she asked, disgusted and confused.

"Sure," he said, walking over the statue of Mary praying. "Catholic, right?"

Kylen placed his hand on the head of the statue and looked at them, amused with himself. Ruth was trying to wrap her mind around it, but she gave up. She joined him and put her own palm against the cool, smooth granite. Nate sighed and followed suit.

They spun and sputtered through a long tunnel of red strobing light that made Ruth's head hurt. Her stomach turned as she tried to close her eyes, but the light strobed against her retinas just as intensely whether her lids were open or closed. They seemed to slide through the tunnel forever. It was much longer than was comfortable and about ten times as long as her trips to Purgatory. A carnival ride gone bad.

When she was sure she was going to vomit, they crashed to a stop at a dusty crossroads. Red fog hung low as far as she could see, which wasn't very far at all.

Nate landed hard but stood up quickly, dusting red clay off his jeans. Kylen frowned as he looked down the road at the red glow in the cloud-covered horizon.

"A crossroads demon is coming our way. I'll do the talking," he said, walking forward to meet it.

The two of them stayed put, happy to let Kylen handle it.

Ruth couldn't hear what was being said, but the demon was nothing like the black smoky mist she'd seen stream from Kylen's body. This creature was a nightmare incarnate. Skeletal, almond-shaped eyes gazed at them appraisingly as it chatted with Kylen, blinking vertically every few seconds. Shiny black skin draped across its bony form, fitting loosely and bunching in folds and wrinkles at its joints. And the smell. My God, the thing was wretched. The stench emanating from it burned her eyes like mace even though it was a good ten feet away from her.

It seemed to be familiar with Kylen. No obvious alarms sounded. Kylen looked back and pointed toward them occasionally, making the demon laugh. A sound she hoped never to hear again. When the demon lurched in their direction, Ruth jumped. Nate held his ground, unflinching. The creature cackled as if it had cracked itself up and turned, retreating back into the red fog. Kylen returned to the crossroads.

"What was that all about?" Nate asked gruffly.

"He's a crossroads demon. He makes deals. I made one." Kylen stared ahead down the road.

"What kind of deal?" Nate pressed.

"The Boss can't leave Hell without a host body. I told him I brought him two willing hosts."

Ruth shuddered. She knew he'd only told the demon a story to get them past it, but she felt more vulnerable than ever. She swallowed down the lump in her throat and looked at Kylen.

"Which way now?"

"Forward." Kylen scanned the shallow horizon as the echoes of screams drifted toward them on a smoky putrid breeze. "We need to find a hiding place where Nate can do his thing."

He turned right and headed toward the red glow of what appeared to be a city or at least a fortress of some sort. Turrets appeared high above the horizon through breaks in the fog. They were walking in the direction of the screams.

They continued on the desolate red desert road, away from the one creature they'd encountered so far. The fog parted before them as they made their way forward, and it closed behind them. It appeared virtually impenetrable to the left and right of the highway. She was pretty sure she didn't want to know what it was hiding. They walked nearly a mile before they felt comfortable enough to venture off the road and into the thicker fog so that Nate could attempt his location spell.

She didn't know if magic sent a signal or left a trace, but she prayed it didn't raise any alarms. Nate squatted, arranging four blue candles around his body and lighting them. He filled a goblet three-quarters of the way up with water from a bottle out of his pack, then removed a twisted bundle of dried herbs.

"Sandalwood and thyme," he explained, lighting them with a match. Closing his eyes, he took a deep breath and began to chant, "Let the water reveal to me the location of Deacon. Let the water reveal to me the location of Deacon."

He opened his eyes and leaned forward, peering down into the goblet.

"Ruth, give me your hand." Brandishing a small pocket knife, he drew the blade across the pad of her index finger, letting the droplets of blood fall into the goblet. As he swirled the water with his finger in a clockwise motion, he repeated the chant three more times. The water settled, and he startled, his eyes wide and excited.

"I see him! He's in a very plush room. It looks like a suite of some kind. Lots of gold statues and crap. It looks…expensive, luxurious. There's an open balcony. No other windows or doors." Nate leaned back and looked up into Ruth's wide eyes.

"Did you see it, too?" he asked.

"No, all I can see is water. You're amazing, Nate!"

Gathering up the candles and the goblet, Nate stuffed them back into his pack.

"There's only one place like that: the Palace…where there are hundreds of balcony rooms." Kylen smirked. "I don't suppose Deacon's grown his hair out real long like Rapunzel?"

"Not hardly," Ruth said. She was pretty sure her smile wasn't fooling anyone.

Nate wasn't even trying for levity. She knew he was ready to get out of there, and the sooner the better. She was in total agreement, but they weren't leaving. Not without Deacon.

Kylen led them back to the road and they continued on toward the red light. Another half mile and Ruth smelled death.

CHAPTER THIRTY-SEVEN

The closer they got to the source of the light, the higher the ceiling of red and gray fog lifted. Still, the landscape was barren before them with the exception of a red stone castlelike structure that was slowly rising on the horizon.

"That's it up ahead," Kylen confirmed as they marched forward. They kicked up small clouds of red dust with every crunchy step, and Ruth felt as though her pores were coated in the toxic stuff. The small breeze died and the only sound was of their shoes on the crushed rock road and the muffled din coming from the palace.

"Is that ..." Ruth started to ask, turning to Kylen.

"Souls of the damned making payment on their contracts." Kylen pushed ahead.

"Lovely." Ruth shuddered. No wonder Kylen hadn't wanted Kara to spend eternity down here. She was fairly certain they hadn't even seen the worst of it, and she was already disgusted and terrified. The entire place emitted a vibe of foreboding and repulsion. Each step forward was protested by her inner voice, which was urging her to turn around.

She looked at Nate. His eyes were huge and bright, searching the horizon in all directions like a wary animal. He was spooked for sure, but he kept moving forward. She knew his courage sprung more from a desire to protect her than concern for Deacon. Suddenly a physical pressure overtook her and her thoughts took a dark turn. What if Deacon wasn't being held against his will? What if he had somehow come willingly or changed his mind once he got here and wanted to stay?

What if just entering this place changed you? She shuddered again.

No, he wouldn't choose this. He's a good man. Or reaper or whatever he is now. He's good, not evil. This is a place for evil.

She wanted to block out the growing cacophony of voices crying out in anguish. None were distinguishable, but the sentiment of each was easily recognizable: pain, agony, fear. And the smell…rotten eggs and roadkill on a hot summer day.

"Do you feel that?" Ruth asked. Nate nodded.

It occurred to her they could perhaps shield themselves at least somewhat from this place with their own energy shields. She hadn't experimented enough with other colors but the orange had always made her feel better before. Maybe with Nate and Kylen's help, they could create a force of their own to deflect the doom that was threatening to overcome them.

"Stop!" Ruth reached for Kylen's and Nate's hands. "Let's try to create a barrier of energy around us. I can't stand this place. It's sickening me. Kylen, can we do that? Create a shield of some sort?"

"No idea." Kylen closed his eyes, and a faint orange glow began to envelope him and flow through him. Ruth did the same and envisioned that glow emanating from herself. Nate did his best to manipulate his own sulfur and brown aura to a healthier color. As the orange light surrounded them, the relief was immediate and physical.

"Damn, that's better," Nate said, breaking out of his funk.

"Good. Me, too. Kylen?"

"Peachy."

* * *

They walked on for what seemed like several miles, enveloped in their manufactured auras. Nate maintained his with only an occasional push or touch from Ruth. He was getting stronger despite his reluctance to admit it. His calling was still unclear, but he'd already proven himself useful more than once with the powers he had. Who knew what other resources lay within him, waiting to emerge.

There was nowhere left to hide, and the closer they came to the palace, the more the fog began to dissipate. The place looked like an impenetrable fortress, complete with a moat of what appeared to be flowing lava.

Wonderful, Ruth thought.

A guard stood post at the main entrance. It was small and toadlike, an imp like the one Ruth had run through with a fire poker in her living room only a few days ago. It seemed like an inadequate guardian for such a tremendous palace, but then again, Ruth assumed that not too many folks were hot to visit this place of their own accord.

Kylen sent them both a look to indicate he would once again do the talking.

No problem, she thought. She didn't know if the imp could sense the energy they were generating, but she wasn't willing to extinguish it. She was pretty sure things would only get worse the closer they came to the source of all the evil and suffering.

Kylen walked forward, indicating that Nate and Ruth should stay behind. They did. She couldn't hear what was being said but caught enough to recognize that it was in a language she didn't understand. Kylen apparently still knew fluent imp. The imp stepped aside, and Kylen motioned for them to advance.

Ruth walked forward, and Nate stuck close by her side, clearly intent on keeping his body between Ruth and the imp. The slimy stunted creature was only as tall as Nate's midthigh, but he kept a wary distance from it nonetheless. They walked in together through twenty-five-foot-high iron gates into the Palace of Hell.

* * *

Once they were well past the lone guard, they made their way down a long black marble entryway toward a spectacular viewing balcony.

"That seemed a little too easy. Where is everyone or...thing?" Ruth asked, glancing around the interior, looking for any sign of life or danger.

"No one uses the front door. See that chimney over the arena? That's where the official residents arrive from Purgatory, then they drop into the pit. They call it... the meat grinder."

"And the unofficial residents?" Ruth asked.

"A few levels below."

"So they aren't all that worried about trespassers?" she asked, amazed.

"Hotel California," Kylen said, walking toward the railing. "You can check out anytime you like, but you can never leave."

Nate rounded on him and jerked Kylen back by his shoulder. "What the hell is that supposed to mean?

We're stuck here? We can't leave?"

His face was full of rage, and he was clearly ready to toss the reaper over the railing. Ruth managed to squeeze her body between the two men to defuse the situation. "Kylen, tell us that's not what you mean."

"Would it have made any difference? Would you have decided against coming? Would you have let me come and look for him alone?"

"No," Ruth said decidedly. "I would have found a way."

"Exactly. Stubborn woman." Kylen scowled.

"Have you managed to trap us here, asshole?" Nate asked.

"I have no idea. This is my first trip since the exorcism. All I'm saying is that it's typically a one-way trip. Most of the 'people' who come here are untethered souls, demons or imps. Not visitors. No one is beating down the gate to get in or hadn't you noticed the scant security? One imp? Guarding the entrance to Hell? They don't worry about souls escaping because it's not possible." Kylen backed away and peered down into the red abyss below.

The orange glow diminished around all of them. Nate seemed to be the most affected by the lack of happy juice.

Ruth put her palm on his chest and gave him a push of OJ. "Nate, we'll get home," she said. "As soon as we find Deacon, we'll figure it out. I promise."

"Don't make promises you can't keep." Nate stepped away from her to peer down from the balcony, as well. "Shit."

Beneath them was a sea of naked, writhing bodies, climbing and crawling over one another through a flood of red mud and worse things. One face would rise and cry out only to be pushed down into the muck by another creature, over and over again. There was no way to tell how deep the pile of bodies went. The palace curved to the left and the right like a stadium and continued in what appeared to be a circle.

It was so vast that Ruth couldn't see across to where the circle should be completed. Spaced along the continuum were many smaller balconies like the one where they were standing. Each one had a front-row seat to the first circle of Hell.

After they all watched the sea of humanity for several moments, hypnotized, Kylen shook his head, as if he was trying to clear it from the fog of self-reflection.

"And that's only the first circle," he said, breaking into their reverie. "There are eight more. They only get worse."

Ruth couldn't imagine anything worse. She certainly didn't want to see it for herself. She wrapped her arms around her chest and turned her back to the railing, willing the infernal noise to stop.

Kylen led them from the viewing balcony, and Ruth took both men's hands in hers. Instantly their energy joined together again, shielding them with orange light that lessened the impact of the foreboding pressing against them.

"We need to find Deacon," she said, squeezing their hands, "and the sooner the better."

"How do you suppose we do that? Every balcony looks the same. There must be hundreds maybe thousands on each side of us, and that's only as far as we can see into the red fog," Nate said.

"Were there any distinguishing features about the balcony you saw? Anything at all that would make it stand out?" Ruth asked, hoping against hope that he would say yes.

"No. They all look exactly the same."

"Do the spell again. Look for something you might have missed," Kylen said.

"I'll try."

"That's all we can ask, Nate," Ruth said. giving him a smile. "Let's do it…now."

* * *

Deacon couldn't rest, but he felt strong and ready for whatever came his way next. He couldn't even imagine what Ruth was going through, worrying about him. He hated the entire situation for her sake more than his own. And what was happening to all the souls that were piling up while he was detained? Ruth couldn't possibly reap them with her limited training. Would they send a replacement? What would that mean for them? So much was unsettled and this derailment wasn't going to make things any easier.

It occurred to Deacon that perhaps that was the whole point of his incarceration. To take him out of the game for a while so Camael could do…what exactly? If Deacon were home with Ruth, he'd be collecting souls as usual, and he'd begin training as a Powers with Grim to prevent demon infiltrations into the human world.

What if Camael was planning something bigger? What if he was planning on unleashing a few dozen or hundred or thousand demons on the earth while Grim was occupied with Seraph duties and Deacon was imprisoned? Who was guarding the border?

No one. That's who.

Deacon's heart sank. Of course that was it. The demons could easily find bodies to inhabit. There were plenty of unsuspecting humans ripe for the picking. And once that happened, there would be plenty of souls piling up to harvest while he was trapped here. He didn't know how long he'd been down here, but with the hit-and-miss job he'd been doing lately, he was at least a hundred souls behind.

Easy picking for a few dozen demons.

Surely he wasn't the only one who had figured this out. Surely there must be experts and guardians to make sure things like this didn't happen. Checks and balances and all that crap. The burning pit in his stomach told him something else.

He *was* that check and balance.

He was the one who was going to have to clean up whatever mess Camael planned to make. And the best way to do that was to prevent it from happening in the first place.

Deacon crossed over to the bed and stripped the sheets and coverings from it. He grasped the drapes hanging from its four posters and ripped them free, too. After gathering every strip of cloth he could find in the suite, he knotted them together into a rope and secured it to the balcony. He flung the bulky makeshift length over the edge. If he couldn't flash out of here, he'd find another way. He wasn't going to stay in this room for one more minute. He was going to break free before all hell broke loose.

* * *

Nate set up his spell once again on the black marble floor and began reciting his incantations. Ruth and Kylen looked on expectantly. They had to figure out a way to narrow down their search. They couldn't exactly go from balcony to balcony. For all they knew, the balconies could go on to infinity.

Nate swirled the water with his hand and watched as the surface cleared.

"Well?" Ruth asked, scanning the perimeter.

He sucked in a deep breath before speaking. "He's made a rope of sheets and bedding. It's thrown over the side of his balcony. We should be able to see it."

"Do you see Deacon?"

"Yes, but he's not going to be there much longer. We need to move, now!"

They scanned left and right but didn't see the colorful rope hanging from any of the balconies in sight.

"Which way?" Nate asked, as he finished gathering his things and stuffing them back into his pack.

"Nate, take Ruth and go to the right. Flash to the farthest balcony you can see, and I'll go left and do the same. Repeat until we find him."

"How can we flash here, Kylen? How can it be consecrated?" Ruth asked.

"Oh, it's consecrated. Just not to the God you've been praying to. Besides, Nate can flash from unconsecrated ground, yes? And I... Let's just say I'm pretty sure they haven't pulled my membership just yet or we wouldn't have made it this far. I would suggest we hurry."

Kylen pulled his white shirt off over his head and ripped it down the middle. He tied the two ends together and wrapped them around the balcony railings.

"So we can find our way back," he said, securing them tightly. "If you find Deacon, flash back here. If you don't find him, but you make it all the way around without seeing him, stay put until we can rendezvous. Then we'll move on to Plan B."

"Do we have a Plan B?" Nate asked, snugging his backpack straps up tightly.

"Not yet. Let's go."

Kylen disappeared before their eyes. Ruth took Nate's hand and together they flashed to the farthest balcony she could see. The suite was dark when they landed. There was no door but the red light from below cast an eerie glow a few feet into the interior. They didn't dare venture in any farther. Ruth cast her eyes to the right. Nothing. No rope. She looked at Nate and closed her eyes, and they flashed again. They flashed at least a dozen more times when they landed hard on yet another balcony. Ruth's ankle twisted, and she crumpled into a heap. Nate was bending to help her, when he suddenly did a double take.

"Look, about ten balconies down! There it is," he said, pointing the way.

"Oh, thank God!" Thunder rolled in the distance. Ruth gave Nate a questioning look but jumped to her feet. "Let's go!"

They flashed to the balcony where the rope dangled.

"Deacon!" Ruth yelled, running into the suite. "Deacon!"

* * *

Deacon turned to find Ruth standing in the middle of the living area. She was covered in a fine red dust, her hair wild and backlit with red light. Nate stood behind her on the balcony.

What fresh hell is this? he thought, facing them both.

Of course this would be the next temptation—the promise of escape, of being with Ruth again. Camael must have seen the rope hanging from his balcony.

So close!

He couldn't see what lay beyond the rope, but he was willing to take his chances and at least try to swing to the next balcony. Maybe he'd be able to flash from another cell. Anything but stay here another minute. Ruth advanced toward him, and he drew the shiv from its sheath, keeping his hand behind his back. How many more demons was he going to have to kill before Camael stopped sending them?

Obviously they were disposable.

"*Hurry,* we came to help you. Nate's here and Kylen is still looking for you, but he'll probably find us soon!"

She ran to throw her arms around him. She felt so good. She even smelled like Ruth.

All the right things. But of course, Kara had seemed right, too. At first.

He didn't embrace her. He stepped back instead, not wanting to be cornered. The one that looked like Nate lingered on the balcony, eyes affixed to the horizon.

"Hurry up, Ruth, let's get back," he said, pulling up the rope.

"Deacon, let's go. We need to hurry. No one knows what we're up to yet. Let's keep it that way," she said, reaching for him.

"I'm not going anywhere with you, Demon." Deacon sliced the knife around in a wide arc and slashed it across the side of her neck.

"Deacon, NO!" Nate yelled, spanning the distance between them. He tackled Deacon, and the two of them rolled across the floor in a struggle. The knife slid out of Deacon's hand and skittered under the bed. Nate punched and swung at him until he stopped fighting, and then he pulled back to help Ruth.

"Shit, Deacon, what's wrong with you? Ruth, Ruth!"

Blood spurted out the side of her neck to the beat of her heart. Her eyes were wide and shiny with tears, and her skin was changing color before their eyes to a ghostly white. Nate put pressure over the wound and began to summon what energy he could muster, trying to push it into Ruth.

Deacon looked on in horror as he began to realize that they weren't demons. They weren't temptations sent for him. They were *real*. They'd come to save him, and he'd maybe killed the one woman in the world he loved.

He reached for her, but Nate growled at him and sent him away.

Deacon refused to watch Ruth bleed out in Hell's penthouse. He would save her, no matter what it took.

* * *

A noise on the balcony drew his attention.

Kylen?

He had no idea how they'd found him. And what the hell were they doing with the demon Kylen?

"What the fuck happened?" Kylen asked, joining Nate at Ruth's side.

"That asshole cut her carotid artery. That's what happened."

"I thought you were demons. I... They've been trying to tempt me." His voice faltered, and he bent at the waist, grabbing hold of his knees in anguish. "I thought you were another temptation." He lurched forward, trying to draw closer to her. "Ruth, I'm so sorry. I didn't know. I didn't know."

Kylen placed his hand over Nate's, and together they generated a bright green glow that lit up Nate's entire arm and curled around Ruth's head and neck. Nate continued to add what energy he could summon. Ruth's eyes rolled back in her head and her body convulsed once, then again. She went rigid before collapsing in Nate's arms. Nate pulled his hand back from her neck wound. The bleeding had stopped, but Ruth was unconscious. He carefully laid her down on the bare floor before looking up at Kylen. "Now what, genius?"

"Now, we get the hell out of Hell." Kylen stood and turned to look at Deacon.

"Are you solid or do we need to worry about you stabbing one of us again?" he asked, staring him in the eyes. Deacon quickly realized his mistake. This wasn't the demon Kylen, this was just Kylen.

"I'm sorry. I can't... I ..." He broke off.

Ruth opened her eyes with great effort and looked up at him.

"Deacon," she said weakly, smiling at him as if she'd just realized he was in the room.

"Let's get out of here," Kylen said. "No time for more happy juice until we're safe. She'll live if we can get her home and heal her." He looked at Deacon. "You coming or what? We didn't make this trip for laughs, asshole."

"I can't flash. There's some barrier. I've tried at least a hundred times."

"Well, you haven't tried it with Nate here. You're too…affiliated with Team Light now. Now get out here, and let's blow this joint," Kylen said. Nate bent to scoop Ruth up in his arms.

The four of them stood on the balcony together. Nate held Ruth as Deacon and Kylen each took one of her hands. "We need out of here now, Nate. Not back to the portal but all the way home. We don't have time to dicker with the guard or the crossroads demon. We need a straight shot," Kylen said, staring at Nate.

"I can't do that," Nate said, gaping back at him.

"Do you want Ruth to die here tonight?"

"Of course not," Nate said, confused.

"Nate, you're the only one of us with an aura of your very own and a downy white soul. You're the most alive of any of us, so you have the loosest tie to the afterlife. *And* you can flash from anywhere. You're going to be the one who gets us back, or we don't get back at all. Now get your mojo on and take us home."

* * *

Nate looked down at Ruth and could feel her life force ebbing away. He was not going to lose her. Not now. Not here. Closing his eyes, he cleared his mind of everything, erasing the desperate cries from the abyss, the red fog, the rolling thunder crashing ever closer, and pictured them home in Ruth's house, the four of them. Safe.

There was no room for doubt. No room for error. He closed his eyes and summoned every god and goddess he and his coven had ever prayed to—the old and the new alike—for strength.

A warmth began to overtake him and radiated from him. His entire body tingled and his skin prickled as every hair follicle became a sharp pin stick. Suddenly, he was being pulled up and up and up, sweeping through the long, dark tunnels. The air grew cooler and lighter as they rushed along, and when he opened his eyes they had miraculously landed in Ruth's living room once again.

He fell to his knees with Ruth in his arms, her eyes closed once again. She'd lost so much blood. Deacon silently took her from his arms, and Kylen led him into the makeshift setup in her junk room.

After taking a moment to recover, Nate raced to the refrigerator and retrieved the O-negative blood he'd brought from the hospital in case he'd need it for Kylen.

"Warm the blood to her body temp…carefully," Nate commanded, passing the bag to Deacon.

He held the bag in his hands and pulsed an orange glow through it before handing it back to Nate. Kylen stood waiting as Nate began to administer the transfusion to Ruth.

The three of them surrounded her, laying their hands on her limp body. Without a word, they all summoned what remaining energy they could produce, pushing their bright green light into Ruth.

The last thing Nate did was close the circle of protection around them, and then they all lay like loyal dogs around the floor of her bed, praying she would wake.

CHAPTER THIRTY-EIGHT

Ruth smelled bacon. And coffee. Pretty much her two favorite things to wake up to these days. Oh, and maybe Deacon. He was pretty okay to wake up to, as well. She rolled over on her side and reached across the bed for him. Instead, her hand slipped off the edge and into thin air. She kicked a foot out in the other direction only to find the same thing. Thin air.

Confused, she opened her eyes, squinting into the sunlight that was streaming in through the window. She was disoriented. This was the junk room. Okaaaay.

More confusion.

She sat up too quickly, and her head went swimmy. She was yet again hooked up to an IV. This time an empty blood bag was attached to one side and the IV was attached to the other. This was getting real old.

"Deacon?" she called out. Within seconds, Deacon, Nate and Kylen all appeared by her side. She lay back, staring up at them in confusion.

"Thank God," Deacon said, leaning down to kiss her forehead.

"Thank Nate." Kylen gave her foot a squeeze. "He's the one who got us home."

* * *

Deacon gave Nate a nod. He had thanked him. Repeatedly. It would never be enough. His unusual combination of humanity and supernatural ability was the only thing that had gotten them *out* of Hell. Not only had he rescued them all from Deacon's Hell cell, he'd also managed, yet again, to save Ruth. The guy really was magic. None of them knew what he was capable of, least of all Nate, but all of them owed him big-time.

Deacon knew one thing: Nate was much more than a healer and a babysitter for them. He was special in ways that were going to be put to the test in the coming weeks.

Ruth had been out for days. Deacon and the others had regained their strength quickly, but they'd continued to pour healing energy into Ruth several times a day. Deacon had traveled to Purgatory to demand an audience with Grim, who had finally and officially been installed as the Chief of Powers, but not in time to stop Camael from setting dozens of demons loose on Earth.

Grim and Deacon had managed to close the St. Agnes portal before the dozens became hundreds, but the damage had been done. It would take them all months to hunt down all the demons and dispatch them. In the meantime, there were so many souls at risk.

Deacon even found it in his heart to soften a bit toward Rashnu after he discovered the protective gift he'd tricked Ruth into drinking. Without that potion, she wouldn't have survived the trip back from Hell. He still wasn't sure he could trust the bastard, but he owed him now, and he doubted Rashnu would let him forget it.

Nate removed the two IVs and Deacon pushed a jolt of green energy into the wounds on both arms. Ruth's skin healed over immediately, the slight bruises disappearing. He smiled down at her, and then shot the other men a look. They both nodded and headed back into the kitchen.

Deacon pulled a chair up beside her bed and took her hand in his, rubbing the smooth palm against his stubble-covered jaw, then kissing it. He laid his head on her chest, and she stroked his hair.

"I'm so sorry, Ruth. So sorry."

"Shh. It's okay, Deacon. See, I'm fine. That's the good thing about us reapers—we're hard to kill." She laughed. "Maybe we need a secret code next time so we can be sure we are who we say we are."

"Maybe so—any suggestions?" he asked, kissing each finger on her hand.

"Hmm, how about *bacon?* Have I ever mentioned how much I love bacon?"

"I like that," he said, raising his head to look into her eyes. "Have I ever mentioned how much I love you?"

"As a matter of fact, no. I love you, too, Deacon Walker," she said, raising her mouth to his for a quick kiss.

"Mmm, now about that bacon …"

THE END

About the Author

Lisa adores beasties of all sorts, fictional as well as real, and has a farm full of them in her Southwest Missouri home, including: one child, one husband, two dogs, two cats, a dozen hens, thousands of Italian bees and a guinea pig.

She may or may not keep a complete zombie apocalypse bug-out bag in her trunk at all times, including a machete. Just. In. Case.

Keep in touch here:

Website: http://lisa-medley.com/books/
Facebook: /lisamedleyauthor
Twitter: @lisamedley
Google+: +lisamedley
Pinterest: medley3
Amazon: http://amzn.to/1axwex7

Don't miss a thing! Sign up for my New Release Newsletter http://eepurl.com/9Zhcz

Other Books by Lisa Medley

Haunt My Heart *A Civil War ghost gets a second chance at love in the 21st century.* - Out now!

Reap & Repent (Book I of The Reaper Series) - Available Now!

Reap & Redeem (Book II of The Reaper Series) - Available Now!

Reap & Reveal (Book III of The Reaper Series) - Available Now!

Space Cowboys & Indians *A sci-fi romance* - Coming in 2015

Reap & Reckon (Book IV of The Reaper Series) - Coming in 2016

THE REAPER SERIES:

The only thing worse than having nothing to live for…is having everything to live for.

A small group of reapers and supernatural beings in Meridian, Arkansas are all that stands between humanity and the apocalypse when a fallen angel stages a demonic invasion. In their battle to save the world, each will meet his or her match, discovering the power of love…and the importance of risking everything to protect it.

REAP & REDEEM

BOOK II OF THE REAPER SERIES

CHAPTER ONE

Kylen kicked the head across the floor of the dark shed with his steel-toed boot. Blood dripped into a pool on the floor from his scythe, which he still gripped tightly with one hand. He straightened to his full height and tilted his neck from side to side, listening to his spine crack and pop. Another demon down.

"You don't have to keep killing them yourself, you know," Deacon said, grimacing at the black ooze spilling out of the severed neck.

"Yeah, I do." Kylen turned and walked to the door, taking a quick survey of the cemetery. A dark, sticky trail marked his course.

"You have to admit, he's efficient." Nate picked up the head by the hair and dropped it into a black garbage bag.

"That's one way to look at it." Deacon pressed his hand, which was glowing with Reiki energy, to the

321

center of the dead male's chest, directly over his heart chakra.

Kylen watched as light radiated from Deacon, encasing him and the body in a soft glow. The demon boiled forth from the dead human host in a thick black torrent of sulfurous haze. Spreading his arms wide, Deacon summoned the stream, which penetrated through his sternum. His body shuddered and the light around him sparked and cracked like the arc of a welder. The glow intensified to supernova status before winking out. Several smaller streams of gray light flowed forth from the ruined body, too, entering through Deacon's mouth.

"Well? Did you retrieve all the souls?" Nate lifted the feet and legs of the body onto the tarp he'd set beside it.

Deacon frowned. "Yes."

"How many?"

"Three." Deacon rose and grasped the body by the shoulders, helping Nate maneuver it. "And the demon."

"I really hate this shit." Nate said, pulling a spool of duct tape from his backpack. They rolled the man tightly in the tarp, taping both ends so that none of the bodily fluids would discharge in transit.

"How many more demons do you think there are?" Nate wrapped the head in a plastic bag and walked toward the door.

"Grim thinks there are at least two dozen more," Deacon reminded him.

"Great. Slow and steady wins the race, yeah?"

"I'm not sure we have the luxury of slow and steady anymore. At this rate, we're never going to find them all. There's already way too much collateral damage. This many missing humans in town won't go unnoticed much longer. We need to find their exit portals and shut down the rest of the demons. Sooner would be better than later."

Kylen waited in the doorway, dividing his attention between the business in the shed and the cemetery grounds. Deacon was right of course. They needed to close the portals. Permanently. As it was, they were playing a game of supernatural Whac-A- Mole. Close one portal and another popped up. New entrance portals continued to open each week, which then had to be closed by Grim and Deacon. And while one batch of demons gathered their fill of souls before sliding down the small one-way shoots to Hell—the exit portals, the next batch waited for their chance. It had become a never-ending battle and the reapers needed to press on.

They didn't bother cleaning up the black ooze or the blood trail. The only way to make sure the scene was completely clean was fire, but arson would be sure to draw more attention to the mower garage by the edge of the cemetery than a few stains that could easily be oil or fuel. None of them were concerned about the law. There were far worse things for them to worry about.

They'd burn the body at home, and then bury the ashes and bits of bone. Just as they'd dealt with the other eleven. This host's disappearance would never be explained. Good thing, since the guy's head was detached.

* * *

Nate continued to insist they could at least *try* to save the hosts, but Kylen was adamant that it was in no one's best interest. After all, the hosts were only human. A demon's essence burned through a human body like dry tinder. If a host did manage to somehow survive the first twenty-four hours, their delicate psyche would be so damaged that there wouldn't be anything left to save. Without the demon to animate them, they would be nothing but a babbling husk.

Kylen knew a thing or two about possession.

He'd spent the past hundred years with a demon riding his body. Being a reaper had its perks as well as its challenges. One perk was that it was damn difficult to die. As long as a reaper fueled enough and kept his head, he was immortal, so Kylen's body could have withstood the demon's toxic venom indefinitely. The downside was that it was damn near impossible for a reaper to kill himself. The demon had always kept Kylen's body nourished enough to maintain the necessary energy flow, and though Kylen had occasionally been able to break through and wrest control from the demon, it had never been for long enough....

Kylen had possessed the will. Just not the means.

Then he had finally been freed, and somehow he had survived both the possession and the freeing.

Physically.

Most days, he wished he hadn't.

"Let's get out of here." Deacon hoisted the wrapped-up body over his shoulder and left the building, crossing the invisible barrier onto the consecrated soil of the dark cemetery. "Ready to go home, Kylen?" He placed his palm on the nearest headstone, and Nate followed suit.

"I can't wait." Kylen placed his hand on the stone as well, and the three men began to shimmer as they were drawn into the consecrated subway.

* * *

Ruth Scott sat drumming her fingers on top of her kitchen table, impatient for the men to return. Dinner had been ready for an hour. Stew simmered on the stove, and she fidgeted with the place settings for the ten thousandth time, rearranging glasses and realigning utensils. It was a useless task. One for which she was way overqualified.

Why they let Nate go on the hunts and not her was a real point of contention. He had way less experience than she did, and she'd proved herself plenty.

After all, she'd helped save both Deacon and Kylen. How quickly they had forgotten. Just because she was a newbie reaper didn't mean she couldn't do what needed to be done. Sure, she'd almost died a couple of times while coming to terms with her new reaper powers, but now they'd had plenty of time to work out the kinks.

Deacon was way too protective. Ever since the demons had been released in the early summer, he'd been on a mission to destroy them. As in a mission from God. She got that. For one thing, it was his job. For another, it was bad for any demons to be let loose on the world, let alone the three dozen that had been hunting the streets of Meridian. Very bad. But how was she ever going to be tough enough to face the danger that lurked at every corner unless she had more *experience?*

She wasn't afraid. She'd spent most of her life being afraid that people would discover her ability to see auras and use it against her. Back then she'd had no idea why she could do what she could do and what it all meant. Because of that fear, she hadn't really lived her life at all.

Until Deacon. Over the past few months, Deacon had trained her how to be a reaper. With a renewed sense of purpose and the encouragement of one fine man, she'd stopped thinking of her ability as a handicap and started appreciating it for the gift that it was.

But now she was sitting in her tiny rock-sided house, keeping the home fires burning while the men were off fighting the big bad demons. Well, that was going to end. Tonight. They were going to have to cowboy up and get over their ridiculous worries. She would be a prisoner in her own home no longer.

Besides, Nate couldn't even *see* auras, souls or demons for God's sake. Since returning from Hell, he could see the Reiki energy when one of them—or he himself—manifested it. Otherwise, he was useless as a reaper. Of course, he did have a nifty way of using his magic to trap the evil bastards from time to time. The demon trap burned into her living room floor was evidence of that. Also, he and Deacon were the only ones who could travel through the invisible reaper freeway without the aid of consecrated ground *and* he was an EMT, which had already come in handy way too many times for comfort. None of them were invincible. At least not completely.

She grumbled to herself over the injustice of it all as she pushed her dinner around her plate, and she was still fuming when they landed in the middle of the living room.

With another body.

Perfect.